Tempted by a Cowboy

Tempted by a Cowboy

VONNA HARPER
MELISSA MacNEAL
DELILAH DEVLIN

KENSINGTON BOOKS
http://www.kensingtonbooks.com

APHRODISIA BOOKS are published by

Kensington Publishing Corp.
119 West 40th Street
New York, NY 10018

All Kensington Titles, Imprints, and Distributed Lines are available at special quantity discounts for bulk purchases for sales promotions, premiums, fund-raising, and educational or institutional use.

Special book excerpts or customized printings can also be created to fit specific needs. For details, write or phone the office of the Kensington special sales manager: Kensington Publishing Corp., 119 West 40th Street, New York, NY 10018, attn: Special Sales Department, Phone: 1-800-221-2647.

Aphrodisia and the A logo Reg. U.S. Pat & TM Off

ISBN-13: 978-0-7582-3451-3
ISBN-10: 0-7582-3451-1

First Trade Paperback Printing: July 2009

10 9 8 7 6 5 4 3 2 1

Printed in the United States of America

Contents

MUSTANG MAN

VONNA HARPER

Dedication

Harry, thank you for jump-starting me in writing *Mustang Man*. Harry, a true cowboy and horse wrangler, recently joined other wranglers in turning wild mustangs into trained mounts ready and willing to do whatever their new owners require of them. I'm grateful to him for everything he told me about the experience.

The West's wild horses have long run free. Currently some 33,000 are on Bureau of Land Management land. Unfortunately, they are overrunning that land, forcing BLM to make some hard decisions in an effort to ensure their future. Some of these mustangs find themselves under the guidance of caring experts dedicated to humane treatment and training.

Several competitions such as Mustang Challenge in Sacramento and Extreme Mustang Makeover in Ft. Worth provide an opportunity for wranglers to demonstrate their expertise in lively competition. Following the events and judging, the mustangs are auctioned off to new and appreciative owners.

I'm delighted to play a small part in sharing that experience with readers.

1

Dust swirled around the legs of the two dozen mustangs trapped in the large corral. Beyond the wood enclosure waited the typical high desert offerings of dried grasses, hearty shrubs, low hills, and endless miles of wilderness. Occasionally, one or more of the wild horses stopped its uneasy movements and lifted its head to stare at the horizon.

From where he stood on the other side of the corral, cowboy and horse wrangler Miguel Perez easily read the mustangs' body language. Born free, they wanted nothing more than to return to the land of their birth. But it wasn't going to happen because they'd been on acreage that was the responsibility of the Bureau of Land Management. After due consideration, the bureau had declared that there was too much horseflesh for the acreage.

"I don't like it any more than you do," Miguel informed them, speaking from the depths of his heart. "Wild's all you've ever known. No matter what happens out there, you believe you should be allowed to live the way nature intended." Not taking his eyes off the thousands of pounds of hearty and well-fed horseflesh, he fell silent.

An ache ground through him, burning his eyes and making his fingers clench. Restless in a way that had been part of him since early childhood, he absorbed the mustangs' energy.

In his mind's eye, he slid between the wooden slats and approached the tall black stallion with the lightning-shaped blaze running down his face and flowing mane and tail. Seeing the human approach, the stallion would rear, his eyes showing too much white, nostrils flared. Standing his ground, Miguel waited for the animal to settle. Then he'd stepped forward and placed a calming hand on the stallion's muscled neck.

It's all right, all right. Everything's changed for you, but you'll survive. We're in this together, you and me. I understand you, and you'll come to understand me. To trust. To love. Maybe even to comprehend that I had no choice but to step into your life.

The grind and groan of an approaching vehicle pulled him back from his thoughts, but as a dust-caked BLM truck bounced into view, he left a small part of himself with the stallion he'd already named Blanco in honor of the white blaze. The journey toward their becoming one had begun.

After stopping some thirty feet away, the truck's driver silenced the engine. As the mustangs had done when Miguel had pulled in with his truck and single-horse trailer, they galloped to the far end of their enclosure. Both truck doors opened. Miguel took quick note of the driver, a tall, robust man in a standard brown BLM uniform who appeared to be in his early forties. His thinning hair was close-cropped and his boots, although dirty, were sturdy looking. Then he turned his attention to the passenger.

He hadn't expected to see a woman out in the middle of nowhere, especially not one about five and a half feet tall with slender arms and legs and a double handful of long, dark hair that she'd caught at the nape of her neck with something he couldn't see. Her close-fitting uniform revealed never-ending curves. His first reaction was that BLM needed to hire sturdier women for the physically demanding work.

His second spawned from his cock. He couldn't remember the last time he'd had sex, several months for the simple reason that managing ten thousand plus beef cattle on a massive and remote ranch didn't lend itself to frequent interactions with the opposite sex.

As the two closed in on him, he read her name tag: DAWN GLASS. She looked like a dawn all right, with lively hazel eyes that swept over her surroundings and then settled on him. Appraised him. Everything about her expression said she loved and embraced life. She was either deeply tanned or, like him, came by her dark coloring naturally. But whatever her nationality, she wasn't Hispanic. He would have known.

"You must be Miguel Perez," the man whose name tag identified him as Brod Swartzberg said. "From what you said, we figured you'd be the first to get here."

Miguel had called the number he'd been given via cell a couple of hours earlier to make sure he had the location right. At the time he'd spoken to a man, probably Brod, which had added to his assumption that he'd be working solely with men. From the way Dawn studied her coworker, he concluded Brod outranked her. As for why she'd chosen a career devoted to managing public lands mostly in the middle of nowhere instead of availing herself of civilization's comforts . . .

"How many others are you expecting?" he asked, directing his question at Dawn.

"Today, three," she said, still meeting his frank gaze. "A couple more tomorrow and what, five or six next week. We were hoping for a greater response to the program, but it's a large investment in time and effort."

Miguel knew that she was talking about the program in

which qualified horse trainers had been invited to compete to see who could do the most with a wild mustang within a set time frame. Although the wranglers would be financially reimbursed to a certain extent, she was right, only a fool would get into the competition for the money.

Money had nothing to do with his reasons for having come here. Doing what he could to ensure a future for at least one of the mustangs drove him.

"How long have you been here?" Brod asked. "Long enough to get a feel for the animals?"

A "feel" for horses, as the other man called it, came as naturally to him as breathing. It was human beings he wasn't sure he'd ever figure out, not that it mattered. "I'm interested in the black stallion, the one with the white blaze."

Dawn and Brod exchanged a look. "Are you sure?" she asked. Once more her gaze leveled on him, and her eyes darkened, letting him know she was trying to dig beneath his surface. "This herd's been here nearly a month, long enough for them to get used to hay and for us to study them and ensure their health. He's the resident stud, probably sire to the majority of foals."

"That's what I figured."

She didn't understand his decision, or more likely, she didn't understand him. But she wanted to. Otherwise, she would have dropped her gaze, right? Wouldn't have sent a sensual zinging his direction.

Dawn Glass wasn't a beautiful woman, not in the way of the creatures who wound up on magazine covers. Her hands, although small like the rest of her, sported a number of tiny scrapes and scars. They were strong looking in keeping with her muscled forearms and what he could see of her thighs and calves. He didn't think she was wearing makeup and was close enough that he'd be able to smell her perfume if she was wearing any.

A woman who didn't think of herself as one, or so deeply female that the exterior package didn't matter? There'd been a zing, right? It hadn't all been his imagination, or had it?

What was he thinking? Hadn't he just allowed as how he didn't *get* humans? His interest in what made her tick was a by-product of having gone too long without sex and standing nearly toe to toe with a ripe example of the other half of the human race. Her breasts, although his fingers itched to explore them, didn't appear to be overly large, and her pants didn't tightly cup her crotch. She wasn't giving him a come-hither look or planting her hands on her hips, no moistening of her lips. Still . . .

Damn it, he was here to pick up a mustang to take back to the spread west of Yreka where he'd given the last three years of his life. No way would she let him throw her into the trailer and haul her there with him.

"You're experienced?" Brod asked. "Of course you are or you wouldn't be here. Even before I was assigned to the mustang project, I was curious about what it takes to change a bronc into a child's saddle pony. More guts than I have."

Shrugging, Miguel turned his attention back to the corral. As had happened when he'd first seen the wild horses, his heartbeat kicked up. In his mind's eye, he saw his beautiful and equally wild mother sitting high and proud and fearless on a bare back. Galloping full-out, she lifted her head and laughed as the wind threw her hair in an ebony stream behind her.

Untamed. A creature of the land.

Like him.

"You're committed to the natural horsemanship's gentling techniques?" Dawn asked. "I know you had to sign the contract saying you'll adhere to every aspect of the approach, but if you have the slightest hesitation about what you're being required to do—"

"Hold up, Dawn," Brod interrupted. "There's no reason for

us to get off on the wrong foot with, what did you say your name was? Sorry but the trainers are all running together in my mind."

Extending a hand in the man's direction, Miguel introduced himself. After shaking Brod's hand, he turned toward Dawn. For just a moment she stood with her arms by her sides and her head tilted to the side. Then she placed small but strong fingers in his paw. A current of heat raced through his heart and headed south. Even when they broke off the contact, she kept her gaze on him.

Heat, everywhere. A wildfire waiting for the wind to turn it into a monster.

What was she looking for, maybe trying to reconcile herself to his Hispanic heritage? Maybe trying to make sure he wasn't lying about his commitment to natural horsemanship? If she went back with him, she'd soon understand how foreign the concept of breaking a horse's will and spirit was to him.

"You didn't answer me," she said. "You're completely on-board with the program?"

"Why don't you watch and find out."

Damn but Miguel Perez had a scrape-the-nerve-endings voice, Dawn acknowledged. The wind's love affair with his ink-black, nearly shoulder-length hair wasn't helping her maintain her equilibrium and she wasn't about to acknowledge the effect his molded-to-his-hard-ass-jeans was having on her libido. If their handshake had gone on any longer, she'd have been forced to press her thighs together.

Turning her face into the hot breeze did nothing to cool her cheeks. She could only hope her tan hid her flush. From the moment she'd spotted Miguel standing alone and self-contained near the corral, her day had spun in a full circle. Yes, she was ac-customed to living and working in a male-dominated world. Yes, she'd been the recipient of more than her share of come-ons and responded to a handful of them. But seldom did she feel as if she'd been sucker punched.

Turned on and hot to fuck.

Primitive to primitive, no boundaries established and no quarters given. Going at it, just the hell going at it.

Teeth clenched in defense against the primitive bitch who'd suddenly made an appearance between her ears and thighs, she worked at making sure her eyes weren't bugging out of their sockets.

Male. Five hundred percent male. Dark and strong, right at six feet with a sinfully flat belly. Shoulders broad enough to hold their own against any and all bucking broncs, eyes straight out of midnight, a simple blue T-shirt too damn in love with that solid chest and washboard abs. And the jeans, the damnable jeans. And a cowboy's thighs and calves beneath the denim.

"The stallion you're interested in," Brod said, sounding a thousand miles away, "is on the upper end of the age we prefer to work with. The vet tried to look at his teeth to get a more exact age, but he wasn't having any of that."

After a quirk of his mouth she felt in her belly, Miguel started toward the corral. Against everything that made any kind of sense, she studied his stride or rather what walking did to his buttocks. Only belatedly did she think to catch up with her supervisor who was following Miguel. By the time she reached the two men, Miguel was lifting a leg in preparation for climbing over a rail and entering the corral.

"What are you doing?" she blurted, her four years with BLM and the last four months devoted to the mustang project kicking in. "Are you crazy?"

He swiveled toward her, leg hooked over a rail and hands on the one above it. The sun settled on his features, giving them depth and stealing her breath. "Getting to know my horse," he said.

"On foot, without a rope, alone?"

He answered her concerns without saying a word. *I know what I'm doing,* his eyes said. *And I don't need or want you questioning me.*

But if he got hurt, if he wound up with broken bones and a bleeding body . . .

Remember what I said, his eyes responded. *I don't need you. Or anyone.*

2

The moment he was inside the corral, the enclosure became Miguel's world, or rather the horses did. A part of him remained aware that Dawn Glass was watching his every move, judging him as a woman does a man. But these moments were for Blanco and him; everything else could wait.

The broncs were still in the far corner, most clustered behind Blanco. Because there were no foals in the group, he concluded they and their mothers had been separated from those that had been selected for the training program and hopefully remained free. Only a half dozen were stallions, the rest yearlings or barren mares.

Step by measured step, he approached the stallion. Instead of retreating, Blanco stood his ground. Whether he was deliberately putting himself between the human and his mares or more curious than the others didn't matter.

"You're beautiful," Miguel told him, his voice low and confident. "Wild but no longer free. You don't understand what's happening, and you don't like it. But it's going to be all right. You're safe with me. Safe." As he spoke, he wondered if Dawn

Glass understood that his words had been carefully chosen. Blanco's coat was glossy despite a few scars on his shoulders and rump, probably from fights with other stallions.

"All this change, particularly the confinement, is confusing and frightening, but you'll learn to trust me, and once you do, you'll relax."

Now paying only small heed to what he was saying, he continued speaking to the stallion. The two of them shared the same gaze, the same energy, even the same air. In the distance, the desert Blanco had always known waited, but as long as the stallion listened to the human, the desert wouldn't call to him.

By moving smooth inches at a time, Miguel came within three feet of Blanco. He continued talking, his voice as musical as his throat could make it. Even as he chose soothing sounds designed for a wild animal, he wondered if they would have the same effect on Dawn Glass.

Because he didn't know any other way, he'd approach her as he did a horse, slowly so she'd have time to get used to his presence. He wouldn't make any sudden moves, and although he ached to clench his arms around her and seal her body to his, he'd hold off.

She wasn't wild, not the way Blanco or he was. A modern woman accustomed to assured and modern men, she'd have certain expectations. But because he had only scant understanding of, and interest in, those expectations, he'd rely on what he knew. She'd become *his* wild mare, driven into *his* corral and nervously awaiting *his* next move.

Although he could throw a rope over her, he wouldn't. Instead, he'd slowly close in on her. He'd give her time to get used to his presence, his smell and movement, the dark messages in his eyes, his muscles and body. Bit by bit, she'd stop thinking about breaking free. Her system would begin to react to his male reality, her nipples hardening and sex heating. No matter whether she leaned into him or turned her back on him, when he reached for her, her body would spark.

In his grip, his grasp and control, she'd cease to be who her name tag said she was and sink into instinct. Woman, reacting to man, skin on fire and heart racing, lungs expanding in a desperate effort to bring enough oxygen to her system.

What are you doing? she'd ask.

Showing you what it is to be a woman.

And because those were the words she'd long been waiting to hear without knowing it, she'd melt into him. Surrender her body to him. Strip off her clothing and spread her legs for him.

And he'd bury himself in her. Turn his selfhood over to her.

Not that simple, damn you!

Propelled by years of experience, Miguel extended his hand palm down toward Blanco. Throwing up his head, Blanco back stepped. Then, perhaps prompted by his engrained curiosity, the stallion again held his ground and slowly extended his head.

"You're beginning to understand," Miguel crooned. "I'm casting a spell over you. It's nothing to fear and has nothing to do with ropes and saddles. We're getting to know each other. Because of what you are, the concept of someone having control over you is foreign. But you're intrigued by what I am and the potential of learning something new under my guidance. From now on you'll have no reason to flee anything which is your nature. There aren't any cougars or wild dogs where I'm taking you, no harsh winter storms or iced-over grasses. In summer, you'll enter my barn whenever you want to get out of the heat. There'll be fresh water and ready food, always. No more endless travel in search of something to fill your belly. All those benefits and the only thing you have to do is turn yourself over to me."

When Blanco exhaled, warm, damp air stirred the hairs on the back of Miguel's hand. In his mind, he'd been talking to

Dawn Glass, not a mustang. He who knew not damn enough about seduction had approached her as he would a horse. He'd used the same words, taken the same amount of time, given her the opportunity to study him.

The result would be the same. By the time he was done with her, she'd lower her head and allow him to place a halter over her head and behind her ears. She might start when he fastened a rope to the halter, might even try to break free. But he'd have snaked the other end of the rope around a post. Whether she stood passively or fought the restraint, he'd have her. She'd belong to him.

And then?

Shocked by the strength of his urge to see if she was watching, he forced his attention back on Blanco. Just because the stallion was acting as if he'd been hypnotized hardly meant a lifetime of instinct had fallen away.

"I'm the most confusing two-legged creature you've ever come across, aren't I?" he asked the horse. Measuring his every move, he turned his hand over so his fingers curled upward. "Probably the first who hasn't forced you to do something you don't want to. That's never been my way with horses. It never will be."

Blanco closed his loose lips over Miguel's fingers. His teeth scraped Miguel's nails. "You don't want to bite me, last thing on your mind. All you're interested in is a touch and a taste of me, do you understand?"

The stallion's lips closed against Miguel's fingers, spawning the question of how he'd react if Dawn Glass and not a horse was doing that to him. "Sorry, a momentary lapse there. Lost my train of thought." Pulling his fingers free, he lightly ran his fingertips over a satiny nose. Blanco snorted but stood his ground. "Good boy, darn good. We're making progress. There's a saying among humans, something about catching more flies with honey than vinegar. I'm honey, patient sweetness."

A feathery stroking motion over the dark nose prompted a sigh from Blanco. "We understand each other," Miguel whispered. "That's what it all boils down to, I know a hell of a lot more about you than I do the human race. Sometimes I think I was born half horse. At least I'm in the right career."

Dawn was far enough away that she caught only bits and pieces of what the horse wrangler was saying to the strangely passive stallion. If a year ago someone had told her she'd be working with horses, she'd have told them that wasn't going to happen in this lifetime. Not only hadn't she known squat about the creatures, she'd thought her degree in earth sciences would have gotten her involved in the geothermal energy development taking place on BLM land.

Well, goes to show how many unexpected turns a life can take. Like now. This morning when she'd rolled out of bed in the five hundred square foot cabin she currently *lived* in, she'd thought the day would be about watching tobacco-chewing old wranglers wrestle broncs into battered horse trailers. Her concern would revolve around making sure the wild beasts received humane treatment while hopefully keeping enough distance from said wranglers that she wouldn't know how many days they'd gone without a shower.

Instead, her attention and nerve endings were glued to a dark complexioned and fearless man, a man with shoulders designed for a physical life, and hips and legs designed to short-circuit any woman's mind and body.

She more than admired what he was doing; she was in awe of his courage. Beyond that, she ached to be privy to the communication between man and stallion. As for the top of her list—a night with him. The two of them alone and naked, no reservations, single-minded and hot to trot.

No trying to fathom the attraction, no need for explanations.

Just heat.

Hell, she didn't care where he'd come from or what he'd do once he'd picked up his charge. She wanted, no, she *needed* to be anywhere alone with this man who made her think of a Plains Indian with the courage and skill to run down a stampeding buffalo while his legs wrapped around a mustang's heaving flanks.

Taken unawares by the warmth sliding from breasts to belly and from there to her pelvic region, she gave up. Vehicle sounds behind her warned that others were approaching, but Brod would have to deal with the other trainers because Miguel belonged to her. For as long as he was remotely near touching distance, nothing else mattered.

If it was night—why the hell was the sun still up—the shadows would keep the secrets of what they were doing. There'd be no need for words, no sensual dance, nothing resembling taking time to get to know each other. She'd unexpectedly and deliciously become a mare in heat. A stallion, what she needed was a stallion! She'd lift her tail and turn her rump toward the stud.

Wise in the ways of brood mares, he'd cover her. Hard and fast, no questions asked and no quarters given. They'd squeal together, hooves pounding the ground, his greater weight settling over her hindquarters and his impossibly long cock reaching between her splayed legs.

Union, hot seed shooting into her and making her scream, his deeper bellow exploding around her.

"Dawn? What are you doing?"

Cheeks and throat on fire, she looked over her shoulder at her supervisor. His arms were folded over his chest and his body language disapproving.

"You're the one who said I needed to learn everything I can about this natural horsemanship business." Hopefully she wasn't stumbling over the words. "From what I've seen so far, I'm not going to get a better example than what Mr. Perez is doing."

Her explanation must have made an impact because although Brod scowled a little, he shrugged and headed for the pickup and trailer that had just come into view. Hoping to recover her equilibrium, she watched Brod for a few seconds. Then, because she couldn't do anything else, she again looked at Miguel.

Although he still stood within punishing hoof distance of the maybe thirteen-hundred-pound stallion, he was watching her. No hat shaded his features. Quite possibly she'd lost the ability to read anyone's expression, but if she hadn't and she was right, Miguel Perez thought of himself as a stallion. A stud who has found a mare ready and willing to be serviced.

Moving with a grace, power, and danger that loosened her bones, he left the black bronc and started toward her. She, who'd never seen a cougar approach its prey, felt like a deer trapped by one. Only, even if she'd been equipped with four swift legs, she wouldn't have run.

How could she when the most alive man she'd ever seen was only a wooden fence away from her?

"Did what you see answer your questions?" he asked.

Somehow she bit back a stupid "huh?" Unfortunately, she couldn't think of a single rational word. Any moment now he'd slide that masculine leg of his between the corral boards. The rest of his body would follow and then they'd be standing together—lordy, would they!

"You were adamant that I follow protocol with regard to training techniques," he continued. If he was deliberately testing her by keeping distance between them, it was working. "I figured giving you a physical demonstration was better than signing a bunch of forms."

She'd gone to work for BLM for a lot of reasons, most related to her interest in geothermal energy sources. Experience had taught her that ideology and a massive governmental agency didn't always go hand in hand. Otherwise, how could she explain her current assignment? But she still believed that rules and regulations were all that stood against lawlessness, or specifically mistreatment of the mustangs.

This afternoon, however, going over the regulations with Miguel was the last thing she wanted to do. Stammering a bit, she said something about assuming he'd thoroughly read through the agreement he'd sent in.

"Did I memorize it, no. Do I understand the rationale for turning mustangs into participating members of society? The answer you expect from me is, yes. If they remain wild, they'll breed themselves right out of the land allotted to them."

"The answer you think I expect from you? What are you talking about?"

"If the mustangs still had natural predators such as wolves, and civilization wasn't closing in around them, they'd have enough room."

"Are you blaming the BLM?"

"I'm simply saying this didn't have to happen." He indicated the fencing. "There should be alternatives to taking away their freedom."

"Such as?"

His silence left her with too many questions and too much curiosity about where he was coming from.

"How, ah, how did you get interested in horses?" she lamely came up with.

On the heels of a low chuckle, he slipped his beautiful body out of the corral and planted it next to her. "I was born on horseback, nearly. Being with them made my mother's world go around. I caught the fever."

His gaze said volumes about that fever, either that or— lordy, could his thoughts be on her and what they could and would do if they had this place to themselves? Arms and legs suddenly numb, she worked at a nod. "Did you have any formal training?"

His second chuckle didn't carry the same warmth the first had. "Formal training's for those who don't have it in their blood." He glanced back at the mustangs, then fixed his compelling dark eyes on her.

She was swimming, drowning, surrounded by heat and energy. Her reaction made no sense! She spent her days in the company of men. Her present assignment had brought her into contact with men who lived on horseback and thought nothing of doing whatever it took to round up wild-eyed mustangs. The majority of those cowboys were lean and hard, made for jeans and boots, totally at home with their saddles and the mounts under them.

What was different about Miguel? Was it his ink-dark eyes, his fearlessness around the herd stud? Maybe something else, an air of mystery, the untamed aura.

And maybe she was simply so damn horny that anything with a cock would turn her on.

"Ah, what about your father? Was he into horses?"

"I never met him."

His soul-deep statement weighed on her. She came from a intact family that consisted of professional parents and two older college-educated brothers. Her parents were happily entrenched in their careers and not yet thinking ahead to retirement. Their home was nearly paid for. They took vacations in places like Hawaii and France, grumbled about taxes and got involved in local politics. Her father had been a school board member while his children were growing up, and her mother had done the PTA thing.

In contrast, Miguel of the hard-as-hell body didn't know the man responsible for his being alive.

"I'm sorry," she said and somehow her fingers were on his forearm.

Showing no emotion, he looked down at what she'd done.

The federal employee in her knew she'd crossed a line she had no business crossing. The woman pulsing deep inside didn't give a damn.

"Don't be," he muttered. "My mother and I did just fine on our own. She never turned to a man for anything, never."

Something in his tone warned that that was a place he didn't want to go, but damn it, everything about this rugged man fascinated her. She who'd always believed she was drawn to intelligent and intellectual men was unbelievably turned on by the most physical male she'd ever met.

Whoever had just arrived must have gotten out of their rig because she could hear Brod talking to someone. Masculine voices floated off into the air. In contrast to her absolute lack of interest in them, she couldn't get enough of looking at this man who'd been raised by a woman who understood horses at the most fundamental level. Miguel Perez was Mexican, which meant his roots were probably in the country to the south even though he had no accent. Were he and his mother U.S. citizens? Why had she raised her child far from their heritage, if that's what had happened? And why did his background matter to her?

"Does, ah, does your mother know what you're doing? Sorry, that didn't come out the way I intended it to. You certainly don't need her permission. But you're hardly going to get rich training a mustang. The small amount we give you won't cover the horse's feed let alone everything else."

"I'm not interested in rich."

Okay, now what? Her hand was still on his forearm and he'd done nothing to shake her off. Maybe he was only being polite, figuring he needed to be hospitable to the federal employee who had the final say in whether he'd be taking Blanco home.

She hoped it wasn't that.

Hoped he needed the touch as much as she did.

Not dropping his gaze, he covered her fingers with his own. Lightning struck her and was that a clap of thunder? "Who knows what you're doing with your life?" he softly asked. "Your husband?"

She tried to swallow, failed. "No husband."

"I didn't think so."

"What makes you say that?"

The faintest of smiles lifted the corners of his mouth. Then his too-kissable lips settled again. "Let's not beat around the bush. The air between us is too damn hot not to acknowledge."

The air wasn't the only thing that was hot. Just trying to come to terms with what he'd said about the mutual attraction had her on the brink of panting. Never, absolutely never had she stood next to a stranger and been about to burst into flames.

3

Idiot. One hundred percent idiot.

Even as he chastised himself, Miguel knew he wasn't going to release the federal employee's hand. Living and working with animals had conditioned him to measure his every move against those that had or hadn't worked in the past. A quick study, he couldn't remember the last time he'd made a mistake with four-legged creatures. Unfortunately, he couldn't say the same about his track record with women. Not only were they much more complex than broncs, he tended to get sidetracked by the question of what they'd be like in bed.

"What about you?" she muttered, looking as unsure as a child standing alone at the side of a freeway and as excited as a girl on prom night. "A wife?"

What had they been talking about? That's right, marital status. "No wife. Nothing close."

"Oh." She let the word stretch out. "So . . ."

Lowering her head, she stared at her slender fingers bracketed by his darker and larger ones.

"If you're looking for me to explain this"—he gently squeezed—"it isn't going to happen."

"I didn't expect you to, hell I don't know what to expect."

In some respects her honesty made what they were doing easier to comprehend. Hopefully the way she was positioned shielded their intertwined hands from the others. The other BLM employee—he'd forgotten his name—was engaged in conversation with the two newcomers, but any time now they'd head for the corral.

"I spotted a hay shed." He jerked his head to the left where a weathered structure stood surrounded by brush. "Let's go there."

She tugged lightly, then stopped trying to free herself. "What?"

"I want to explore this *thing*, and I think you do too."

Although she kept her gaze downcast, he believed he understood her inner battle. If she called a halt to the energy racing between them, he'd honor her decision, but it would be damn hard.

"I shouldn't. This could get me fired."

"I'm not telling."

Her sigh came from someplace deep inside and added to his nearly raging need to fuck her. Still not looking at him, she shook off his grip. His heart settled painfully in his chest. Then she started toward the shed and everything lit up. Mindful that the others might be taking note, he waited a moment before trudging after her. As he did, he shrugged as if exasperated by what he was being asked to do.

The shed, which was some hundred feet away from the corral, was large enough to hold a stake truck full of hay bales. Right now it was about half full with a couple of open sleeping bags on one of the bales. Although there were walls on three sides, the back was open. By the time he came around to the rear, she was sitting on the top of a two-bale stack. Her hands were folded in her lap, her knuckles white.

Incapable of speaking, he stopped with some three feet separating them. A living force tried to pull him closer, but he didn't dare give into it, yet.

He'd come to the Litchfield corrals because he believed he owed it to the mustangs. Meeting a woman who appealed to him had been the last thing on his mind, but he had. She was here, looking up at him, her crotch nearly in alignment with his cock. Her legs were clamped together, for now.

Waiting for his eyes to adjust to the shadows, he mentally went back to getting ready to leave the Yreka area cattle ranch this morning. He'd slipped his wallet into his back pocket with little thought to its contents. Hopefully there was a rubber in there.

The moment she came into focus, protection became the last thing on his mind. He didn't understand, flat out didn't comprehend. Women had moved through his world, most of them average, a handful blessed with extraordinary bodies. At first he'd chased after them with a stallion's single-mindedness. What rested between their ears hadn't mattered, only the external package and willingness to share said package with a horny cowboy. Fortunately, since his teenage years, either he'd learned how to tamp down his libido or life had smoothed out. His world no longer revolved around sex, which meant he could concentrate on what he was being paid to do.

Except today.

"You're staring at me," she said, her voice low.

"Am I?" Gripping self-control with a tight fist, he slid closer and rested his hands on her knees. She jumped, and her now-taut thigh muscles stood out against her practical attire.

"We shouldn't—ah shit, what am I—they could come in any time."

Tightening his grip a little, he inched her legs apart. "Then we need to get at this."

He half expected her to bolt like an untamed filly. If she did, he wouldn't have to labor under the complex issue of what the hell they were suppose to do and say. Instead, speaking volumes in the move, she leaned back and planted her arms behind her.

"I'm scared," she said. "No, not scared. Shaking and wondering what in the hell I'm doing. I'm sorry, I keep saying the same thing."

"That's all right."

"Is it? I just wish I understood . . ."

"It's the same for me."

Her slight nod might be the most graceful thing he'd seen in weeks, certainly the most mesmerizing. "I don't know what's going to happen," she admitted. "Maybe I'll panic and—we are thinking the same thing, aren't we?"

Women had always been able to talk rings around him. Where he considered himself lucky to come up with a sentence, they seemed to have no trouble carrying the conversation ball. Being with a woman who appeared to be no more articulate than he should be a relief, but what if silence stretched on and on?

"Sex," he came up with and then wished he could punch himself. "This is about sex."

"Oh, yes. Of course." She leaned back a few more inches.

Her slacks had looked reasonably loose fitting when they'd been standing outside. Now the fabric strained against her crotch. Wishing his hand was there, he increased the gap between her legs. A pink tongue moistened her lips. Releasing her right knee, he ran a forefinger over her lower lip. Her eyes glassy, she licked his nail. Sensation raced up his arm and sent his heart to boiling.

"No time," she whispered. "It's insane to even think we have time for—"

"We'll make it happen."

Her nod struck him as part quiet acceptance, part panic. The sense of unreality continued to coat his every breath. This was a dream, a delicious dream! He was on the brink of waking up, and once he did, she'd be gone. Maybe she was a figment of his imagination.

He'd withdrawn his finger while she was talking, but she'd left her mouth parted and he had no choice but to slip his thumb between the scant space. She helped by sucking him in and closing her lips around him. Lifting her head a little and turning it to the side, she granted him a faint smile. In his mind, his cock was buried in her sex. A universe away from wanting the union to end, he pushed deeper. He'd fuck her mouth with his thumb, start slow but build up until they were both starving for the real thing.

Her lips closed down. He was trapped.

Do you know what you're doing? he wanted to ask. *How close I am to losing it?* His cock, smashed against his jeans, pulsed. He needed to adjust his clothing, to reposition his cock, but doing so meant pulling out of her mouth or releasing her knee, and he couldn't do either of those things.

Groaning, she tongued him out of her and began working her lips. "Sorry but those are muscles I never use that way." Then she leaned forward so her arms no longer supported her weight and massaged her mouth. "Good idea, lousy execution."

He would have laughed if he could have wrenched his mind off his cock. The damn thing was on overload, responding in ways it hadn't since he was seventeen. One moment he believed he had a handle on things, the next he'd reached out and snagged one of the sleeping bags. "Stand up."

"What?"

"For just a moment."

Looking confused, she scooted off the hay bale. After shaking out the bag, he spread it so she'd be protected from sharp pokes. Then he grasped her around the waist and helped her back up. Not waiting for a thank you, he took hold of her shoulders and pushed her away from him. He held on long enough to help her ease onto the hay, then worked himself into the gap between her legs.

Grabbing her wrists, he positioned her hands against her belly and leaned over her.

"What's that?" she asked, indicating her crossed wrists. "A cowboy move? Got me lassoed?"

The idea of wrapping her in lengths of rope had him increasing the pressure on her wrists. Going by the smoky look in her eyes, he didn't believe she had any objections.

"Okay, okay." She sighed. "So you don't need a rope."

"Not this time."

"This time? Let's don't go any further than right now, all right."

Because he wasn't sure where this moment was going to lead he had no objection to that boundary. Besides, her breath kept reaching his eyelashes and distracting him. At the same time, the scent of hay seeped into his pores. Hay was part of his world, woven into endless days spent on horseback with a horse's muscles under him and the animal's warmth part of him.

Releasing her wrists, he slid his fingers over her inner thighs. She moaned and turned her hips to the side. When he began working his thumbs up the sleek length, she straightened and stared up at him.

"Do you trust me?" he asked.

She laughed, a short, sharp sound. "Miguel, I don't trust myself."

Her fingers clenched and relaxed, clenched and stayed like that. Her gaze spoke of excitement and disbelief, making him wonder if she could read the same expression in him.

Holding his breath, he continued his exploration. *Hurry, damn it, hurry,* the adolescent in him screamed. At the same time the horseman who'd spent as long as it took to gain an animal's trust knew to hold back. The two emotions warring, he arched his pelvis at her.

The moment his trapped and hungry cock touched her inner right thigh, a jolt lifted him onto his toes. He couldn't remember what he'd been doing with his hands, what, if anything, she'd said about this raging river current between them. He heard nothing except their breathing, saw only her wide and barely comprehending eyes.

He asked himself if he'd survive.

4

This wasn't happening, it wasn't! No way in hell was she sprawled on her back with her legs gaping wide and a black-haired stranger closing in on her pussy.

Thank goodness for clothing! Thank goodness for a throat and a tongue and the ability to order an end to this insanity.

But although the woman she'd always believed she was put the right words in her head and the necessary strength in her muscles, she couldn't lift her hands off her belly or get her mouth to open. It had been so easy a few moments ago when she'd sucked on his finger and thumb but now . . .

Sucked on him? Her?

A shiver running through her, she blinked until he came back into focus. She didn't believe his hands had moved in the last few seconds. Just the same, he'd left her with the promise and threat of what he planned to do next. And because she absolutely and completely hated waiting, she straightened her legs and pressed them against his thighs.

What did he want, for her to encourage him to continue, maybe beg? She could do those things, if she could speak.

Clothes, gone. Hay, replaced by a soft bed. Other people, non-existent. Only her and Miguel—and the mustangs of course.

"I want to see you ride. To watch as you turn a mustang from something wild to . . ." Her mind shut down. Untangling her fingers, she massaged her belly. Her slacks had become a straightjacket, thick fabric tight around flesh that longed to be free.

To be touched.

"Where are they?" she asked.

"You want—"

"Check, please."

Spinning on his boots, he quickly covered the distance to the opening. Then he disappeared, leaving her to fight a thousand battles with her nerve endings. All too soon he was back, shadows hiding his expression.

"What?" she demanded when he remained silent.

"By the corrals. They didn't see me."

In other words, the two of them were off the others' radar scopes. Just the same, urgency nibbled at the nerve endings already on overload.

"We're going to do this?" she asked. "Just like that? Now?"

"I want. Do you?"

With every fiber of my existence, stronger than anything I've ever felt. "Yeah."

His arms were by his sides, ready for action and yet patient. But the bulge in his jeans spoke of single-mindedness. "You don't sound convinced."

"What do you want?" she snapped, wanting to pummel him and wrap her body around his at the same time. "A written invitation?"

Not dropping his gaze from hers, he cupped his cock. "This doesn't give a damn about invitations, but I need to be sure. Otherwise . . ."

Otherwise, he risked a rape charge. Were the tables ever

turned, a man insisting that the woman had been the aggressor and he'd been taken against his will? What did it matter?

"This feels unreal," she admitted. "As if some part of me I didn't know existed is responsible." Without knowing it was going to happen, she was on her feet and her fingers were at her zipper. A current ran from throat to thighs and back again. If she wasn't careful, she'd collapse.

Watching her fingers, his nostrils flared and his eyes narrowed. "Wait."

"What?"

By way of explanation, he reached into a back pocket and pulled out a thin leather wallet. Even before he opened it, she knew what he was going to do. Just the same, when he held up a small foil-wrapped package, her heart skittered and her temple throbbed. More proof of what was going to happen.

"I wasn't sure," he told her. "Before things went any further—"

"I should have thought of it." Her throat dried.

Damn it, every word was so incredibly hard, nearly as difficult as pulling the zipper all the way down and unfastening the button at her waist. She started to tug down, then stopped, exhausted.

"What?" he asked.

"I'm just—I don't know."

He muttered something unintelligible that suddenly endeared him to her. Until this moment he'd been little more than a walking, talking testosterone package to her. Now he was becoming human. Although she didn't believe he could be as overwhelmed as she felt, neither had he planned and plotted this *encounter.* She just wish he'd explain why she was so hot to have sex with a complete stranger. With him.

"Either we're going to do this or we aren't," he said. "Which is it?"

If she walked away, she'd spend the rest of the day and many more wishing to hell she'd allowed him into her. Her body would pulse with frustration that made concentrating on anything else impossible. On the other hand, the next time she looked in the mirror, she wouldn't drop her gaze in embarrassment and confusion. She wouldn't stare at her features and ask herself where the inner slut had come from.

Slut? Was it really that simple?

Or was Miguel Perez something she'd been looking for her entire adult life?

Safety or risk, civilized or wild?

"We do it," the wild slut said. "Fast. No explanations, nothing."

"And no regrets?"

She couldn't think about tomorrow, couldn't put her mind on anything except the heat flooding her being. Feeling as if she were having a heart attack, she yanked her jeans and panties down around her knees. Her legs threatening to quit on her, she leaned against the sleeping bag-covered hay.

Not once breaking eye contact, he unhooked his jeans and freed the zipper. Her lips went numb as he exposed himself and sealed his massive looking cock in latex.

No backing out now, no *what was I thinking, I'm outta here*. There was only pressing her buttocks against the bag's waterproof covering as he closed the distance between them.

Outside, a horse whinnied. A whispery sound from the opposite end of the shed made her wonder if a mouse was responsible. Thanks to the lack of a fourth wall, the air wasn't stale and smelled equally of hay and desert.

Then he closed his hands around her waist and lifted her onto the bale and only that mattered. His rough fingers on her bare middle sent heated shockwaves to every inch of her being. A sudden and powerful weakness stripped her, and if he hadn't helped her stretch out on her back, she would have collapsed like a puppet with the strings cut. Now she was staring at the tin roof, seeing nothing of him, arms outstretched and fingers clawing at dry hay.

Dangerous. The man could be the most dangerous human to walk the planet and she was exposed to him, helpless.

And ready. So damn ready that hot juices flooded her and her nipples felt as if they'd been tied in knots.

The rough and warm hands responsible for the shockwaves were now on her hip bones. The way he ran his fingertips over her belly, he *had* to know what the touch was doing to her.

"So pale," he muttered. "Your skin where the sun doesn't reach is so pale. And soft. Incredibly soft."

Unable to remember the last time she'd felt utterly feminine, she took hold of his wrists. Her thumbs pressed against his veins. When he stopped his exploration of her stomach, she guided his fingers under her top and along her ribs. Her breath whistled, and her hips twitched. She was floating, swimming without having to expend the slightest effort. If only they had the day for this.

Perhaps he read her mind about time because with a deep sigh, he reversed direction. Her belly should have remembered what his touch felt like, but the moment he trailed a fingernail there, she gasped and arched her back. Trying not to pant took all her concentration.

"Sensitive?" he muttered.

"You know the answer to that."

"Yeah, I do. And I'd give a year of my life to explore that sensitivity."

Before she could guess what he had in mind, he leaned over her and ran his tongue where his nail had been.

"Oh, God, God!"

His hand closed over her mouth. He was right, absolutely right! She needed to be quiet. But damn it, he was still tonguing her belly and the taut flesh over her hip bones, compelling her to try to bite him. Still gagging her, he blew a long, moist breath along her pubic hair.

Something white and swift surged through her. She started to thrash her head from side to side but stopped when he pressed down on her mouth. He'd repositioned himself so he was on her left side with his body pressed against her outer leg. Maybe she should have scooted away from him, but even though he was driving her crazy, freedom was the last thing she wanted.

Breathing noisily, she released his wrist and grabbed a fistful of coarse hair. When she tugged, he tried to straighten, prompting her to increase her grip. He might have imprisoned her with his hot, knowing strength, but she was no helpless captive. Far from it, she could give as good as she got.

Or not.

Although she still had hold of his hair, he didn't seem to care as he bathed her middle. When she stopped squirming and concentrated, fully, on the damn-wonderful sensation, he ran his teeth over her flank. Her flesh quivered. Nerves short-circuited.

She nearly screamed when he let go of her mouth. Then he gripped the fingers tangled in his hair. Understanding that he wanted freedom, she complied. Not knowing what to do with her hand, she let it fall back to her side. Immediately her fingers started digging into the hay again.

"I hear voices," he whispered. "Constant. Not coming closer."

"Yet," was all she could contribute. Because she couldn't remember how to blink, her eyes burned. She couldn't see him.

But she could feel, oh, yes!

What was he doing now? Oh, right, pulling her pants down around her ankles. A wave of embarrassment began and died because what did it matter what her clothes looked like? It didn't, not at all because—

Oh, shit. Because those wonderfully calloused fingers were at her core. Despite their roughness, they slid easily over her wet labia. He didn't say anything about the absolute proof of her arousal. Instead, he simply explored. Explored and glided. She stopped trying to hold still. Keeping her teeth clenched against a river of excited cries took all her strength but not her concentration.

That, of course, remained on his wonderful and overwhelming hand.

Torn between wanting him to continue and the need to finish what they'd begun before they were discovered, she parted her knees as much as the restraining fabric around her ankles allowed. Next time—what next time?—she'd strip herself naked down to her socks or even better, let him do the deed.

Maybe he needed more room. Maybe he simply enjoyed controlling her. Either way, he pressed against the insides of her knees, exposing her even more. At the same time, he pulled her toward him a few inches. A moment later he flattened his hands against her inner thighs. Without knowing how it had happened, her hands were in her hair and pulling hard enough to bring tears to her eyes.

Something hard and alive brushed her clit.

"Oh, shit!"

"Shh. Quiet."

"I can't help—"

The touch returned, lasting longer and reinforcing what she already knew. His cock was against her, promising the world.

"When you come," he asked, his tone deeper than earlier, "are you loud?"

"Sometimes."

"You can't be this time."

She knew that, damn it, knew everything except how to rein in her body. Although it might be a lie, she told him she'd remain silent. Knowing he expected her to climax spoke not of his confidence in his sexual prowess, but of his understanding of her deep-riding hunger and need.

Of course he understood. After all, hadn't she done everything except rip his clothes off and throw herself at him?

Blindsided by the question of why she needed this particular man so badly, she ground her teeth together. Neither that or her grip on her hair lessened her need.

He was what, wild? Unknown. The mysterious stranger. Sex on two legs. All that and more. A tornado.

And she needed him as much as she did air.

"Hard. Fast," she got out. "Now. Now!"

Instead of the well-primed organ her sex wept for, he gave her another taste of those work-honed fingers of his. This time he went beyond a quick but practiced exploration of her labia. This time a finger slid into her. Fast. He'd buried himself in her pussy as far as he could before her brain registered what had happened. He'd impaled her. Just like that. Taken liberties. Taken control. Taken over.

Panting open mouthed, she relaxed her grip on her hair because once more her system demanded she thrash her head. She thought she heard him grunt but whether in amusement or from his own arousal, she couldn't tell. Didn't care.

He rotated his finger, roughness sliding over satin. Mewling like a lost kitten, she propelled herself toward him, stopping only when her ass reached the end of her perch. She mewled again when he pulled out, then sucked in as much air as her lungs could hold because he'd replaced his forefinger with the middle one. Once he was again in all the way, he cupped her mons in his palm.

He seemed to be everywhere, in and around her, positioned between her legs with his breath flaming her cheeks.

"Now, please," she bleated. "Oh, God, please."

His rapid breathing had matched hers, but now the tempo seemed to increase and, was he trembling?

He uttered something that might have been a curse. Then, although she believed with every fiber in her that he wanted to go on manhandling her, he drew his finger free. Anticipation bled through her. Releasing her hair, she reached for a masculine arm but only succeeded in raking it. His tension rolled over her, and she couldn't breathe. *Be silent. Not a sound.*

The slick-on-slick touch again, her clit on fire. Raking his arm once more, she struggled to arch her back off the hay. She might have succeeded if she could have concentrated.

But there was that touch, cock pressing against her sex as if asking permission. The only thing she could do was toss her head and arch her pelvis toward him. An image of what she was doing and how she looked briefly swamped her. Then his cock stretched her, invading and gifting, and her world began and ended with him.

Something crawled up her throat, prompting her to jam the side of her hand in her mouth. She bit down, only dimly feeling pain. Knowing she wouldn't scream out what they were doing.

Fucking. Splayed like some obscene display on a desert day. A stranger humping her, pushing deep and full and wonderful until his cock was everywhere. He wasn't just in her pussy, no, not just that.

He'd invaded her being, spreading hot and delicate tissues until she didn't know where she let off and he began. It didn't matter. They'd become one, fused.

And moving.

By gripping the sleeping bag with strong fingers, she managed to remain in place as he plowed her. Concerned a cry might escape now that she wasn't gagging herself, she clenched her teeth as she'd done earlier. Mostly she met him thrust for thrust, determination for determination. Sweat bloomed along her sides and at the base of her throat. The small of her back was drenched.

His low, deep grunts carried notes of desperation. Catching his mood, she surrendered her body and will to the white force. Her climax was right there, sudden and strong. For once she'd been given no warning, no time to anticipate. Instead, the explosion loomed over her, a tidal wave. She couldn't run from it, couldn't hold it back.

Surrendering to the damn-wonderful inevitable, she threw herself into the churning current. Caught in its grip, she could only fight to breathe as it slammed her here and there, going on as never before, starting to settle only to rise up and shake her. Her jaws ached, and her fingers threatened to cramp. She couldn't see. Couldn't hear.

But feel, oh, yes, she could! And when his body first froze and then shook and his breath bled over her exposed middle, she knew he'd found his own release.

He was still inside her, still panting as rapidly as she was when her world started to come back into focus. Without her being aware of it, he'd slipped his hands under her ass and positioned her for maximum ease of entry. Although the position might have contributed to her over-the-top climax, the small of her back was beginning to protest.

Letting go of the sleeping bag, she pushed herself into a semi-upright position with her arms braced behind her. He stepped back, freeing his still-swollen cock. Looking at her, he stripped off the condom. Then he pulled up his jeans and shoved the condom in a pocket.

There was something final about his gesture, a return to sanity and civilization. She should do the same thing, cover herself and present herself as what she'd been up until a few minutes ago, a professional.

Instead, the delicious ache in her sex held her. She looked

down at what she could see of herself. Embarrassment nibbled for a moment, then faded as surely as her climax had.

She should say something but what? And why wasn't he speaking?

Lifting her gaze, she studied a man with his shirt barely tucked in and his zipper undone, a man with flushed cheeks and a chest that rose and fell in double time. What had she thought a few minutes ago, that he was wild?

The untamed was there all right, along with hints of the desert that surrounded them and the mustang waiting for his touch.

Almost as if Blanco knew she was thinking about him, a loud, proud whinny cut through the air. The sound both thrilled her and sent a chill through her. The first time she'd seen the stallion, he'd been galloping along a rise with his mares close behind. His tail and mane had floated behind him, and he'd carried his head high and proud.

She'd never forgive Miguel if he destroyed that spirit.

Not knowing what to do with her thoughts, she got off the bale and hauled her clothing back into place. She kept her gaze locked on Miguel, quaking a bit in reaction to his intense stare. Putting herself together took too long because she couldn't concentrate on what her hands were doing, but finally she'd done everything she could to make herself presentable.

"I'll leave first." His voice carried no remnants of the sex-charged tone that had played a part in flinging her over the top. "Give me a couple of minutes and then come out."

What he'd proposed made a thousand kinds of sense. Why then did she hate hearing those words? Before she'd come up with an answer, he'd spun on his heels and was heading toward the opening. She watched with her lips parted and her body humming.

She didn't want to feel like this, damn it! To still have so little control.

But could she expect anything different, she chided herself as he disappeared. The sun was touching him again, and the wind brushed over his exposed flesh. Thinking of those things made it all too easy to place him in the role of rugged cowboy. Everything about him was designed for an outdoors existence. What woman wouldn't be drawn to a man who embraced, and was embraced by, nature? He had no use for fashionable clothing, no interest in popular cars or "in" entertainment establishments. He'd probably never gone to a hair stylist or considered buying modern male grooming products.

Despite what constituted a great deal of his appeal, the question she had to face was whether those things had blinded her to a simple truth. She'd thrown herself at him and he'd used her need to his advantage.

Used her.

Filled with equal parts of regret and denial, she ran her fingers through her hair and started after him.

The sudden sunlight made her squint and hold up her hand to shade her eyes. When her eyes had adjusted, she saw that all of the men were standing outside the corral. Miguel must have just spoken because they were looking at him and nodding. Putting an end to the distance between them was harder than she wanted to admit. At the same time, she could hardly wait to be close to him so she could feel his what, his sexual appeal?

"Where'd you go?" Brod asked when she was close enough that they could carry on a conversation. "One minute you were here, the next—"

"My fault," Miguel supplied with a too-casual shrug. "I wanted to see the feed you'd been giving the mustangs. It's good quality stuff."

Brod's expression said he didn't quite buy the explanation, and she could only pray she didn't look too disheveled. Fortunately, the others who'd come to pick up a mustang were interested in what Miguel meant by "good quality." Leaving them to discuss the merits of various grades of hay, she positioned herself so Brod was between her and Miguel. Just the same, something she didn't want to name reached out from the man she'd just fucked to stroke body parts that hadn't fully recovered from the urgent coupling.

Hoping to distract herself, she studied the mustangs. Many people who knew nothing of wild horses beyond their mystique believed they lived a precarious existence, but these were well fed with glossy coats and healthy muscles.

She wanted to see Miguel on horseback, barefoot, leaning over a straining neck as the stallion under him raced for the pure joy of life.

Even more, she wanted to be the one under him.

Caught unawares, she turned her face into the wind in a determined effort to cool her inflamed cheeks. Her pussy remained imprinted with his feel, and if she'd been alone, it wouldn't take much to work herself into another climax. Even better would be a night with the near stranger who'd stormed into her world and taken over everything.

All except for having to face herself the next morning.

"If I was a betting man, I'd say the Mexican's going to blow away the competition," her supervisor said after the wranglers had departed with their new charges.

"What makes you say that?" she asked as the two of them headed toward the cabins where they'd been staying since the mustangs had been rounded up.

Brod shrugged. "Let's call it instinct. There was something about the way he studied the broncs, as if he was trying to get inside their heads. Especially the one he chose."

She'd noticed his intensity of course. She just hadn't thought of what he was doing in that light. "I wonder what he found."

"More than most people would suspect. I've been involved with mustangs long enough to realize they don't survive and thrive unless there's something going on between their ears. The Mexican gets that. My guess, he knows how to make the most of his stallion's intellect."

"His name is Miguel Perez," she said, her tone sharp.

Brod shot a glance in her direction. "All right, Miguel Perez. He made quite an impression on you, didn't he."

Because it hadn't been a question, she wasn't sure whether he expected a response. Unless he pressed the issue, she wasn't going to say anything. They were nearly at the cabins. Once there, they'd go their separate ways. She'd be alone with her emotions and still-hungry body.

"My guess," Brod continued, "he's spent more time around animals than humans. He sure as hell thinks and acts like one."

"How can you say that? You only spent a few minutes with him."

"Same with you, right?" This time she couldn't fathom the look he gave her. "What I'm saying is, why do you care about what might be my half-baked attempt to psychoanalyze him?"

"I didn't—"

Brod held up his hand. "Look, I'm sorry I said anything. I wish all the wranglers we'll be dealing with are the best. Lord knows the mustangs need this new lease on life. Otherwise, we're going to have to make some decisions about them none of us wants to. I'm just glad it isn't me trying to domesticate them."

Relieved to have the conversation take this turn, she agreed with him. Then, although she was too restless to think about settling down, she went into her cabin. It had always struck her as barely large enough to accommodate one person. Now the walls closed in around her as never before.

The reason was both simple and complicated. She felt swamped by what she'd done in that hay shed. The near whore who'd invited a stranger into her body wasn't her. Never had been, never would be.

Except this once.

Once.

"I don't know why the hell it happened," she told Miguel even though he wasn't around to hear her. "What lasso you threw over me. But I'm not some untamed bronc you brand and—"

Unable to finish, she opened the small refrigerator only to slam the door. Suddenly she felt sorry for Blanco. No matter how much the stallion craved his freedom, he was in Miguel's clutches. Miguel's eyes would probe his heart, and Miguel's mind would reach deep into his soul.

Thank God she wasn't a mustang.

5

Blanco stared at Miguel from under the longest, darkest lashes Miguel had seen in years. Three days ago he'd placed the stallion in the spacious wooden corral where he worked and then had left him alone so the mustang could become accustomed to his new surroundings. Although there were no other horses in the corral, nearby enclosures held cow ponies. Because Blanco had spent his entire life with a herd, it was vital for the mustang to be close to others of his kind.

He entered the corral carrying nothing but a long, slender pole which he held casually at his side. Blanco had already galloped to the far end of the enclosure and stood on wide-spread legs, poised to jump in whatever direction seemed safest.

"Shhh, big boy," Miguel crooned as he approached an inch at a time. "Shhh, nothing to be afraid of. Nothing to want to stomp into the dust."

Apparently not buying into his logic, the stallion reared.

"Shhh, no need to do that. In case you haven't noticed, I'm not a cougar. Just an ugly cowboy hauling this." He shook the pole, careful not to lift it above the horse's eye level.

Even as he'd headed toward what he'd labeled his salvage project, his mind had been not on the mustang, but the woman he'd met the day Blanco had entered his life. In truth, Dawn Glass hadn't been out of his mind since he'd first laid eyes on her.

Amend that, fucked her.

Damn it, he didn't want or need that! As foreman of the massive D&B Ranch, his duties and responsibilities kept him on his feet from dawn until well after dusk. Year around, more than a dozen cowboys answered to him. Beyond that, the well-being of more than ten thousand cattle and twenty-some working horses depended on the decisions he made, to say nothing of the amount of sweat that ran off him.

He loved his life. Looking after livestock came as naturally to him as other men were drawn to trying to make fortunes. Although he'd put enough away from his earnings to buy his own spread—which he would when he found the right one—he didn't give a damn about getting rich.

What it all boiled down to was, everything revolved around horses. Yes, the cattle paid the bills, but they didn't own his heart.

"Shh. Shh." Keeping his muscles relaxed, he closed more of the distance between himself and Blanco. Although his voice was lower than his mother's had been, like her, he relied on the same calming sound. Being captured had been traumatic for Blanco, and he'd come away from the experience believing all humans yelled and made loud noises. First order of business was to show the stallion that there was another way.

"Shh. We're doing this together, this getting to know each other business. I'm on your side. It might not look like it right now, but I have your best interests at heart."

Apparently he'd made an impact with Blanco as witnessed by the way the horse lowered his head a little. Less white showed in his eyes than before. Dawn hadn't been anything like the wary, yet curious bronc, but he'd intrigued both of them. He just didn't understand why the woman had been drawn to him.

Again irritated for letting himself get distracted, he slowly held out the stick. Inch by inch it neared the mustang's withers. The moment the stick touched Blanco's shoulder, the stallion snorted and his loose skin shivered.

"Shh. Nothing to get riled up about, just this cowboy trying to get on your good side. Let me take a guess. You'd love to be scratched there." He guided the stick over Blanco's withers. "Ah, feels good, doesn't it. Used to be, you could get your mares to do a little nibbling and licking in the spots a guy can't reach."

At first Blanco's stare said he didn't trust the human any further than he could kick him, but as the seconds ticked on, he relaxed until his lower lip sagged. In no hurry, Miguel rubbed along Blanco's back until he reached the solid rump. By then, Blanco had all but closed his eyes and was breathing slow and deep.

Damn it, why did he have to imagine Dawn Glass's hands running over him? Why not some powerhouse of a woman? But no, his mind, and more, was putting the woman he'd fucked the other day in that role.

Giving up, he let unaccustomed fantasy take over. He'd been out on the range all day rounding up strays and repairing fences. By the time he reached home he was tired and hungry and feeling every one of his thirty-one years and then some. Muscles he could ignore most of the time ached, and the only things he wanted in life was a beer, a shower, and dinner, in whatever order they came.

But when he stepped into his place, he realized he wasn't alone after all. *She* was waiting for him, naked as the day she was born, rose and lavender-scented oils on a table next to his bed.

"I've been waiting for you," she said. "Lie down. I know what you need."

Blanco snorted, bringing him back to the here and now. He'd stopped moving the pole over the horse, something Blanco obviously didn't approve of. Shaking his head, he went back to work, but as he picked up his singsong monologue, the image he'd shaken free of returned.

In the time he'd been gone, the spent cowboy he was had removed his boots, jeans, and shirt, and was stretched out on his belly on clean sheets. Dawn stood over him with her soft, warm hands spread over his lower back. She began kneading motions he felt clear through to the other side. Much more and staying on his belly, or specifically his hard cock, would be out of the question.

Another snort from Blanco. Another shake of his head. Even as he again administered to the mustang, he had no choice but to acknowledge the pulsing knot between his legs.

"Shh. Shh. A piece of advice for you, Blanco. Don't ever let a mare get under your skin. Use them for what nature intended but never let it become more than that."

Apparently Blanco agreed as witnessed by the way the mustang's head bobbed up and down. The difference, one of them anyway, between horses and humans was that mares and stallions weren't wired to commit to each other.

"It's a damn good thing I'll never see her again," he said, tugging on his jeans in a less than successful attempt to give his cock more moving room. "And if things get upside down and I do, I'm going to keep my damn hands off her. Not let her get anywhere near me."

Only three of the wranglers who'd accepted the training challenge had dropped out of the program. One had had no choice when he broke his leg. Another turned his mustang back in, citing lack of time. The third had lost custody when a local vet had called BLM about the wrangler's rough treatment of a two-year-old mare he owned.

None of the three had been Miguel.

Dawn hadn't expected anything different from the man she had no intention of seeing again.

Sacramento was hot, the sky hazy. Still, as she drove toward the fairgrounds where the Mustang Challenge was being held, Dawn paid little attention to weather conditions. Instead, she once again asked the same question she'd been putting to herself since requesting a week's vacation.

Why was she doing this?

The simple answer, of course, was that in the hundred days since she'd last seen Miguel, she'd thought of him every one of those days. More to the point, he'd been part of her nights. Even now with traffic hemming her in on all sides, a too-familiar heat stabbed at her pussy, prompting her to squeeze her legs together.

Damn, but the man had taken hold of a certain part of her anatomy.

All right, so much for the simple answer, she acknowledged as the driver ahead of her touched his brakes, prompting her to do the same. Hadn't she resolutely reminded herself that she wasn't hardwired for one-night stands? She could count her lovers on the fingers of a single hand, proof that she didn't believe in bed hopping. Not counting Miguel, her sex partners had become so after lengthy lead-ins during which she'd gotten to know them as human beings. Even when her libido argued that knowledge didn't have to come before scratching certain powerful itches, she'd held true to her personal code.

She was a *good* girl, maybe a little repressed in terms of today's free-swinging single scene but able to face herself in the mirror. At least she'd always been able to until—

Activating the left turn signal, she started to pass the vehicle ahead of her. She didn't finish her thought until she'd settled back in the right lane. Okay, the deal was, even after one hundred days, she had no logical or sane explanation for why she'd let Miguel Perez jump her bones.

Or, despite the modified missionary position, had she jumped his bones?

Too complex. Too technical.

She was here to see what he'd accomplished with a wild stallion, that's all. A bit of a busman's holiday, something to take back with her and maybe share with future mustang wranglers. She had no intention of letting him know she was here, none at all.

Maybe.

"No *maybe* to it, Dawn!" she chided herself aloud. "No playing with fire and that man's a pyromaniac where you're concerned. You ain't got a lick of sense around him."

Nothing except fascination for a man who in many ways was as wild as the horse he'd taken home with him.

And she didn't need wild.

It scared the hell out of her.

Although he'd never been to the Sacramento fairgrounds, as Miguel stood on the bleachers overlooking the riding arena where he and the other wranglers would start competing tomorrow, his thoughts kept straying from his surroundings. After getting Blanco out of his trailer and into the stall that had been assigned him, after making sure the stallion had adequate feed and water, he'd decided to familiarize himself with the setting. A handful of other wranglers were doing the same—lean, solitary men in western garb staring down at the large, empty enclosure.

Surely they were thinking back over the past three-plus

months, mentally replaying the time they'd spent with their mustangs, questioning some aspects of the training, feeling pride in other areas.

They weren't fighting distraction, especially not *that* distraction.

Determined to get a handle on his mind and body, Miguel reminded himself that he hadn't heard from, let alone seen, Dawn Glass since the day he'd taken possession of Blanco—the day he'd insanely fucked the BLM employee.

As a teen, especially in the year following his mother's death, he'd gotten drunk. More nights than he wanted to admit, he'd chased one beer with another until he'd either passed out or thrown up. Finally, he'd faced facts. His damn-stupid behavior was going to land him in a world of trouble if he didn't get a grip.

Well, he'd gotten a grip on his drinking.

And fortunately, he'd regained sanity after one round with Dawn Glass. He wouldn't make the mistake of a repeat performance.

How could he?

They weren't even in the same part of the state.

According to the copy of the events' agenda she'd been given when she'd walked onto the fairgrounds this morning, the first day's events would begin with a veterinarian examining all forty of the mustangs who'd been entered in the Mustang Challenge. They'd be checked for body conditioning, which constituted 20% of the total score, and when that was over, the in-hand competition would begin. Fortunately, the flier explained that in-hand meant each horse would be ridden through the same obstacle course and their efforts compared.

The stands were still filling and she was able to find a seat in the front row. Wondering if Miguel might look up and spot her almost had her scrambling higher, but she wanted the best possible view. She tried to settle in and relax, but her hands kept sweating and she'd give a great deal to be able to press those sweaty hands against her crotch.

Damn it! Knowing she'd soon be seeing *him* shouldn't be doing this to her.

But it was.

Her thoughts jumped and started, turned and stopped. Time passed. More and more people moved in around her, reminding her of how claustrophobic she'd felt on the freeway. When were things supposed to get started, damn it! Waiting for Christmas morning back when she was five and six hadn't been any harder than this.

Then, suddenly, energy filled the air. Shivering despite the heat, she stared at the open gate at the far end. A horse led by a wrangler wearing high, narrow-toed cowboy boots approached the gate. Then they were inside the arena. A single glance had already assured her that this wasn't Miguel. Just the same, her heartbeat quickened, and the delicious ache between her legs had her squirming. Soon, soon!

Horse and trainer after horse and trainer came into view. According to the announcer, the vet had already made his examinations, which meant the action would soon begin. Her eyes ached from staring, and her muscles burned from the tension she couldn't shake off.

Then it happened. If someone had held a gun to her head, she couldn't have said what made him stand out from the others even though they all wore Stetsons. Yes, his body had been carved by a physical existence, but his wasn't the only one. Like other wranglers, he carried himself with a self-confidence she would have given a great deal to emulate right now. Although he didn't look behind him at Blanco, she sensed a connection between the two.

Beyond working with the stallion, what had he been doing for the past hundred days? Her study of his application and the recommendations that had accompanied it had told her he was the foreman of one of the largest cattle ranches in northern California, maybe the whole state. The ranch owner and a local vet had been unanimous in their praise for Miguel's ability to work with horses. What was it the vet had said—something about Miguel being part mustang.

That was his appeal—his appeal and what caused her heart to leap in something that might be fear. He might not have been born in the wilderness the way Blanco had, but he understood the stallion on a level she could only struggle to try to grasp. He'd gotten not just into Blanco's head, but the horse's soul as well.

Just as he'd done to her.

Clapping coming from all around brought her back to the here and now. She'd been so intent on finding Miguel that she hadn't paid much attention to what was in the arena. Now she saw that an obstacle course had been laid out, and the first horse was getting ready to go through it. The course included a number of rails laid out on the ground only a few inches apart, a line of barrels of various heights, several tires, a haphazard arrangement of hay bales, and something resembling a goalpost with long, bright plastic streamers hanging from the top.

The first horse, led by its handler, did a great job of stepping over each rail one at a time. It balked at squeezing between two closely placed bales and refused to have anything to do with going under the goalpost streamers. The second horse reared when its handler tried to get it to place a front hoof in the tires, and like the one before it, said "to hell with that" about the flapping plastic.

Maybe that opinion was catching as witnessed by the reaction of the mustangs that came after. It didn't help that the wind was blowing, causing the streamers to dance crazily. Just the same, she was impressed by how patient the wranglers were and the way the horses extended their heads toward them for a reassuring pat.

Miguel, finally Miguel!

And Blanco looking as free as he'd been before his capture, without so much as a halter let alone a lead rope.

A couple of wranglers had taken their charges through the obstacle course without ropes on their halters. Neither had been completely successful, but her admiration for what they'd accomplished gave her a good idea of what Miguel and Blanco would have to do to win the competition.

Even before horse and man reached the starting line, something shifted in her. She no longer sat looking down at the action. Instead, she was beside Miguel, taking Blanco's place, feeling the invisible connection between the two. Miguel's self-confidence and belief in what Blanco was capable of seeped into her. In her heart of hearts, Miguel became a thousand years old, an ancient soul. He had no existence beyond the bond he had with Blanco—with her.

In a dim way she realized the stands had hushed as everyone watched man and mustang work together. "He's a stallion," someone behind her whispered. "And with all those mares here . . ."

Belatedly, she realized that the speaker had been talking about Blanco and not Miguel. But as Miguel stood near Blanco, mouthing something or making quiet hand gestures, she wondered if there were any difference between the two.

Not where she was concerned.

She, a woman in heat, had been turned on by a two-footed stallion.

"Ladies and gentlemen, give this wrangler and his charge a hand," the announcer said unnecessarily after Blanco had walked unhesitantly through the dancing plastic streamers. Fighting the urge to jump to her feet, she joined in the enthusiastic applause as Blanco rubbed his forehead against Miguel's chest.

Smiling for the first time, Miguel reached up and scratched between Blanco's ears. And Dawn, who couldn't have taken her eyes off Miguel if doing so blinded her, felt the communication everywhere.

Touch me! Let me feel everything.

He hadn't yet returned to the spot where he and Blanco were supposed to stand when they weren't going through their paces, when Miguel sensed something he hadn't been aware of back when he'd concentrated on keeping the connection with the mustang. At first he told himself he was simply responding to the audience's positive reaction to Blanco's performance, but this wasn't just approval, simple respect. Something deeper was at work.

Somewhere.

Looking up with a hand on Blanco's neck and his Stetson shielding his eyes, he scanned the crowd. There were so many people and so much movement, how could he—

Her.

Not blinking, he intensified his gaze. Dawn Glass was surrounded and yet she stood out from the others, her own gaze more intense than anyone else's. He'd told himself she wouldn't be here, that she had better things, more important things to do with her life than to watch the challenge. They'd had what, only a few minutes together. No way would she drive for hours, rent a motel room, and spend days in this flat, crowded city.

But she had.

Blanco's skin rippled, taking a little of Miguel's attention off the only member of the audience he cared about. Not sure how long he'd been standing there staring, he started walking, making clicking sounds as he did. He returned to his assigned spot and resolutely studied the next competitor instead of doing what had to be more dangerous than stepping in front of a Brahma bull—look at her again.

He didn't know what her game, her intent was. But he wasn't some damn stud.

He wasn't!

6

The day's events were over, Miguel and Blanco the hands-down winners of the initial competition. But although Dawn acknowledged a quiet pride in their accomplishments, that pride was complicated by everything else she was feeling—especially deep inside her core.

In deference to the heat, she'd worn shorts and a short-sleeve blouse. Accustomed to her uniform, the change had increased her awareness of herself as a woman. Either that or the moment of eye contact between her and Miguel was responsible.

Damn it, she had no business heading toward the long structure she'd learned contained the stalls the mustangs were being kept in. Granted, other people were milling around them so it wasn't as if she'd stand out, but unlike a number of the others, she wasn't related to a competitor or considering buying one of the mustangs.

Was she the only one more interested in the wrangler than his charge?

Judging by a trio of early twenty-something women in

skintight jeans and western shirts with more buttons than necessary open, she wasn't alone in her focus. She'd heard of sports
groupies so it wasn't a stretch to realize that wranglers held the
same sexual appeal for certain women.

So that's what it all boiled down to, did it? This journey of
hers had nothing, or rather little to do with Miguel Perez as a
separate human being. He was a cowboy, macho male to the
max, at one with open plains and part of the heritage of the old
west.

No, she argued with herself as she reached the extensive stables, she wasn't some airhead broad seduced by the allure of the
West. Then what was she?

Too many damn complicated questions!

Her legs were unsteady and her palms sweaty as she called
up the courage to look in the first stall. A horse was standing
there munching on hay and looking nothing like Blanco. And
no wrangler, mostly no wrangler.

The trio of young women about twenty feet ahead of her all
giggled at the same time, and she felt ridiculous and a bit like a
stalker. A stalker after the man who'd spread her legs, once.

The air smelled of horse and hay, and as she made her way
down the long line of stalls with the top half of their doors
open, she mentally went back to the time she'd spent with the
recently captured members of Blanco's herd. Even with the
desert and isolation and dust, she'd fallen so in love with the assignment that she'd put in to be part of what might become its
next phase. Although what was under consideration was con-
troversial, she believed the mustangs' future depended on it.
Had Miguel heard about the plan, and if so what had his reaction been?

"Dawn?"

Her name, on his tongue, sounding like liquid fire. Licking
at her skin and spreading deep. Touching a place maybe only he
knew about.

She turned without conscious thought. From what she could tell, he'd been in the stall but coming out when he spotted her, either that or something about her had telegraphed her presence to him. Not wanting to have that much power, she waited while he locked the half door behind him. Sticking his head out the opening, Blanco whinnied. The sound echoed inside her.

"I saw you," he said, his hands at his sides, straw sticking to his jeans and boots.

"I know you did."

Nothing. Not another word between them, only sensation like a building mountain storm and her pussy on fire and instantly hard nipples pressing against her bra. He was everything her imagination had remembered, and more. Rugged like faded barn wood and strong as an ancient oak. Again she was stuck by the agelessness in him, the conduit running from the settlement of the West to the present day. She guessed he'd had to force himself to drive his truck and trailer onto the freeway and head south into civilization. Unlike her, he probably hadn't checked into a motel but was staying on the grounds near his horse.

A horse he'd soon turn over to someone else.

"You did incredibly well today," she managed.

"Not me, Blanco."

"He wouldn't have known what to do if it hadn't been for you. Getting him to walk through those streamers, and without any ropes, how did you accomplish that?"

"Blanco and I understand each other," he said, glancing at the stallion. Then his attention was back on her and she felt as Blanco must have the day his freedom had ended—trapped.

Deliciously trapped.

"The two of you think the same way?" she asked, hoping her attempt at a light tone would get her through the next few seconds. And after that?

"I let him inside my head."

Shouldn't it be the other way around? Gaining Blanco's trust and obedience by getting inside the stallion's primitive mind? But the truth was, she didn't know enough about what natural horsemanship gentling constituted. If she could get her mind, emotions, and body off the moments they'd spent fucking, she'd ask him to educate her.

Instead, she stared up at him while her legs trembled and heated. This was why she'd come here, the only reason. She *had* to see him. Touch him. Have sex again. Maybe even kiss him.

"Tomorrow's the riding competition," she heard him say. "Will you be here?"

As long as I'm alive. "I'm planning on it."

"Good."

So far he'd seemed to have no difficulty keeping his end of the conversation going. Now that had changed, making her wonder what was going through him. His thoughts had to be on her, but did he want to go on talking or were there other things he'd rather be doing, another woman—

A cold river of emotion forced her to widen her stance. What a damnable fool she'd been to think other women didn't want him. The presence of the attractive young women she'd just seen were proof of that.

"Ah, I didn't mean to—you must have plans for tonight."

Instead of replying, he stared at her, his gaze so intense it burned her. She was so damn transparent and pitiful! A sex-hungry broad who'd driven hundreds of miles for a second chance at meaningless sex. Ashamed, she wiped her hands on her hips.

"You, ah, you said you learned your horsemanship from your mother. She must be proud of you."

"She was."

"Was? Is she—dead?"

"Yes."

"I'm sorry." Did he expect her to say anything else?

"So am I."

"She must have been young."

"She was."

"What—happened?"

"She was thrown."

"My God."

"It shouldn't have happened, but it did."

Was he telling her that working with horses was inherently dangerous or that his mother had made a mistake that had cost her her life? Incapable of forming the words that might lead to an explanation, she stepped toward him. Half believing he'd shake her off, she reached for his hand. He let her take it, and when she lifted his hand and pressed it against her breasts, his darkening gaze sucked her in.

"Were you there?" she asked, pulling his strength into her.

"No. But even if I had been, it wouldn't have made a difference."

As she stood with his still fingers on her breasts and their legs inches apart, he spun a brief tale of a remarkable and wild woman whose life had ended on a trail leading up a ski mountain in the middle of summer. She'd been hired by the ski resort to take a trio of pack horses carrying repair equipment to the top of the mountain. The pack horses had been hers but not the mare supplied for her to ride. The mare had belonged to one of the resort employees who'd assured her that it had been on the trail numerous times and could be trusted to lead the pack animals.

What the mare turned out to be was terrified of the cougar they'd encountered.

"No one was with them when it happened so I don't know all the details," Miguel quietly said. "When Mom didn't show up they went looking for her. They found her, dead. Against a boulder."

Sensing how hard it was for Miguel to know his mother had died alone, she kissed his knuckles. Heat-energy still hummed over her nerve endings, but the sensation was blunted—for the moment—by her determination to comfort him, if that's what he wanted from her.

"How do you know a cougar . . ."

"From the scratches on the horse's flank."

"Then it was more than her being thrown," she said, wondering if that made a difference. "The horse she was riding was being attacked. It panicked."

He was still, too still. Although there was a graceful fluidity to the way he moved, it seemed to her that until this moment he'd always been in motion. This contrast was saying something she didn't understand, or did she?

"What bothers you is the idea that she was killed doing something you believe she was born to do, isn't it?" she asked.

More silence from him kicked up her heart rate. She waited for him to jerk free, to retreat to wherever it was men went when they wanted to protect their emotions. She shouldn't have intruded on his personal emotional space! Should have kept their relationship physical.

"I'm sorry," she started, then shook her head. Yes, their relationship had been purely physical and wanting to recapture that was why she was here. But right now sex wasn't enough. "No," she amended. "I'm not. I was going to say I had no business trying to analyze what you've been through, but from what I know of you, that's the only conclusion I can come to."

"You don't know me."

Damn him for being such a macho male! For locking up his emotions, or trying to. "No, I don't. Not all the way. But—"

"I don't want to talk about it, all right?" he said and pulled free. "My mother died years ago. Let her stay that way."

7

Miguel had stepped back into Blanco's stall, closing the half door behind him as he did. At first Dawn simply stared at where he'd been while the warmth left from his hand on her seeped out of her and into the early evening air. She felt adrift and lost, rejected. Just the same, she couldn't let things end like this.

Pulling courage from deep inside her, she walked over to the stall and pulled on the door. It opened too easily. Studying his back and outstretched hand on Blanco's neck, she stepped inside. He didn't acknowledge her, but his awareness of her presence played out in the rigid set of his shoulders.

"I'll apologize if that's what you want," she said. "But I think we'll both agree it's the truth. Your mother should still be alive, not dead at the hands of something she loved so much."

"It doesn't matter, not after all these years."

"Maybe. Maybe not. Miguel, please look at me." The words said, she wished she could take them back. Even with her eyes still adjusting to the shadows in here, he was the most incredibly put-together man she'd ever seen. A true cowboy, his legs were slightly bowed, his ass and thighs hardened by the lifestyle that had chosen him.

Wild.

Then he faced her, Blanco right behind him as if they were one and the same, and she couldn't think. Yet felt. Everything.

There it was, raw sex slamming into every particle of her being and her longing to stretch out her arms in welcome.

He felt the same thing. He had to! Otherwise, why was he closing the distance between them and taking hold of both of her wrists? Placing one over the other, he secured them in a single paw. The rough calluses at the base of his fingers took her thoughts back to the only other time they'd been on her body and how much she'd loved the sensations.

"You came alone?" he asked.

"Yes."

"Good."

In the silence that followed, she weighed the emotion behind the single word. She'd been hoping to have time alone with him and for no one from work to know what she was doing. Did he understand how vulnerable she felt?

On the brink of asking the same of him, she reconsidered. If he was here with another, like a woman, he'd let her know. Otherwise, she'd take whatever he gave her.

On the tail of a low snort from Blanco, Miguel brought her hands down by his right side. The move pulled her off balance, compelling her to shuffle closer to him to keep from falling. Her thighs kissed his.

Electrified by the contact, she sucked in a breath in an attempt to put distance between them. Then, giving into the insanity that had brought her first to Sacramento and tonight to his turf, she eased against him. His free arm went around her shoulders.

"I didn't know if I'd ever see you again," he said.

"You could have called, said something."

"So could you."

True but what would she have said after "hello." *Could you please come fuck me? Meet me in a motel room? Tell me how to stop obsessing about you?*

"I thought about it," he was saying.

"So did I." *Endlessly.*

She was trying to think what to say next when he released her hands and spread his fingers over her throat. With his arm still around her, she felt caught, not trapped but closed in on. Surrounded by *him*.

The stall was too small. Blanco took up too much room and might demand even more. They couldn't possibly have sex in here. Could they?

A mix of nearby male and female voices supplied the answer. Whatever groping might take place in here wouldn't go beyond that. There'd be no undressing, no end to the ache that was everywhere and everything.

"I'm not used to thinking so much about a woman," he said, still holding her in his strange embrace. "I didn't like feeling like that. That's why I didn't call or come see you."

"The solitary cowboy then? Free to ride the range unencumbered?"

"Maybe."

As when they'd been talking about his mother, she'd gotten too close. Even with his hands on her, she felt him drawing away. Damn him, if this was how he reacted every time a woman breached his personal space—

Confused, she pulled his hand off her throat. He could have resisted of course, but he'd let her have her way. In this.

"Where are you staying?" she asked. "On the grounds?"

He nodded. "There's a camper on my pickup."

Large enough to accommodate two people? "Oh."

After a moment, he placed both hands on her shoulders and

held her at arms' length. She felt small again, and alive. Terribly alive. Horny and vulnerable. About to combust.

"What are you looking at?" she demanded, unable to take any more of the stare she couldn't fathom.

"You. Trying to figure things out."

"What things?"

By way of an answer, if that's what it was, he marched her backward until her spine pressed against the wall across from where Blanco continued to observe the two humans in his space. Miguel released her but only so he could flatten a forearm over her breasts and hold her in place. "I want you here, right here. Not moving until I've figured out what to do with you."

She could do that, do anything he wanted. It wasn't dark yet, but if he told her to strip down to nothing, she wouldn't think of the consequences beyond what the sight of her might do to him. How strange to care about nothing except him.

And liberating.

Blanco gave another of his short, soft snorts. She would have laughed if Miguel hadn't pressed his free palm against her mouth just then. Although she guessed he was warning her to say nothing, she couldn't help nibbling on his baby finger.

His chuckle, the first she'd heard from him, made her smile. Knowing they had precious little in the way of privacy was both disconcerting and exciting. Of course Blanco had a clear view of whatever took place.

She was trying to look over her shoulder at the mustang when sudden, unexpected pressure against her mons lifted her onto her toes. Miguel had released her mouth and now cupped her sex, or rather what he could reach of it through her cotton shorts. "That was . . ."

"What? Don't you want me to?"

"I do, Miguel, I do." Sighing in expectation and pleasure,

she settled back down onto the balls of her feet. His forearm still pressed against her breasts; she'd have to fight him if she wanted to free herself, not that she had any interest in doing so.

How long had she waited for him to touch and control her like this, months. Thousands of months.

Eyes blurring, she stared at the ceiling she couldn't have described if her life depended on it and gave into his touch. Became his touch. He no longer simply rested his forearm against her breasts but had rotated his arm and now covered one breast with his palm. The other palm, of course, continued to shelter and tease her crotch. Both hands were moving, kneading her clothing and beneath that flesh in danger of melting.

Her mouth dried. In contrast, her sex juices drenched her underpants. She dimly acknowledged how quickly they'd gone from a simple "hello" to groping—or rather her being groped. But she wouldn't have come here if she hadn't wanted this or something like it to happen.

And more.

Once again the nearby speakers' voices filtered into Blanco's stall. Someone said something about rusty tasting water. Another someone agreed.

"We can't—" she began.

"I know."

Because she couldn't do anything on her own, she waited for him to lay out what they needed to do and where they should go, but he continued to hold her suspended somewhere on the downhill side of sanity. Yes, she was still in danger of melting, but it had become more than that. A single flame and she'd go off like a rocket.

"My life's pretty solitary," he told her with his breath warming the top of her head. "Not much interaction with the opposite sex."

Because you're as wild as the land you roam. "I'm surrounded by the opposite sex, not that it matters."

"No work-related affairs?"

"None." His hands and arms had gone still on her. "Most are married. Those that aren't—there's never been anything. No spark."

"Not like what's happening between us?"

"Not remotely," she admitted, suddenly on the brink of laughter. "This *thing* we have going defies description."

"Yeah, it does." Leaning over, he placed his lips against the top of her head.

The unexpected whisper of intimacy relaxed her, soothed a little of the energy snapping throughout her. She tried to imagine them years down the road when looking at each other didn't send them racing for the nearest bed. Instead, they'd curl up together on the couch to watch TV.

No, they were far from that.

Needing something she couldn't define, she ran her fingers over his arms. Next she slid them under his shirtsleeve where powerful muscles reinforced what she knew of his life.

"I love it that you're a cowboy," she told him. "The time-lessness, the permanency of what you do."

"Permanency?"

"You don't agree?"

"I wonder, will my son or daughter be able to earn a living the way I have, or are things changing too much? Like the mustangs, will they be corralled?"

"You think they shouldn't be?"

"I want them left alone to live the way they have for hundreds of years."

"That's not possible."

"Isn't it?"

Was this the time to tell him about the BLM program she'd signed on for? Yes, but if she did, it might ruin everything between them.

Maybe because he continued to trap her with his unmoving

body, she left off her exploration of his arms and remained silent. Taking hold of his shirt, she tugged it out of his waistband. She touched his warm, naked sides.

"Careful," he groaned.

"You're telling me to be careful, after this?" She pushed her hips toward him.

"I'm just warning you."

"And I'm doing the same."

When he didn't reply, she risked touching him again. No, she wouldn't say anything that could jeopardize these moments. Later, much later. He shivered, and his breath snagged. Taking pity on him, she increased the contact so hopefully her touch no longer tickled. With his lower body angled away from hers, she could only guess what was going on between his legs. Hoped it was what she needed.

Blanco stomped his foot and snorted, loudly. Laughter fueled by nervous anticipation escaped her lips. "I think he wants us to leave him alone."

"After what he did today, he deserves the rest." His fingers still trailing over her mons, Miguel took a miniscule step backward. "It isn't much, but my camper's private."

"I'm sure it is," she managed, unable to drag her fingers off a part of his skin that hadn't been rubbed rough by the elements.

8

Miguel was careful not to touch Dawn as he led the way to the collection of campers, trailers, and tents at the far end of the fairgrounds. Because he'd fed, watered, and rubbed Blanco down before she'd shown up, he only had to make sure the stallion was settled in for the night before going to bed himself. At least that had been his plan before the woman who'd taken up too much of his thoughts had made her presence known.

He was a fool, a damn turned-on fool!

Pulling his keys out of his back pocket, he unlocked the camper door. Instead of climbing into it, however, he pushed the door open and stepped back to let her go first. If she couldn't handle the cramped quarters, now was the time for her to say.

After a brief hesitation, she brushed past him, climbed the three steps, and entered the small, metal structure. Staring at her neatly rounded ass, he forced himself to come to grips with reality. She, the only woman he'd ever fucked within a few minutes of meeting her, had come looking for him. She'd seen what he'd accomplished with Blanco and hopefully understood how proud he was of the intelligent stallion. More to the point of the moment, she'd endured his adolescent groping of her in Blanco's stable. Even more to the point, she'd agreed to come here.

Yeah, he was a fool! A mature man would have handled things differently, damn it! Instead of zeroing in on her shorts-shielded crotch, a male worthy of the label would have taken her hand, asked her out to dinner, something, anything civilized.

But he hadn't.

Because?

Shaking his head, he trooped in after her, switching on the light as he did. She was standing next to what passed for a table with the world's smallest stove and built-in refrigerator on the other side. Behind her was a double bed, elevated so it fit in the part of the camper that sat on top of his truck's cab.

Unwanted nerves clamped hold of him. He couldn't remember the last time he'd questioned his ability to satisfy a woman, maybe not since his teens. His confidence between the sheets had almost nothing to do with the size of his cock, which he figured was in the average range. He had confidence in his body, specifically its ability to perform whatever his lifestyle required of it. He was in good physical shape, lean where he understood women wanted men to be lean, muscled in the appropriate places, flexible. His endurance held him in good stead through days that sometimes lasted twenty hours.

Looking at Dawn Glass, however, he knew those things weren't enough. If tonight was going to be what they both needed and deserved, he'd have to bring more to the table. As for what that *more* was—

"I'm shaking." Her voice had gone up a little. "I feel like a freshman girl on prom night."

"I've never been to a prom."

"No kidding." Her smile started tentative but then grew. "Why not? I'd think the girls would be asking you."

"I had to choose between spending money on everything that went with a prom and feeding our horses."

"Ours? Your mother's and yours you mean?"

Even with memories of the relationship between mother and son getting in the way, he remembered to nod. He wasn't sure he wanted to be talking about this, but for one of the few times in his life, words were easier than silence. After all, a few minutes ago when he hadn't known what to say around her, he'd wound up with his hand between her legs.

Like he had the right.

"I'm trying to understand the ah, relationship the two of you had," she told him, her hands interlaced over her lower belly and his attention speeding to that part of her anatomy.

"We were in life together. For the most part, it was just the two of us, doing what gave us a sense of pride and completion, even if we weren't getting rich."

"Working with horses, you mean?"

Again he had to remind himself to nod. Strange, he couldn't remember the last time he'd told anyone about life with a parent who'd given birth to him when she was sixteen and needed him as much as he needed her. Maybe never.

"I wish you could have met her." He meant it.

"I wish I could have too. From what I've seen of your skill with horses, she taught you well."

"There was little teaching. Just following her lead and loving it as much as she did."

She was the one doing the nodding now, the movement slow but steady. Her gaze remained fastened on him. Seeing beneath the surface? "Thank you for telling me that."

Say something, like, you're welcome. Like I needed to. Instead, he wrapped himself in familiar silence. He'd said only the half of it when he'd let her know his camper was small. His need to bury himself deep and dangerous in her grew.

"I'm not much good at small talk," he admitted.

"The strong, silent cowboy." Reaching out, she stroked the side of his neck. "That's all right. We aren't here for small talk."

What are we here for, beyond the obvious? he wanted to ask. *Do you understand? Can you explain so I will?* "I'm sorry." He indicated the surroundings, but his mind and more were on the lingering sensation her touch had spawned. His hard-on had bloomed the moment he'd recognized her. Now her fingers had stroked his skin and his entire body had burst into flames.

"What are you sorry about?" she asked.

"That it's so cramped."

Her mouth twitched. "It's better than a bale of hay."

Grateful for her attempt at levity, he nodded agreement. "Did—I hope that didn't cause you any embarrassment."

"My supervisor didn't say anything, but I think he had suspicions."

Had holding up his end of a conversation ever been this hard? If he'd always been this tongue-tied around the opposite sex, no wonder he'd never asked a girl to the prom. Even as he pondered the possibility, memories of the feminine bodies he'd wrapped his own around and entered reminded him it hadn't been like that.

Just now. With her.

She wasn't touching him, but it wouldn't take much, another lifting of her arm, soft and warm fingers pressing against veins and tendons. And him shooting off like sparks from a campfire.

Sparks. Fire.

An unexpected film hazed his view of her. If he hadn't noted earlier that she hadn't cut her hair since he'd last seen her and it was no longer contained at the back of her neck, he would have no comprehension of what it looked like. Needing more, he reached out and stroked the rich brown mass. It reminded him of a newborn foal's satiny coat.

Foals fresh from their dams had no fear. They trusted whoever touched them, bonded with who or whatever their eyes
first lighted on. Dawn was much more complex, and yet he
could dream. She'd look at him and her flesh would respond
and she'd want him. Always want him.

Fisting her hair, he drew her close. She smelled of something
feminine, perfume probably. Had she chosen the scent for him?

Wondering if he'd ask, he kept up the pressure until her
breasts stroked his lower chest. He shivered, then released her
hair so he could rest first one hand and then both on her frail-
seeming shoulders. After spending so much time with livestock, had he really forgotten what a woman felt like? Maybe
only she could make him feel like this, strong and protective
and vulnerable all at once.

"You asked about my supervisor," she said, her tone husky.
"Whether he suspected something was going on between us.
What about here, you? Does anyone care that I came in here
with you?"

Fighting his raging body, he told her that although his path
had crossed with several of the competing wranglers over the
years, he didn't see how any of them would care what he did
with his personal time or who he did it with.

"I envy you," she muttered. "I think. Between my cowork-
ers and the public, I feel as if I'm always under a microscope."

"Then do something else."

Although she laughed, her eyes didn't carry the same message. Then her expression sobered. "It's hardly that simple. Besides, who said I wanted to change?"

He'd been wondering if she'd become immune to his fore-
play, but as she looked up at him, he knew better. Her somber
expression darkened and grew smoky, and he believed in every
pore of his being that she was deliberately exposing herself to
him or at least trying to. What was it she wanted to reveal?

Releasing her shoulder, he placed his hand under her chin.

She stood still as a moonless night for maybe three seconds, then turned aside and reached for her blouse.

"I want to get naked," she said. "After that I'm not sure."

Unwilling to release her, he ran his hand down her arm. Her long, slow shudder resonated throughout him, nearly spawning a like reaction. Still, driven by years of solitude and self-reliance, he waited for her to make the next move. Would she kiss him?

What Dawn wanted was for Miguel's expression to change. It remained neutral and unemotional when she couldn't believe he felt that way. Every time she reassured herself that they were finally together and on the brink of having sex, she had to battle down her need to rip off his clothes. Although they hadn't used them, a couple of the wranglers had worn spurs. What she'd always associated with the cowboy life now struck her as cruel, and she was deeply, deeply glad Miguel's boots were unadorned.

She also wanted them gone. And not just his well-worn, faded, and comfortable looking boots. It was beyond time for him to shuck out of the jeans he wore as if he'd been born to them, to free himself from the long-sleeve shirt with the pearl buttons. A man who no longer wore his Stetson didn't need clothes.

Instead of doing those things for him, however, she set herself to unbuttoning her blouse with fingers that felt swollen and bruised. He watched her every move, not twitching a muscle himself. The cab-over was small and claustrophobic, and yet it was all she wanted. They were together in this confined space, their bodies speaking and sex waiting like spring sunlight.

She came to the last of her buttons with no memory of how she'd accomplished her task. With her throat seared and hunger clawing at her sex, she should be ripping the unwanted garment off her shoulders and kicking away her shoes. Why then was she staring at his chest and remembering how dark and deep his eyes were?

"Do you want me to—" he started.

"No." Ducking, she would have evaded his outstretched arm if not for the metal walls. As a result, his fingers scraped and seared. "I want to do this." *To prepare myself for you.*

Because she'd said what she had, she now had no choice but to slip out of the blouse. She'd planned, she thought, to throw it on the bed, but the table was closer. Maybe when *this* was over, she'd ask about the papers stacked on the table. His responses might bring her into his world and allow her to share it with him.

And then she'd sit across from him or maybe next to him or even on his lap and tell him what was being planned for other wild stallions like Blanco. Instead of calling it messing with nature, he'd listen, ask intelligent questions, agree.

Later. Maybe.

9

Even as she kicked out of her shoes, Dawn again wondered why Miguel hadn't gotten in touch with her. Why her world hadn't meant enough to him.

Then she was standing barefoot on worn, dusty linoleum and the answers didn't matter.

Throwing back her shoulders so her breasts jutted against the practical bra at him, she started to reach behind her for the fastening, but his fingers curled inward and his nostrils flared, and she tackled her shorts instead. The waistband was tight, prompting her to suck in her breath and concentrate on relieving the fastening of its burden. The sudden loss of pressure around her waist brought a sigh of relief. She rubbed the marks the fabric had left around her middle. That done, she pushed the shorts down over her rounded hips.

Hers weren't a cowgirl's hips. Instead of a lean, hard length stretched over firm muscles, hers were what her mother had called childbearing hips. Content as she was with what nature had designed her for, she couldn't help wondering how she stacked up against the women he saw on a daily basis.

But hadn't he told her that he spent most of his time alone?

Weary of her self-absorption, she let the shorts drop to the floor and stepped out of them. Mindful of the dust that had sifted in, she leaned over and picked them up. They landed on top of her blouse next to the papers of his life, and there she stood in her underwear, her panties' crotch soaked and her nipples stabbing at her bra. She felt fifteen and virginal.

"Your turn," she managed.

"Not yet. I want to see you naked."

For the first time, she silently finished. Their previous coupling had been fast and furtive, cheap if she was being honest with herself. As desperate as she was for him to fill her aching hole, she needed tonight to last longer. Willing strength into her hands, she again reached behind her and unfastened the bra. She gave momentary thought to turning things into a striptease, but she shook too much to be able to carry it off. Still, she managed what she hoped was a bit of a flourish when she tossed the garment on top of the small pile she'd created. Happily free, her breasts jiggled in time with the movement. Gravity hadn't yet had much impact on them, and she often went about braless when she was alone. Her earlier uncertainty about his reaction to her less-than-perfect body evaporated.

She was woman, sex on two legs.

Burying herself in the belief, she slowly, outwardly calmly drew her panties down over her womanly hips. When the satin reached her thighs, she sucked in her stomach and shimmied, encouraging the bit of nothing to slide the rest of the way down. At the last moment, she leaned over and grabbed so the final piece of her clothing wouldn't land on the floor. Free. Her fingers on her damp, warm crotch.

"There," she said unnecessarily when nothing stood between him and a study of everything she had to offer. Her skin fairly danced with need and yet she wasn't in a hurry to end the sensation. Anticipation painted every inch of her being.

Waiting for him to join her in nudity.

He did so with an economy of movement she'd spend the rest of her life envying. Every move he made had purpose, and his hands were steady, his eyes on her even when he lifted one leg at a time and pulled off his boots. This wasn't a striptease. Instead, he shed what he had no need for. But while he might envision disrobing as nothing more than a necessary task, those spare movements of his resonated throughout her. By the time he was naked, she'd forgotten what she'd told herself about savoring every moment.

She needed him now, hard, hot.

Looking around, she tried to come to some decision about how they'd address both their needs, but there was nothing seductive or sensual about the space. At least the window over the sink was open. Otherwise, they'd have already used up the air in here.

"The bed," he said.

Of course. Why hadn't she come to that conclusion? The answer came in the form of the rock-hard rod that defined the man she shared the air with. How could she possibly put one and one together when the only tool she could ever want waited for her? Belatedly catching up to his suggestion, she ordered her feet to traverse the maybe five feet to where he'd spent last night. But between anticipation and wondering if the sheets smelled of him, she couldn't command a single muscle.

"What?" he asked. "Second thoughts?"

"If I had any thoughts, I wouldn't be here."

Frown lines carved the space between his eyebrows. "Why not?"

"Because you're a stranger, and I don't fuck men I don't know."

"You already did."

No arguing that. And no denying how desperately she

needed to repeat the act. As he'd done in the brief past they shared, he kept staring into her eyes. His dismissal of the rest of her prompted the question of what she'd have to do to change that, but even more important was discovering why he was studying her the way he was.

"What do you want me to say?" she asked. Of their own volition, her fingers laced over her lower belly. Now the heels of both hands brushed loosely curled pubic hair and spoke volumes to the flesh beneath.

"Nothing, now."

Instead of pondering what he meant by "now," she caught hold of the word "nothing." So she was nothing except a body to him, was she? Available and eager. Hot to fuck the rugged horse wrangler she'd chased for hundreds of miles.

He was still tearing her apart with his stare when her feet pointed themselves at him and she took one step followed by another. A half stride brought her body to body with him. Her fingers trailed off her mons, reached for the most important thing he would bring to the elevated bed—if they got that far. All she could bring herself to do was lightly stroke the sides of his cock with electrically charged forefingers.

The rough fingers she hadn't come anywhere near purging from her mind despite the three months she'd had to do it in settled over her shoulders. He couldn't have reined her any more in if he'd used a lasso. She lost awareness of the slightly stale and overly warm air, the outside sounds of humans and horses. Her world, that's what he'd become.

As his hands trailed over her collarbone and headed for her free and eager breasts, her own fingers began their exploration of him. How sleek and soft his flesh was, strength draped in silk. Blood-swollen veins cried out to be touched and soothed. He was uncircumcised, a decision his mother had undoubtedly made long before he'd been capable of having an opinion. Whatever the reason for her decision, she thanked the dead woman who'd charted her own course and brought her only child on it with her.

A shiver claimed her, stole her thoughts and brought her head up. His fingers were on the move, just grazing her own swollen flesh and tightening her nipples almost painfully.

"Oh, God," she breathed, torn between needing relief from the mind-blowing touch and longing to press herself against him.

His fingers were so slow, the contact so light she couldn't find the line between reality and imagination. Much as she wanted to do the same to him, her fingers wrapped around his cock and she simply held him, embraced, encompassed.

There was so much to him, strength and length and width, his cock sometimes resting like an exhausted captive in her gasp, sometimes jerking within her crude embrace. His short, sharp gasps fed her own arousal.

"Oh, God," she repeated.

Then the rough finger pads that came close to being her undoing caught her nipples between them, and she made a sound she'd never heard.

"With me, Dawn?" he muttered. "You're with me every step of the way."

Although she wasn't sure she understood what he was saying, she responded with a nod. Still studying his now-blurring features, she slid a hand under his cock. Her fingernails kissed his balls.

"Shit," he gasped. The grip on her nipples tightened.

Spurred on by the delicious pain he'd inflicted on her, she opened her mouth to tell him she agreed. Instead she growled. There was nothing ladylike about the sound. He sucked in his belly and held it. If he was trying to put distance between them, he had a fight on his hands because right now his cock belonged to her. *She* supported the weight of his sex. *She* was responsible for keeping it at full attention. And only she could take the single drop she'd discovered on his tip and spread it over his head.

"Shit, shit," he muttered.

She'd thought, actually thought she might have won this round when he dipped his head and fed her right breast to himself. His teeth raked her nipple. Growling again, she swayed dangerously. She must have slackened her hold on him because suddenly her fingers were empty. Although she immediately reached for him, he released her breast and spun her around so her back pressed against his chest. The cock she'd lost rammed into her backside.

When she tried to arch away, tried to put even the slightest bit of distance between herself and what had the ability to tear her mind to pieces, he looped an arm over her breasts. Knowing she couldn't break free, she nevertheless demonstrated she wouldn't easily surrender by twisting from side to side. He put an end to that nonsense by delivering a teasing slap to her buttocks.

"What the hell was that?" she demanded.

"Getting your attention. I do have that, don't I?"

Not waiting for her response, he again sealed her against him. As his arm flattened her breasts, she sighed in delicious surrender and leaned her head against his shoulder. She saw nothing. The hand now keeping her in place slid over her pelvis, pushing a groan from her. In her mind's eye, she'd become a hobbled horse incapable of moving its roped front legs more than a few inches. Whoever had captured her had left a lasso around her.

Now that she was his, what did he intend to do to her?

What indeed?

Even before his hand settled over the join between her legs, she'd widened her stance. Whether her eyes were closed or simply incapable of focusing she didn't know, but how could she be aware of anything with her pussy trapped under his rough heat?

"Mine," he whispered against her ear.

"That's what you think?"

"I'm simply picking up on the messages you're giving me. And feeding off what comes naturally to me."

For a moment she couldn't fathom what he was talking about, but as his hold on her pussy became more all encompassing, she decided he was referring to the way he made his living. Ropes and fences were a way of life to him, his means of controlling and protecting the livestock he was responsible for.

All right, so she'd become his livestock, had she? A mustang mare he'd roped and hobbled and might soon brand.

Brand? Was that what was happening? Her cunt was trapped beneath his greater strength and knowledge about her. She couldn't begin to think how to move her arms or legs let alone free herself, but then she didn't want to.

Instead, every part of her being sank into pure, primitive sensation. He'd caught her arms against her sides. She couldn't put her mind to lifting her head, and her legs had reached the end of their strength. It was all about the arm over her breasts and the hand looped over a thigh and between her legs. Spreading her. Testing her. Slipping into her sopped opening and giving her his finger to feed off.

That was her growling again, her eyes focused on nothing, her legs strong and spent at the same time, repeatedly struggling to suck him into her center. And when he let her know he was in charge of that journey, her head rolled to the side. Her fingers fisted, relaxed, fisted again. Her pussy endlessly bathed his hand.

"Are you with me?" he muttered. "All the way. Nothing coming between us?"

"What—are you talking about?"

"Assuring myself that I have your full attention." As if punctuating his statement, he reached even farther around her hip and parted her sex lips.

Oh, God! "You do. You do!"

"And you want this as much as I do."

"I wouldn't—damn it—wouldn't be here if I didn't."

"Good." That said, he nibbled the ear he'd been speaking into.

Unable to handle the assault, she struggled to free herself, but he easily held her in place, and his finger remained against her entrance. She was going to die, goddamn die right here and now.

Her rebellion over as soon as it had begun, she sank into him again. She made no attempt to close herself off from him. But instead of pushing his advantage, he seemed content to bathe his finger in her slick offerings. Just as she'd spread his pre-cum over his flesh, he coated her labia and washed her pubic hair. Not caring the slightest what she sounded like, she welcomed each and every touch with a groan or sigh.

"Everything happened so damn fast the first time." He spoke with his mouth against her ear again and his breath tickling and tantalizing her sensitive system. "I wanted it to be different this time."

Hadn't they already touched on this subject with her questioning how he'd been sure there'd be a repeat performance? What had his response been? Maybe he'd begun and ended as he was doing now by stroking her labia and clit until her climax burned a heartbeat away.

"I can't—I'm going to—"

"I want to feel you come." Once more he slipped between her sex lips. "Feel you shudder and hear you scream."

"I don't—scream."

"You're going to tonight."

Yes, damn it, yes! Slam me up against insanity and show me how to live!

Like putty and butter rolled into one. Everything about her existence was wrapped against the finger sliding past her hot, swollen defenses and stepping into her innermost cave. He deserved as much as what he was giving her, but his turn would have to wait for her to finish climbing the mountain called arousal. Her head had never been heavier, and closing her mouth had never been a more impossible task. If anything, her nipples were more tightly knotted, and she doubted any bra's ability to contain her painfully swollen breasts.

Damn but she loved her woman's body! Loved the wise finger now pumping her.

For an instant she feared her knees were giving out on her. Then she realized they were simply obeying commands from a part of her that was all instinct and need. Although he continued to finger-fuck her, instead of simply letting him do it, she sank down and rose up, cunt muscles tight around the delicious invasion and dragging him with her. Faster and faster her knees and hips worked, frenzy building, flames licking so damn deep she wondered if the top of her head might blow.

"Slow down, slow down," he chanted. Even as he spoke, she sensed his frenzy build. His hot energy swirled around her, adding to what had already reached combustion stage.

Even so, she tried to tell him how impossible putting on the brakes was, but instead of words, a series of far from ladylike grunts spewed from her. She lived through, and for, the pleasure nibbling at her edges.

"Can't help it, damn it! I can't stop—" No longer interested in trying to form words, she squeezed her eyes as tight as possible. Her awareness spiraled down, centered in and around her pussy. Her spine arching, she surrendered.

Crying something obscene and honest, she dove into the

whirlpool. Muscles twanged. Her knees locked, and her pussy refused to release him. Her climax rocked her; sweat ran down her sides. Some bitch of a woman was screaming. A man's voice joined the torrent of sound.

Even as her climax faded, she acknowledged Miguel's role. Yes, the months of celibacy factored in, but she'd released some of her tension via her limited supply of sex toys and batteries. The climaxes she'd experienced at her own hands had been little more than puffs of steam escaping a volcano.

Miguel had uncorked the volcano.

And still she wasn't done.

"That was—incredible," she admitted.

"My neighbors will probably agree."

Far from embarrassed, she laughed. And because his finger remained inside her and his arm still captured her breasts, she couldn't take her thoughts beyond this place and time.

"Your turn," she said, her eyes opening.

"Only if you join me."

His voice had smoothed out, lost a little something. Unable to process the change, she opted for standing on her own feet and slipping out of his embrace. Her pussy continued to hum. Already she needed it filled again but with his cock this time. What a bitch she'd turned into, an animal in heat.

10

At least Dawn's ability to see had returned. Magnificently naked, he stood with his arms uneasy at his sides and the fingers of his right hand glistening with her arousal. He glanced over at the bed and then looked at her again.

Letting her body speak for her, she made her way to the bed and hoisted herself onto it. She scooted over to the far side where a long, narrow window provided a less-than-expansive view of the area set aside for RVs.

After what might have been hesitation on his part, he climbed up next to her.

Even before he could settle on his side next to her, she reached for him. Draping her arm over his shoulder, she eased her length against him. He hadn't bothered with a bedspread, and the wool blanket under her abraded her sensitized flesh.

"You need a woman's touch in here," she said. "Someone to put up curtains and figure out a color scheme."

Instead of picking up on her attempt at humor, he wrapped a powerful arm around her. His cock waited between them. As it slid over her thigh, she realized he'd put on a rubber. Grateful because he'd been tending to business instead of questioning whether he should join her, she reached under his length to stroke his balls.

"Shit," he hissed, jerking.

"What?"

"Hair trigger." After a long, slow, but not calm breath, he continued. "I haven't felt this close to the edge since I was seventeen. The things you do to me . . ."

What things she nearly asked, but the tension riding through him supplied the answer. Remembering her own overwhelming and unreliable hormones at seventeen, she lifted a leg and draped it over his hip. She compensated for the loss of his scrotum by running her hand first over his shoulder and then what she could reach of his side.

"Careful," he warned.

"Why? Not as in control as you'd like me to believe?"

"I never said—"

"That's not the point." Taking pity on him, she ceased her movements but kept her hand against his lean side. He was so warm and strong.

"Then—what is?"

Although she tried to recall what this excuse for a conversation had been about, her thoughts refused to go any further than skin against skin. Climaxing had been a mistake because instead of feeling satisfied, she wanted more.

Wanted everything he had to give her.

Not that she'd been able to hold back.

"On your back," he muttered. Putting weight to his words, he rolled her away from him. Then because she was jammed against the cab-over's wall, he tugged her close before climbing on top, spreading her legs and making room for himself as he did.

Despite the nearly useless window, enough illumination from the nearby neon lights gave her a semiclear view of the masculine form over her. If he felt the strain of supporting his upper body, his expression didn't show it, but neither did he look calm. Running her knuckles over his biceps brought her the truth. He held onto self-control with iron hands.

Lifting her head off the bed, she ran her mouth over his chest. Groaning, he stared down at her. In an instant of insanity and weakness, she came within a breath of kissing him only to lose courage. Much easier than what she'd long considered the ultimate in intimacy was bending her knees in a silent invitation for him to settle completely into the space she'd created.

His head and shoulders were within a half foot of the ceiling, giving her a fleeting image of them rolling off the bed and crashing to the floor during their energetic coupling. Was this, really, that different from sex on a hay bale?

Damn it, she didn't want to be thinking thoughts practical or otherwise. Didn't want to ask how deep her insanity ran. What she needed was to have her pussy filled. Determined to reach her goal, she again pressed her lips to his chest. He tasted of the way he'd spent his day, horse and physical effort, leather and hay. Needing more of his world, she licked the space between his pectoral muscles.

Expelling a harsh breath, he reared up. His cock slid from her slit to her mons. "Damn it, Dawn. You're playing with fire."

"I love fire."

"Then you're going to get it."

Heat whipped through her, took her from logic and intellect to something raw. Slipping her arms around his neck, she pulled her upper body against him. Her muscles trembling from the strain, she held the contact, felt his life strength. The only thing she didn't do was kiss him. He made no move to do so himself.

When trembling became pain, she reluctantly lowered herself back onto the bed. Her head pounded. *Do it, do it!*

Movement from him splintered her silent refrain. He was sliding down, settling himself more fully into the space they'd both had a hand in creating. His features blurred and then all but disappeared because she could only do one thing at a time, and that was anticipate. Offer herself to him.

Still bracing himself over her but now with a single arm, he slid a hand under her buttocks and lifted her. Closing her eyes in anticipation, she rolled her crotch toward him. Her wet, warm, and swollen cunt twitched. One second passed and then two. Losing track of time, she could only wait.

He touched her, his tip barely kissing her labial lips. When he pulled away, she cried out. Shocked by the desperate sound, she ground her teeth together.

Then he touched her there again, not a quick kiss this time but more, determination meeting willing surrender.

"Yes," she whimpered. Although every inch of her being ached to suck him into her, until he'd given her enough to hold on to, she could only wait. Ache and anticipate. "Miguel?"

"Quiet."

His command was too damn complex. Unable to think how to tell him that, she gave herself over to what little of his cock he'd gifted her with. Damn his self-control! How could he possibly stand keeping himself at her entrance?

"What are you doing?" she demanded. "If you're trying to drive me crazy—"

"I'm not."

Then what? But he'd begun to tremble, negating the need to ask. Gathering her strength again, she pulled up so her breasts rubbed his chest. Fiery pins and needles attacked her nipples. Still clinging to his neck, she nibbled his chin. His mouth was so close, desperately so.

"Shit! Shit," he gasped.

"Who needs to be quiet now, who?"

Instead of answering, he pushed forward and into her. Just like that, a single smooth movement and he'd filled her. Her inner tissues wept and rejoiced. Strength flooded from her. The rough blanket scraped her back again.

"Yes," she muttered. "Oh, God, yes."

Much as she wanted to give him everything he deserved, at first all she could do was focus on their mating. This wasn't a dream, no longer part of the fantasies she'd unwisely fed herself. The real thing, his cock skewering her and her flooding pussy welcoming him, became her world. She cared nothing about their surroundings or Blanco or Monday morning. This was him. And her. Fucking. Both of them weak and vulnerable and strong and brave all at the same time.

Wondering if he felt the same way restored enough of her brain that she was able to respond to his long, hard thrusts. The bed rocked. Maybe the cab-over itself was being shaken.

"Your neighbors. They're going to know."

"Do you care?"

"No."

"Neither do I."

His admission still echoed when he shoved himself at and into her again. This time instead of riding with him, she set herself. The slide of cock against pussy burned her cheeks and clenched her stomach. Eyes resolutely closed, she tossed her head from side to side, feeling, experiencing. He came at her once more, this thrust as long and commanding as those that had come before and yet was, what, more intimate?

When he had nothing more of his hard, hot length to give her, he remained in place, his every muscle trembling, breathing like a racehorse.

"Yes, oh, God, yes," she gasped.

Long after she thought he'd give way, his cock continued to ream her. Riding the current with him, she lost touch with where her body ended and his began. They'd become part of a united whole, strangers bonding in the most primal way.

Except for a kiss.

When, finally, he drew back, she tried to go with him, but with him anchoring her body, she had no choice but to let him go and wait. Anticipate. Her body from the top of her head to the bottom of her feet was on fire. Wanting only one thing in life.

He came at and for her again, plunging deep only to stop and then pick up the pace again, claiming more and more of her core. Owning it. Tension wrapped his body; his breathing picked up.

Hers matched his pace.

"Do it!" she demanded, oblivious to anything except the two of them. "Let go!"

"Yes!"

Determined to feed off everything he was experiencing, she opened her eyes to see him arch up and away from her. He seemed to be trying to free his upper body while what mattered the most remained trapped inside her.

"Are you afraid of me?" she asked.

"Afraid? No. Shit, ah, shit!"

There. A man breaking loose. Losing control and becoming animal. She looped one hand around his neck. The other stole to his shoulders in time to feel them turn to stone. His cock pummeled her pussy.

"Yes!" She scratched his shoulder blade. "Yes!"

Miguel, climaxing. Inside her. His cum trapped by the damnable rubber but every muscle shouting as release shook him. Unexpected tears burned her eyes. Not bothering to blink them away, she stared through the mist at his tortured features.

Still shaking and with sweat blooming everywhere, he lowered himself onto her. His greater weight collapsed her, trapped her between him and the blanket. Sealed them together.

Then he turned his head and sucked a breast into his mouth and she lost it. She screamed and shook as her second climax slammed into her.

Terrified her.

* * *

Nightfall had officially taken over by the time Dawn scooted away from Miguel and climbed out of bed. The last few minutes were less than clear, making her think she must have dozed off. Going by his breathing, she knew he'd fallen asleep shortly after pulling out of her and removing the rubber. He'd muttered something when she'd lifted his arm off her, and his breathing had quieted. He was now awake, or nearly so.

She didn't want him to speak and didn't want to have to open her own mouth.

Deliberately keeping her mind as empty as possible, she pulled on her blouse and shorts without bothering with underwear, which she wadded up and tucked under her arm after sliding into her sandals. Because she had her back to the bed, she couldn't say for sure that he was watching her. Something made her back tingle.

She reached for the door.

"Where are you going?"

"To my motel room."

"Why?"

"Because."

"That's no answer."

Of course it wasn't. What did he expect, a practical and reasonable explanation? "All right," she said and turned around. Thank goodness for darkness. Otherwise, the sight of his naked body would destroy her. "We fucked, got what we both wanted out of the way."

"You're saying that's the only thing you need from me?"

Like I'm going to answer that. "It's all you need from me."

Sitting up, he started to swing his feet over the side of the bed, head bent to prevent contact with the ceiling. "That's what you think?" he asked.

"Yes," she snapped even though she understood nothing of her emotions. "What do you know about me, Miguel? I know about your mother and her influence on you, why you do what you do for a living. You haven't bothered to ask a single damn question about my family, whether I'm happy with my job."

His shadow legs dangled. He'd stopped moving, which should have filled her with relief but brought her near tears. "No," he whispered. "I haven't. Dawn, I—"

"Don't bother. It doesn't matter, Miguel. It just damn doesn't matter." Her fingers ached from clutching the door handle.

"Stop this! All right, tell me about your job."

"I'm excited about something I've been part of since we met, but you won't approve."

"Try me."

How had she let the conversation take this turn? "Blanco was hardly the only mustang stud running free. There are other stallions, too many of them if they all breed."

"Hmm."

"The agency I work for is going to start rounding them up and sterilizing them." She rushed her words. "Once that's accomplished, they'll be returned to their herd. They just won't be able to reproduce."

"What?"

"I know what you're thinking, damn it! Not only are the mustangs losing the land they were born on, now they'll—"

"No longer be able to do what they were created for."

"That's right," she agreed, perversely needing to turn the conversation into an argument. "There's no alternative, don't you understand that? Of course you don't. You want to go back in time, tear down all the fences and make civilization disappear."

"You really believe that?"

"I don't know. How can I when we're little more than strangers?"

Emotionally exhausted, she stepped outside.

11

Miguel was the sixth wrangler to compete in the freestyle event. If anyone had asked her impression of those who'd gone before him, she wouldn't have been able to offer so much as a word because only he mattered.

He shouldn't but he did.

Studying his quiet form as he waited his turn on Blanco's back, she had no choice but to replay what little they'd said before she'd stormed away. It didn't help that their argument, if that's what it had been, had kept her awake most of the night, but at least she hadn't had to look at him. That's what made right now so damn hard.

That's why she'd come here today, wasn't it, because she couldn't head north without trying to get in touch with her emotions. Granted, she'd spoken the truth when she'd chided him for not asking about her life and world, but what did she expect? All told they hadn't yet spent two hours together. And that time had been spent doing very little talking.

The horse and rider ahead of Blanco completed their talent, which included getting the mare to stand on a platform so small her four feet nearly touched. In preparation for Blanco's demonstration, three barrels were rolled into the arena and placed on end in a triangle. She recognized the pattern used in rodeo barrel racing events. Two other competitors had already taken their mounts around the barrels, and she couldn't understand why Miguel had chosen it.

Still . . .

Give me something to take back with me, a memory to last a lifetime.

Like the others, he began by urging Blanco to race at full speed toward the barrel farthest from where he'd taken off. Even as she silently applauded Blanco's speed, she noticed something. Miguel wasn't using reins. Instead, they'd been wrapped around the saddle horn and lay on either side of the mustang's neck. As Blanco neared the first barrel and started around it in a clockwise pattern, Miguel leaned into the turn, one hand cupping the saddle horn, the other resting at his side. Man and animal came within inches of scraping the ground. Dirt flew up from churning hooves.

The turn completed, Blanco straightened and charged the barrel on the left. Miguel wasn't urging his mount on by digging his heels into his sides. She nearly convinced herself that Miguel was simply along for the ride and Blanco knew exactly what he was expected to do. But surely Blanco wouldn't be risking a fall as he raced around the second barrel if his trainer wasn't sending him reassurances known only to the two of them. As before, horse and man completed the turn as one, their bodies dangerously close to horizontal, Blanco's legs churning.

Miguel and Blanco straightened, the marriage between them stealing her breath. Only the third barrel remained. All around her, people had fallen silent, proof that they appreciated how much wordless communication was taking place. This time horse and rider approached the barrel from the right, compelling them to lean low to their left in order to switch to counterclockwise.

Once again she barely had time to question how Blanco had known this turn would be different from the others before horse and rider all but kissed the barrel, Blanco digging his hoofs into the loose ground. She hadn't seen Miguel switch holding on to the horn with his right hand to the left. All she could do was jump to her feet when he reached out and stroked the barrel.

Then he sat straight and still and magnificent in the saddle as Blanco stretched out, mane and tail streaming as he galloped for the finish line. Even before he'd crossed it, Miguel lifted both arms over his head, fists pumping the air.

"That's amazing, ladies and gentlemen!" the announcer gushed over the applause. "Think about that. No hand signals or control, nothing but man and animal with the same goal and determination. I don't need to say this, but I wouldn't recommend trying this at home."

Others laughed, but Dawn could only sink back into her seat, pounding her hands double time as tears ran down her cheeks. *He'd done it!* Gotten inside Blanco's head so the two of them shared the same brain. The same dream.

She was so caught up in admiration for his accomplishment that at first she didn't realize he hadn't returned to his spot in the arena but was slowly riding past the audience. His expression was somber and tense.

Her heart pounding and her pussy flooding, she stood up again, her arms at her sides. He came closer, then stopped below her. Because she was in the fifth row, she couldn't get to him, and because whatever they might say to each other was personal and private, she didn't speak. Neither did he.

For the first time since the competition had begun, Miguel wasn't with Blanco. Instead, like the other wranglers, he was standing outside the arena near where the auctioning was taking place. He had climbed partway up the wooden fencing and had propped his arms over the top railing, watching. He'd remained near Blanco until the stallion's turn to be auctioned off neared, then had handed Blanco over to one of the assistants. From where she'd been sitting surrounded by those interested in taking over ownership of the formerly wild horses, she believed she could read Miguel's body language. He didn't want to lose Blanco.

The horse ahead of Blanco was bought by a middle-aged woman who'd explained that she wanted a mount for her grandchildren. Unable to handle more of the distance between her and Miguel, she left the stands and made her way to where he was. Then she scrambled up next to him and hooked her own arms over the top.

He was quiet and still, a study in patience. Or resignation?

"If you don't want me here—"

"What? No, not that."

"Then what?"

"I wasn't sure I'd see you again."

"I wasn't sure I'd look you up."

"Why did you?"

"He should bring a good price, maybe the top one," she told him instead of trying to answer his complex question. "After all, he took first place."

"He should."

"You've done an incredible job with him." She was too close to the wild wrangler, their elbows brushing and feet only inches apart. Still, she couldn't make herself move. "I should have told you that earlier."

"Other things got in the way."

"Yes, they did." *And if we were alone right now—*

The auctioneer announced a starting bid of five thousand dollars for Blanco. Elbow against elbow wasn't enough after all. She needed his arms around her, his cock housed inside her, sperm bursting free and flooding her, maybe impregnating her.

Rocked by the thought, she struggled to concentrate on the

bid increments. No fewer than four parties were interested in the stallion. Despite the auctioneer's insistence, the bidders refused to be rushed.

"Could you buy him? He means so much to you that—"

"I agreed to this. I knew what I was getting into."

"But it isn't easy." Risking more than losing her perch, she let go of the railing and touched his arm.

"No." He covered her hand with his, jolting her. "It isn't. I fell in love with him."

Love. "I can see why."

"Blanco wouldn't be alive if he wasn't intelligent," he said, "and he wouldn't have had his own herd if he hadn't proven himself as a stud. He's passing his smarts on to his offspring."

Wondering if he was making a case for why mustang stallions shouldn't be sterilized, she debated telling him that vasectomies had been chosen over castration so at least the horses would continue to exhibit normal social behavior, but he had to know that.

The bidding was up to ten thousand dollars. Two of the original bidders had dropped out but a well-dressed couple and a man wearing a shirt with the name of a Nevada resort and dude ranch on it showed no signs of quitting.

"I wish we'd never rounded Blanco up," she admitted. "He deserves—"

"It's too late for that."

"Are you blaming me?"

"No. I was as much a part of his change as you were."

"But if he'd been left alone—"

"He'll be all right. He understands that humans aren't the enemy."

"Do you think that's enough?"

Still sheltering her hand, he shrugged. "Blanco will embrace whatever comes his way. He loves a challenge. And now he won't have to spend a snowstorm with his back to the wind."

"There's that." Much as she wanted to link her fingers with his, she had to take hold of the fencing again. He did the same.

"There's something I want you to know," he said following a barrage of fast-paced words from the auctioneer. "Despite the way I reacted, I don't disagree with what you and the BLM are going to be doing."

"You don't?" Even with just their elbows touching once more, an even longer zing chased over and then through her veins.

"You were right about one thing, I'd love to go back in time to when there was no limit to the land mustangs could roam, but that's behind us. Just like I can't bring my mother back."

The well-to-do couple exchanged high fives. A moment later, a boy and a girl rushed forward and hugged them. Tears stung Dawn's eyes. Looking over at Miguel, she saw him nod. His own eyes glittered.

"I wish I could have met your mother," she told him.

"I wish you could have too. About last night—"

"I'm sorry." Her arms and legs ached. Any second now, she'd have to climb down and stand on terra firma. "I don't know why I acted the way I did except . . ."

Maybe he could read her mind because he pointed at the ground and started down. As soon as she could get her legs to work, she joined him. And when he held out his hands, she placed hers in them.

"I've been thinking," he began. "You said the things you did and acted the way you did because you were overwhelmed."

"Overwhelmed?"

"By what you were feeling."

She'd been wrong. He did know certain things about her. Vital things.

"It's been intense between us," he continued. "And unless I'm wronger than I've ever been in my life, that isn't going to change." He made his point by pulling her against him. His erection caressed her belly. "Dawn, you weren't the only one who felt out of control. That's why I didn't try to make you stay."

"You—"

"But it didn't take me long to realize I'd made a hell of a mistake." Holding her in place with one arm, he cupped callused fingers under her chin and lifted her head. "I think you felt the same way. Otherwise, you wouldn't be here today."

"No, I wouldn't."

"What about tomorrow and the day after that?"

Her throat aching and her pussy already loose and ready, she answered him, not with words, but action. Standing on her toes, she covered his mouth with hers. Sounds faded away. She no longer smelled anything except him. Cared for nothing except him.

Tasted only his lips.

Tomorrow. Together.

LONG HARD RIDE

MELISSA MacNEAL

1

---

*"**R**aindrops keep fallin' on my head!"*

"Oh, enough already!" As she peered through the fogged-over windshield, Diana Grant jabbed the radio button. The wipers could barely keep up with the beating rain that had pelted her since she'd left the bank ten minutes ago, which seemed only fitting. While her previous chats with the bank president hadn't boded well, this one had sounded the death knell for Seven Creeks Ranch.

Diana blinked rapidly. While it devastated her to hear those final pronouncements about the home Garrison had built for them more than twenty years ago, crashing into another car would only make matters worse. She just wanted to crawl into a hole and die. But it would be another half hour before she got home, the way this rain kept her from seeing out.

Vision. It all came down to vision. And Jerry Pohlsen—Jerry the *polecat* Pohlsen—had eyes only for his own interests. Once the bank foreclosed on her ranch, he planned to finance a community of upscale townhomes and condos that would make Wolf Point, Montana—and his bank—look a helluva lot more progressive. He didn't seem to care where *she* would fit in this picture.

Through the loud, constant downpour the sign for the Wel-Come Inn flashed red and then white. Gossip was the last thing she needed on top of unpaid medical bills and this foreclosure crap, but she simply couldn't drive any farther. Diana cranked the wheel in a hard left and took the cafe's last open parking slot.

She turned off the engine. Sat there, numb, surrounded by the roar of the rain and a lonely desperation like she'd never known. Where had she gone wrong? Why had Garrison's liver transplant and medications done nothing other than drain her and their accounts? Why was her life one huge pile of shit right now? One huge *wet* pile of shit.

God, what she wouldn't give for an escape . . . a good man who would love her and rescue her and take care of her. All these months of being the strong woman who solved her world's problems had worn her way too thin.

Diana yanked her old shades from her purse. It felt good to hide behind dark sunglasses even on a cloudy day, especially when there wasn't a glimmer of light or hope to be seen anywhere.

She shoved her door open and the cold deluge soaked her. Once inside the cafe, Diana paused on the soggy doormat. The tables were all full with the noon rush, as this was the only place north of town to eat. One empty stool remained at the lunch counter, between a guy absorbed in his newspaper and another one with a set of shoulders the size of Montana. A wet, black ponytail clung to the back of his soaked shirt. *A guy like that wouldn't take any crap from Jerry Pohlsen. A guy like that would cure what ailed a needy woman—*

Like he'd even look at you.

Diana shoved her shades back in place and hurried toward the empty stool without making eye contact. Everyone knew who she was. No need to rub her nose in what they'd all heard about the fate of Seven Creeks by now, and about her financial setback. Pity got her nowhere.

Get a Coke and go. Sit in the car until this storm lets up. Why open yourself to condolences or speculation?

"What'll it be, hon?" Gladys, the county's oldest and most cantankerous waitress, gazed across the counter at her. She snapped her gum, waiting.

"Diet Coke. In a go cup, please."

"Want pie with that? Today we've got cherry cheesecake and peach and—"

"*No.* Thank you," Diana added with terse politeness. "Just the drink."

Gladys rolled her eyes and strode to the fountain spigots, filing away this little incident for the local litany about how that Grant woman had no call to be so antisocial or rude.

Diana slumped on the stool. Exhausted as she was, it felt good to remain invisible—or as anonymous as anyone could be here among the locals. The man on her left folded his newspaper and nearly dragged it through the gravy where his meat loaf had been. The guy on her right—

"Is that peach pie you mentioned homemade?" he asked in a low voice. "Peach is my all-time favorite. If it's fresh."

Gladys set Diana's plastic cup in front of her, raising her eyebrows flirtatiously. "Don't even *think* about me passing off store-bought stuff as real pie!" she teased. "Earl'd shoot me!"

"That's for damn sure! Made that pie myself, just this morning!" the heavyset fellow at the grill called out.

The guy smiled lazily. "How 'bout you give me the biggest piece you've got left? Warmed up, with a scoop of ice cream."

"You got it, hon. Comin' right up."

As Gladys bustled away, Diana glanced sideways at the owner of that velvety voice. He wore a striped western-cut shirt so old it was nearly transparent, and so wet it clung to his muscles like white glue. His jaw rippled with an alluring masculine shadow her fingers itched to caress. Those lips made her hungry . . . and she suddenly wanted to be the first bite of the pie, sweet and spicy, that made him smile.

Forget about that! And stop staring!

Diana peeled the wrapper from her straw very slowly. The hands at the end of those wet shirtsleeves cradled a coffee mug . . . long, strong fingers with skin several shades darker than her own. Fingernails clipped short. No rings.

Enough already! Take your Coke and go!

Her peripheral gaze traveled upward to take in his long midnight hair, tied loosely at his nape with a leather thong. Something about the flex of his neck muscles sent her temperature through the roof . . . made her clench where her weight met the stool top.

"Thanks, ma'am," he crooned when Gladys topped off his coffee. He sounded . . . nice. Like the waitress was his grandmother, even though her platinum hair and pale skin had nothing in common with his Native American palette. Gladys must've thought he was nice, too, because after she slid the slice of steaming pie in front of him, she dipped out *two* generous scoops of vanilla ice cream.

God, that looks good. Diana's stomach rumbled as his fork parted the pastry. Peach goop oozed onto his plate. She'd been too antsy to eat breakfast, and an hour in the bank president's office had tied her insides in knots. But now . . . now she could use a good, solid—

"Want some?"

Diana's eyes widened behind her shades. What she wanted had nothing to do with food—*and you've got no business thinking about sex when*—

The guy's lips quirked as he looked at her straight on. He was maybe thirty. Had the same down-and-out air about him she was feeling these days, yet he exuded a cool, calm control. Smooth, smooth skin the color of coppery walnut. He held the bite of pie up for her, awaiting her reply.

Diana sucked hard on her straw and then went into a panic of strangling. Soda spewed all over the counter and she couldn't stop coughing or control the spasms that racked her shoulders— couldn't get any air past the fizzy clot of liquid in her wind-pipe—

"Easy now. Just relax. Stop struggling."

His voice was a silken purr, patient enough to gentle the wildest, most frightened mare. As his ebony eyes drank her in, Diana felt so, so humiliated and stupid. Another sip from her Coke didn't help, and when her next round of coughing kicked up, the tall, dark stranger laid a hand on her back. He placed the other palm lightly against her throat, gazing directly at her.

"Breathe in through your nose and hold it. Gently."

Diana fought the urge to struggle, or to run. Everyone in the cafe was surely watching this lunch-counter drama, but all she could focus on was the overtly handsome face in front of her . . . black eyes that didn't waver . . . the lips that parted slightly as he softly massaged her throat. His palms felt warm and sooth-ing. A strand of wet, black hair fell beside his eye as he held her loosely—yet with total control—between the flats of his hands.

She did as he said, once her frenetic thoughts allowed his words to sink in. Diana relaxed . . . didn't swallow or fight. Just held her breath and sat very, very still, to allow the stray cola to drain down her throat on its own.

And then it did.

Diana swallowed tentatively. Opened her mouth to thank him—

"Don't talk yet," he whispered.

If he was some magical, mystical witch doctor, he was a very, very good one. He knew all the right silences, all the right pauses . . . the perfect touch that allowed his pulse to throb lightly against her throat, where her own pulse answered it and then went into his rhythm.

She let out her breath. "Thank you," she rasped. "I didn't mean to interrupt your dessert."

"Not to worry. Nothing comes between me and my . . . pie."

Diana desperately wished she were the ice cream melting on his plate, being spooned up—

Like he'd want a worn-down woman who resembles a drowned mouse.

Exhaling carefully, Diana focused on the white plastic lid of her cup. Once again she was aware of the clinking of utensils against plates . . . the low chatter of voices, mostly male . . . the *hisssss* of meat on the griddle and the heavy scents of hamburger and bacon grease. Her wet clothes clung to her, yet she felt anything but cold.

The guy beside her might as well have been making love to that slice of pie. His eyes closed with utter enjoyment as he savored each bite. Long, dark lashes fluttered on the tops of his high cheekbones. When he swallowed, his Adam's apple throbbed suggestively, which sent another wave of heat below Diana's belt.

This was insane, to pay so much attention to some stranger—especially considering the *real* issues she was dealing with today! Yet she squirmed; felt tingly when his elbow brushed hers as he dug out his billfold. He tossed a couple dollars on the counter and reached beneath the counter for a black broad-brimmed hat. With a quick nod at her, he rose from his stool.

Diana tried not to gawk as he sauntered toward the cash register at the door. His soaked, faded jeans fit his hips like skin . . . showed off legs that went on forever, to end in square-toed boots that looked saturated. His black hair hung in a thick, wet column down his back—far too blatant to be considered masculine in *this* town. Yet not a man in the cafe would've challenged his sexual preference, and none of the women would've kicked him out of bed, either.

Where are these thoughts coming from? They're going nowhere, that's for sure! With a sigh, Diana followed his backside out the door, where the rain still fell in torrents. The bell above the door jingled cheerfully, and she remembered again why she'd come here . . . and how hanging around would only give somebody a chance to pick at her emotional scabs. They knew her mostly because Garrison had come in for coffee on his way to the farm supply store or the gas station—but that hadn't happened for nearly a year. Maybe they'd let her alone. Maybe her mood remained dark enough to ward off any would-be pity pushers, and that suited her just fine.

She drained her cup and slid off the stool. Dug a wad of bills from her front pocket as she approached the cash register, but then Gladys jammed her ticket down the metal spindle without punching any numbers.

"Your boyfriend picked up your tab," the waitress announced. "Have a nice day now."

2

Diana's jaw dropped. Gladys hurried away to bus a booth on the outer wall, leaving her to wonder how many folks had heard that triumphant tight-lipped remark. The last thing she needed were rumors about a boyfriend in the wake of Garrison's passing—especially with the bank board breathing down her neck about the back payments she owed on the ranch.

But when she opened the door, there he stood. The cowboy glanced her way nonchalantly, waiting beneath the awning. He gave her a sexy, sexy smile ripe with promise—and then a suave nod—before he strode back out into the downpour.

Diana gawked after him. "Hey—hey, thank you!"

Mr. Mysterious glanced back and tipped his black hat, but kept walking.

When he was past the line of parked cars, her senses returned and she didn't give a damn who heard her. "Where's your car? Can I give you a ride somewhere?"

He stopped, silent as an ancient totem in the pouring rain, watching her with those dark eyes.

Had she insulted the man, assuming he'd need a lift? Diana's hand plunged into her pocket for her car keys as her gaze remained fixed on him, immovable and permanent like a post in the parking lot.

Must be a nutcase, to stand out there in the rain, she thought as she opened her car door and dove inside. Yet she recalled his patient way with Gladys . . . his light, effective touch on both sides of her neck when she was choking—

And there was nothing nutty about that, *was there? You were so damn hot you nearly melted into a puddle on the floor.*

She cranked the key and waited for the engine to catch. Pulled out carefully, straight back, so she wouldn't hit him—and then there he was, leaning down to peer through the passenger-side window. Diana fell sideways to yank on the handle. "Get in here! You're getting soaked!"

With a single fluid movement he swung low and into the seat beside her. He closed the door with a solid *whump.* And then it was the two of them in her very small, steamed-up car, separated only by the console. Diana had never felt more at risk in her life—not from a man who'd do her harm, but from a predator of a different sort . . . a sensual, slithering, sinewy male whose intent shone hard in his obsidian eyes beneath his dripping black hat.

"Can . . . can I give you a ride?" she asked again.

His slow smile made her replay that line and hear it for the come-on he took it for. Damn. She'd left herself wide open—and suddenly envisioned herself open beneath his solid male body as he entered her with a long, hard—

She exhaled. Couldn't drop her gaze, and he wouldn't, either. So damn sure of himself, this one was—but then, why wouldn't he be? He was young and hot and powerful—

And you, dear, are old enough to be his mom. Or you surely must look like it. You certainly feel like it . . . and it's been so long since you had a man you might not know what to do with him.

Diana nipped her lip. Tried not to cry, because damn it, over this past year she'd cried a deluge like the one that pounded the roof of her car.

"My truck conked out down the road. Walked into town looking for a repair shop. Got in out of the rain when I didn't find one. Found you instead."

His voice coiled around her insides and squeezed. Her breath came out as a pant despite her attempt at decorum. He'd paid for her Coke. She'd politely—with chaste intention—offered him a ride. He'd gotten in out of the rain. That's all this was.

The heat between them made parts of her flare and smoke. The inseam of her jeans cut into her as her nipples fought her bra . . . *the raggedy-ass bra that matches your cotton panties with the worn-out elastic. You can't let him see that—can't let him—*

She snickered. This tall, dark and arrogant cowboy with the ebony hair plastered to his back wasn't the sort to ask permission. Like she had any more control over what he thought or did than she had over her own wayward body parts right now.

"What're you thinking?"

Diana's jaw dropped and she frantically thought up a lie. "I . . . can't help but wonder why you'd come into *this* town looking for a repair place, when everybody knows—"

His lips quirked. "It's not like I chose where to break down."

Her face flared ten shades of red. "I—that sounded really dumb, to insinuate—"

"You weren't giving me a straight answer." He shifted closer, his obsidian eyes burning with dark fire. "If you'd told the truth, you wouldn't be blushing. But then, I like your face with more color. What I can see of it."

Diana's breath caught as his hands framed her face to remove her oversize sunglasses. The air thickened. She became very aware that she was sitting in the middle of the parking lot with her engine running, where anybody in the cafe could see this man was taking off her—

Taking off your clothes. What happens then?

Her eyes widened with the thought, and again the ruddy young stud in her passenger seat smiled. This time his entire mouth curved . . . lush lips carved into a face of mahogany granite, framed by wet strands of inky black hair her fingers longed to loosen.

"You're gorgeous," he whispered. "You wear your sorrow like a shawl, and I want to peel it away to find the strong, independent woman who waits for me inside."

"I—you can't mean that! I look like a train wreck—"

One long, calloused finger silenced her. "Never a good idea to squawk at a man who's complimenting you."

"But I'm old enough to be your—"

"Age is a relative thing."

"Mother! Or at least your aunt!" she spouted. "And when I asked if you wanted a ride, you know damn well I wasn't talking about—"

"You don't want to take me to a repair shop any more than I want to go there, sweetheart." His voice sounded husky now. His chest rose and fell beneath the shirt that clung to the darker skin beneath its thin old cotton.

She swallowed hard. Gathered her scattered thoughts. "How can you sit here in *my* car and insinuate—"

"You invited me."

Her mouth clapped shut. This desperado had an answer for everything, and he was so damn sure of himself . . .

Who's the desperado? And who's two steps ahead of him, far as the wants and needs he's talking about?

Diana let her breath seep out. Any minute someone would come out of the cafe to see if she was having trouble. And she was. Trouble of the randiest, dandiest kind. Trouble in the form of temptation like she'd never known—even though she was alone now, and it wasn't cheating.

Was it?

"What's your story?" he asked quietly. "Why the shades hiding the red eyes? Why duck into a greasy spoon where you're bound to know folks, without so much as nodding at any of them?"

Her lips parted but the words fled. Just a moment ago she'd seen herself naked beneath this hot young man with the long legs and broad chest, and now her mind returned to the bank: Jerry Pohlsen and his insidious plan for the ranch . . . the house that would echo when she walked in . . . the home she was about to lose, mere months after she'd lost the man who'd built it. "You don't want to know."

"Yeah, I do. You've got a helluva lot more going wrong than a broken-down truck." He tucked her sunglasses into her shirt pocket . . . made her squirm when his fingers flirted with the outline of her breast. Her chest thrust out of its own accord.

His breath whistled between his teeth . . . teeth that looked strong and white against his russet skin. She suddenly wanted those teeth to tease her nipples until they stuck out hard and solid as he sucked them—

Diana gasped and looked away, but the dark stranger placed his hand alongside her face. His pulse raced with hers as he brought his face within inches of hers . . . within kissing distance. His gaze dropped to her lips and then returned to her eyes.

"You ever done it with a total stranger?" he whispered. "Just fast and hard, down-and-dirty fucking? No strings. No rules. No consequences?"

Diana shook her head. Tried to figure out what the hell he saw in her that would make him want—

"My truck quit a couple blocks from an old mom-and-pop

motel," he continued. "If it makes you feel better—gives you an alibi if folks get nosy—you can take me back to my truck. Just a good Samaritan giving a guy a lift on a rainy day. But it's up to you. I'll get out, if you want."

He dropped his hands. Settled back into the passenger seat. Watched her with eyes that missed nothing.

Diana looked over her shoulder to be sure she wouldn't hit anything—except the back windshield was as fogged as the front one. She cranked her wipers up, full tilt . . . let the rapid-fire sound of rubber on glass drown out the anticipation hanging between them like an invisible swarm of hornets. Never mind that the buzz was inside her, driving her nuts. What should she do? As the rain beat against her car, she heard the thrum of his body . . . and her own body's urgent reply.

She took her foot off the brake so the car drifted farther back, past the row of trucks parked along the front of the cafe. She turned the wheel slowly, so the car was pointed toward the road she could barely see through the rain. "Which way?" she rasped.

He smiled and pointed. "Unless there's someplace else you had in mind."

Diana's laugh sounded sharp in the small car. "It's not like I go around looking for places to—"

"Maybe that's about to change. Are you okay with that?"

She stopped at the edge of the graveled lot as a semi roared by, throwing a wave of water at them. "I . . . I guess we'll find out. Won't we?"

3

Michael White Horse sat tightly, trying not to bang his knees against the dashboard every time her car hit a rut. What the hell was he doing, coming on to this woman? Was he so hard up for—

His jeans had the answer to that one, didn't they? He shifted in the worn-down seat, aching with an erection that had nowhere to go. Truth be told, this woman wasn't the type he usually came on to. He didn't feel proud of propositioning her when she looked like she'd been ridden hard and put away wet.

Yet that was exactly what appealed to him: that haunted look in her red-rimmed green eyes told the same story of separation and brokenness that had set him on the road to the rodeo. She obviously needed a white knight, and in his finer moments he took pride in rescuing women who'd succumbed to trouble. Helluva note, that he'd gotten less than a hundred miles before his truck died.

But if he didn't get any further with her, that was even better. Last thing he needed was another woman expecting things he couldn't deliver, or somebody who wanted to be his mother.

She had brought up the age thing, and he wasn't in the mood to quibble. He was just needy enough, just horny enough, to take off some of this edge while he waited out the storm. He hadn't expected her to go along with it, but desperate times called for desperate measures. And this gal knew even more about desperation than he did.

From beneath the brim of his dripping hat, he stole glances at her. Slim, strong arms . . . sturdy hands gripped the wheel to keep the car from weaving all over the road. She sat forward, squinting through the windshield . . . making lines around her eyes that shouldn't be there, damn it. She was too young to be so carved up by life. Had a plain gold band on her left hand, yet her hesitant answers said the man who'd given it to her was no longer around.

Michael's chest tightened in warning. He should thank her and get the hell out of her life. She wasn't the type for one-night stands in cheap motels, and she'd be pissed at him—and at herself—after he rolled down the road and left her feeling cheap. Used. *Slutty.*

But she was no slut. *He* was the one who'd brought this on. "Over there," he said, pointing to the side of the road. "Watch that ditch by the shoulder. It's full of water."

She gazed out more intently, until she caught sight of the abandoned black pickup. "You want to get out?"

"Need something in the glove box. Unless you want to drop me off and then keep on rolling home. Your call."

When she widened those green eyes he saw the proud, strong woman she'd been before trouble struck. She cleared her throat nervously. "This rain's wearing me out. It'd be my luck to ram into something—which is *not* what I need after my meeting with the bank president this morning. And it'll take me an extra half an hour to get home, the way this storm—"

The shift lever vibrated in her grip when he placed his hand on top of hers. "You don't need to justify anything to me," he murmured. "But yeah, it'd be on my conscience if you wrecked before you got home. Wait here."

Michael threw open his door and dashed through the deep puddles and the deluge. He opened his truck, slipped a box from the glove compartment into his wet shirt pocket, and then hurried back to her car. He cussed when he whacked his head getting back inside. "*Shit!* Sorry, I—" He had to grab his hat before he could close the fricking door.

"Ooh, that had to hurt." Her eyes widened with his pain, and again he considered calling this off. She wasn't that kind of woman. Integrity was written all over a face she hadn't covered with makeup. Desperation made a furrow between her brows and his thumb had the urge to erase it.

But when she rubbed his head . . . massaged the pain with fingertips that knew exactly the touch he craved, Michael's breath rushed out. "Jesus, woman—"

"I didn't mean to hurt—"

"If you don't get us across the road to that motel, I'll have to take you in your backseat," he rasped. "And my jeans are so tight and wet I don't think I can yank 'em down in this little space—"

Her giggle filled the small car. It tickled his ears and made his heart bubble over, even though his cock felt like it was caught in a vice grip. Michael stared at her, yet he had to laugh, too. It was a damn sight better than making her cry. "You think this is funny, you little feist?" He didn't miss the way her soft, rounded breasts shimmied as she kept rubbing his sore head.

"The whole situation's ridiculous! Well, *isn't* it?" she asked between snickers.

Her eyes took on a shine and her mouth muscles relaxed. He had no trouble imagining how wet and warm and willing she'd feel beneath him—long as he didn't let their situation *mean* anything. Just sex. Just a wham-bam-thank-you-ma'am and he'd be on his way, knowing he'd gratified her as much as she'd satisfied him today. "You gonna drive us across that highway, or do I have to chase you there?"

Her teeth caught on her lower lip and Michael's insides clenched. He grabbed her head in his hands and kissed her hard, swallowing her gasp as he devoured her mouth. Her lips felt soft and sweet, and the lingering taste of her Coke coaxed his tongue inside her mouth to extend their kissing frenzy. God, she was eating him alive, and all he could think about was getting her naked. When she sighed with surrender, he pulled away. "Sorry, I—"

"You are not."

Michael blinked. He suddenly needed much, much more than a kiss.

She swiped at her window to defog it. "Hope there isn't a semi coming," she muttered, and then jerked him back against the seat when she floored the gas pedal. Seconds later she jerked him again when she jammed the brake at the parking rail that spanned the length of the old has-been motel. The place needed paint but he didn't care.

"Wait here," he breathed, "because if you're gone when I get back, I'll chase you down and take you in the rain."

4

Diana gripped the wheel. She was parked in front of the old no-tell motel she'd passed a hundred times—the place everybody rumored did more day business than tourist trade. She was going inside a room. With a man she'd met fifteen minutes ago. And she didn't even know his name.

It scared her and shocked her—but hot damn, she was *feeling* again! She gazed eagerly through the steamy windshield, watching for him to come out of the office. Better him fetching that key than her, because he wasn't from around here—

How do you know? You've been holed up so long, caretaking and then tending to funeral details—and this business with the bank.

Yeah, a trainload of Chippendale dancers could've moved into the line shack on Seven Creeks, and she wouldn't have known. This hottie with the see-through shirt and midnight hair could've lived around Wolf Point all his life and she just hadn't run into him. Until today.

This fateful fact suddenly seemed like *destiny*. Diana had no idea why, but she sensed her life was teetering on the brink of a huge improvement—

Or a fiasco that'll take you down so fast Hell will look like up. And that doesn't touch what Pohlsen will do if he gets wind of this little . . . affair? Rendezvous?

What was the current term for succumbing to a stranger? A perfect stranger. He might be called a Native American in politically correct circles, but in her imagination he was a hot-blooded Indian who intended to ride her bareback at a full gallop until they both collapsed. Diana squirmed, and when the decrepit storm door slammed behind him, she dashed through the rain to join him under the roof's narrow overhang.

He fumbled at unlocking their door. Number eight—her birth date and lucky number! How had he known?

When she stepped inside he pushed her against the door to shut it. He was on her then: pressed his wet body into hers and found her mouth again, like he had in the car. Diana let him think he was having his way for a few moments. Soft moans escaped her as he kissed her senseless, again and again, with that relentless young mouth that still had so much of life to taste.

When she couldn't hold back anymore, she grabbed his shoulders and squeezed with more strength than she thought possible . . . nibbled and grimaced and groaned as she showed him her hunger and her need and her intentions to satisfy them. He was the perfect height. She stretched up on her toes . . . felt the raw strength in arms that closed around her . . . squirmed beneath the hand that grabbed her ass, which brought her into contact with an unmistakable ridge in his pants.

Lord, it had been so long. What if she'd forgotten the moves? What if he lost interest once her clothes came off?

Diana broke away with a gasp. "You probably think I'm—"

"Thinking is the last thing I want to do."

"I'm some sort of sleaze, or, that I've got no pride, or—"

"I really don't care." He grabbed her head between his long, strong hands to gaze unflinchingly into her eyes. "This'll be clean and neat, get it? No woulda, coulda, shoulda afterwards. I won't promise to call you, and you won't be waiting for me to. Right?"

Diana swallowed, eyes wide.

"*Right?*" he repeated. "No strings, or I won't play."

She nodded quickly. Her body got hot and bothered inside her cold, wet clothes. Her mind raced over the ramifications of this situation, but she didn't want to walk away. Just this once she'd give in to a fantasy most women only dreamed of, with a man like she'd never believed she could attract. "By the way, my name is—"

That long dark finger silenced her. "No names."

This thought barely had time to register before he was kissing her again. His predatory lips left no doubt he'd be fucking her rather than making love.

Again he flattened her against the hard door with his hot, damp body but this time his kiss felt more sensual: still ruthless, far as the price he made her pay with her pride, yet Diana's body quivered as his lips did their business. He held her head in his hands . . . speared his fingers through her damp hair and angled his face to get the rest of her resistance out of his way. Not that she had any.

As Diana melted against him, he fumbled with the buttons of her shirt. He scooped her breasts out of her bra and she sucked air, still caught beneath his lips and his solid body. His palms rasped her nipples as he squeezed and fondled and massaged, and all she could do was wiggle beneath him helplessly. He held her relentlessly against the door, the wolf toying with his tender prey. And when had surrender ever felt so sweet and so dirty?

Her fingers found the leather thong around his hair and untied it. This man's heavy mane sent a primitive thrill through her: under the wetness of the top layer her palms met his smooth, warm neck. On to his shirt snaps she moved, caressing his chest after she popped each one.

Impatient, he jerked his shirt from his jeans and then yanked it off. His chest was smooth and firm, punctuated by two dark nipples and an enticing little ditch that ran between his pecs. He yanked her shirt open, too, gazing hungrily at her bared breasts. Buttons pinged against the tile floor. As he unfastened her bra, his dark eyes riveted on hers. "If I do anything that hurts you, holler," he breathed. "Not my intention to inflict pain. I just—can't hold back much longer."

When had a man ever told her that? And why was *this* man saying it? She didn't waste time pondering such mysteries. Brazenly holding his gaze, Diana peeled off her wet shirt and jeans.

He met her silent bet and upped the ante: struggled with his wet zipper and then revealed red stretch skivvies that bulged indecently with his need. When he slid the box from his pocket and removed a foil square, Diana blinked.

"I may be a dangerous man to meet in a roadside cafe," he purred like a puma, "but this way, you won't regret me when I'm gone, sugar."

Sugar, he'd whispered. The coolest—hottest—endearment she'd ever heard. "Better safe than sorry. It's been a while since I had to think about—"

"No personal information." He ripped the foil between his teeth. "Just here and now. Down and dirty. You with me?"

Why did his words sound so liberating? She knew damn well she'd still be his prisoner weeks from now—and who knew where she'd be living by then, if the bank took the ranch? It was a blessing, this "here and now" a stranger mapped out for her. Easy to agree with.

He scooped himself from his skivvies. Put his fist at the end of his long, thick cock, to slowly shove it between his fingers and thumb. It pointed at her in black latex then, looking unspeakably wicked. "You want that?"

She nodded mutely, engulfed by need and curiosity.

"Bend over the end of the bed. Brace yourself."

Trembling, Diana obeyed. She got only one foot out of her jeans before he slapped her ass and waddled them into position with their pants still around their ankles. As she bent at the waist he prodded her, begging for entry. She reached between her quaking legs to guide him and felt hot liquid trickling over her fingers. Diana cried out as he shoved himself inside her. He thrust again, his breath hissing between his clenched teeth—

And then he stopped. Gripped her hips and pressed his tip against her deepest inside wall. He held it there until her muscles wrapped tightly around him, welcoming his intrusion . . . throbbing with the need to *move.*

"Give it to me!" she rasped. "Damn it, if you're going to destroy me, don't stop now!"

He grabbed her and rocked in and out, fast and hard. She'd never known a man who wanted it so badly, but then, she'd been pretty innocent when she married Garrison. She shut images of her husband out of her mind . . . gave herself over to sensations that might take her over an edge she wouldn't come back from. When her spasms began, low and slow, it was already too late to do anything but surrender.

Her cries echoed in the small, shabby room while her hips went crazy. Behind her, the warrior rode hellbent with his raven hair fluttering around his shoulders. He leaned back farther—farther—until he grimaced and cut loose. For long moments they stood panting, still joined, lost in their insanity. Diana fell forward on the bed and he landed alongside her.

"Holy shit!" he rasped. "Holy *shit*, woman!"

Diana grinned giddily into the chenille bedspread. To this young stud, she probably appeared as faded and worn as this old motel furniture, yet she'd never heard more exuberant praise from a lover. She'd made him work for it, too. Left him breathless. And she had no sense that he'd get up or go away any time soon.

Maybe I haven't lost it, if I turned on a total stranger this way, she thought as she drifted sweetly into oblivion.

5

Michael paused in the bathroom doorway with the wet wash-rag in his hand. She was still sprawled at the bottom of the bed with her jeans and panties at half-mast on one shapely leg. Totally relaxed. Totally sexy. When she met his gaze, she shifted self-consciously.

"Hold still. I'll wipe you off."

Her eyes . . . God, those green eyes that looked into his like a little lost dog's. So trusting. So sweet. She obediently lay still, letting him tug off the wet denim and white cotton panties before he turned her on her back. The bed creaked, and the ditch in its middle became more pronounced, yet he refused to feel cheap about this encounter. He'd taken this woman out of sheer lust and the selfish need to vent his frustrations, but other emotions pulsed in his chest now.

He lifted her leg to stroke her pale skin with the washcloth. She sucked air when he touched her sensitive inner flesh, but she didn't try to break free. Just opened herself, as though she felt too weak or too needy to protest his intimate attention.

Michael cleared his throat. "You got really hot and juicy. Because none of this slickum was mine."

"You made me that way. Bad boy."

He snickered. "Hardly a boy."

"What are you? Twenty-three? Twenty-four?"

He laughed, watching her coarse curls swirl around the washcloth as he wiped her deep pink petals. "Twenty-nine going on sixty. Old enough to know better about seducing a stranger, but still young enough to pull it off."

"Oh, don't pull it off!" she teased. "If you keep wiping me this way, I'll want it again. Real soon."

He glanced up, surprised at her playful tone. Her dark blond hair dangled in crushed waves around her pixie grin, and it did crazy things to him. "You like me rubbing you here?"

"Haven't you noticed I'm not getting any drier?"

When Michael ran a fingertip around the rim of her slit, her hips bucked. She wasn't nearly finished, was she? Might be the type to have one climax after another—and who was he to deny her that? The rain still pelted the roof, so it wasn't like they were going anywhere.

"Ohhhhh." She closed her eyes against a sensation that made her body writhe like a tigress, all sleek and smooth and so damn provocative he had to have more himself. "I feel all loose and rubbery and relaxed," she purred. "I was worried that you'd lose interest when I got naked, because—well, I haven't taken the best care of myself for the past several months. I've been—"

Her fingertips fluttered to her lips. "Sorry. No personal information, right? If I were smart, I'd just lie here and let you think I wasn't all washed off yet."

To tease her—or was it himself he tantalized?—Michael stood at the foot of the bed looking down the length of her body. He kicked aside their jeans and stood where she could give him the same kind of looking-over he indulged in. And damned if her gaze wasn't getting a rise out of him.

Michael focused on her face, holding her gaze while his hand slipped between her legs again. Slowly, slyly, he rubbed the coarse curls in a circle, around and around the damp, deep pink lips that so badly wanted his attention. But he denied her. Chuckled when she shifted her hips so his fingertips found her warm moisture.

"Horny little thing, aren'tcha?" he whispered. Not that he could claim anything different: his cock was half-hard and throbbing again.

"Is that a problem?"

"No way! Nothing on this earth sexier than a woman who wants it—and who goes after what she wants."

"If I'd known I was going to be—well, I'd have shaved my legs," she murmured. "It's been a long while since I had a reason."

"Not to worry," he replied smoothly. "Your legs have more texture . . . more friction. And that's not a bad thing." He grinned, feeling lazy and indulgent. "It tells me you're not afraid to be your natural self—that you don't rely on spas and cosmetics and mirrors to define yourself. You are who you are. And who you are is pretty damn hot, from where I stand."

With that, Michael inserted his third finger. Watched her rise with need as her eyes closed. He was amazing himself with this sort of chatter, because ordinarily he didn't wax too philosophical with a partner—nor was he bullshitting this one for what he wanted from her. Whoever she was, she'd laid it all out on the tacky, squeaky bed without apology or pretense. What he saw was what he got.

When her breath became an uneven singsong, he upped the speed and stepped between her thighs. His cock pointed at the ceiling, red and ready, but Michael had other plans: first he plugged her with his thumb, thrusting deep and hard until her cries drove him half nuts. She was squirming, totally under his control as the bed rocked and creaked beneath her. Smiling, Michael knelt to put his lips where his fingers had been.

She convulsed, eyes wide and mouth open. When her hands came at him, he caught her hips, refusing to let up—bracing for a slap. But no! She grabbed his head! Laced her fingers into his hair and thrust against his tongue, begging for more—yet begging for mercy. "Please . . . please just—oh, don't stop! I need it right there. And harder!"

He surrounded her lush nether lips with his mouth. He'd found this woman's favorite way, and her response was truly an inspiration. She was wriggling and writhing, wrapping her quivering thighs around his head, and then spreading them to press herself harder against his mouth. It wouldn't be long until—

Her scream rose to a wild crescendo. His pulse pounded in his ears—and everywhere else—but he didn't let up. He'd give her something to remember him by, because she obviously wasn't into one-night stands or fucks on the fly. She was a rock-solid, stand-by-your-man kind of woman. Not her fault she didn't *have* a man right now.

As her spasms racked her entire body, she was a joy to watch. So free. So unpretentious. So responsive. How long had it been since he'd had such a lover? Michael shoved the thought aside and focused again on this fabulous woman who didn't realize how hot she was.

Her hands tightened around his face and she forced him to meet her gaze. "My name's Diana. And you damn well better tell me yours, so I know whose name to scream when this all comes back to haunt me. After you're gone."

He suddenly didn't want to think about the *gone* part, but he'd made that rule himself, hadn't he? "Diana," he whispered raggedly. "Goddess of the moon—and certainly goddess of this room," he quipped. He slyly slid two fingers back inside her to watch her jump.

"Forget the diversionary tactics." She brought his face within inches of hers, holding his gaze with eyes the color of a sun-filled forest. "Tell me your name. I promise not to call you at all hours or stalk you on the Internet."

Damn. It would be nice to hear her voice on the phone once he was down the road, wouldn't it? "Michael," he replied. "Michael White Horse at your service, sweetheart."

"Careful there. My heart's been hiding in a dark cave so long, any sign of affection—any endearments—might make me take you more seriously than you intended." She kissed the tip of his nose and then rubbed it, Eskimo-style, with her own.

Michael went all silly inside. He felt like one of the seven dwarfs when Snow White kissed him.

"And meanwhile, since you're not going to hang around, I'll tell you straight out: you give the best damn tongue job I've ever had." Her smile went lopsided. "If I don't live to see tomorrow, I'll die a happy woman."

"Don't talk like that! If you're going to do something stupid like—"

She silenced him with a kiss. A kiss so sweet . . . so lingering . . . yet so innocent, it took his heart a few beats to recover its rhythm. Why was he feeling shaky? Downright *scared*, when she talked about dying?

"I didn't mean to upset you," she whispered. Her eyes were wide and kind, smiling into his. "I've lived with death—the before and after of it—for so long, I no longer fear it. It's like a friend I can count on to do the right thing."

He swallowed. Kept looking into eyes that didn't flinch even when they misted over. He'd never met another woman like Diana. And although the rain was letting up, he wasn't

nearly ready to leave. His mind was spinning in a dozen different directions, and when he could speak again he wasn't expecting what came out.

"Do you think we could talk about that? About doing the
right thing?"

6

Diana's eyebrows rose. Her Native American stud puppy was kneeling before her, rock hard, with lips still shiny from giving her that stellar tongue job. What did a guy like this mean by *doing the right thing?* It was his bravado, his don't-ask-don't-tell declaration that gave her the freedom to be so bold and brazen. If he offered to make an "honest woman" of her—or, heaven forbid, if he apologized for taking advantage of her loneliness—she'd be sorely disappointed.

She liked the woman she'd become with this younger man. She wanted to be this feisty, brazen, she-devil Diana for a while longer . . . for as long as she could string him along. Rules were made to be broken, right?

Still gazing at his cinnamon face between her pale legs, Diana smiled. "Doing the right thing," she mused mysteriously. "What would you like to know, Michael? Is this about my story or yours?"

"Mine. I . . . I just left a job as the chief accountant at my great-uncle's casino, where some of the financial practices are clearly against the law," he began in a quiet rush. "I haven't reported anything yet—don't want to bring the Feds down on my family, you know? But they're calling me a traitor, saying I've not only pissed on them but on the entire tribe. The Indian Nation and all it stands for."

"I see," she murmured. "It's not like you're the first person to sniff at cooked books and smell something rotten. I could tell you a few stories about that myself, but it's still your turn." Diana patted the bed beside her.

Michael slid onto the mattress, and she cradled him against her body. For several moments they lay that way, breathing together. It felt so damn good, having a man hold her. She sighed as she trailed soft kisses over his smooth young face.

"It's just that, well . . ." Michael's hesitation bespoke a heavy burden. "The place started out as a bingo hall, and then the tribal elders got the big-ass idea to build a casino. None of these guys have any business expertise. Some honchos from Vegas helped them set up, but once the big money rolled in, my uncle and his cronies resented outsiders telling them how to run things. So men who'd been marginally efficient at managing a bingo hall that netted ten thousand a week are now in charge of a monster that generates about five hundred thousand a day."

"Holy cow." Diana bit back a remark about what she could do with just one day's earnings. She wove her fingers into Michael's glorious long hair. "So when you saw discrepancies in the P & L statements, or asked where the money was going, they gave you trouble?"

"My uncle accused me of skimming huge amounts of cash. He said I'd picked up too many, uh—Caucasian—habits to be trustworthy, just because I asked to see records of what the slots brought in." He laughed ruefully and nestled closer to her. "I saw those records, all right. They hadn't been filled out for weeks."

Diana considered this. "So the government doesn't audit them, or—"

"Nope. Not on the reservation."

"No one from the tribe ever questions managerial practices?" she continued. "How do they know they couldn't be even *more* profitable if the casino operators knew what they were doing?"

"Doesn't matter. Only the tribal chiefs can remove anyone, and since they're happier than pigs in shit, wallowing in all that money, nobody asks any questions. Except me, that is."

She tightened her arms around him, loving the feel of his sleek body . . . savoring this conversation that had nothing to do with her own iffy situation. It touched her that Michael would entrust such details to her, a white woman . . . but then, people confessed all sorts of things to total strangers they'd never see again. "So you have a degree in finance?"

"I'm a CPA, yeah."

"Surely you could find work just about anywhere then."

He grimaced like a kid who'd bit into a lemon. Then his onyx eyes lit up with a teasing glimmer. "I did the rebellious, irresponsible thing," he whispered. "I used to ride saddle broncs in college. Pretty good at it, too. So I've left the nine-to-five behind to pursue my dream of getting to the PRCA finals in Las Vegas."

Diana's jaw dropped. "You're a pro rodeo cowboy *and* a certified public accountant? Hot damn!" She squeezed him, giggling. "It's *such* a cool thing that you're doing what you really love! You *go*, guy!"

He chuckled and hugged her hard. "It was going so well, too. Until my truck broke down on my first day out."

Diana rolled onto her side to lean into him from a superior position. She indulged herself in another long, languid kiss, losing herself in the warmth of his sensitive mouth.

He lifted her head, grinning. "Not so fast, sugar. You have to share your story now—or you're not getting that cock inside you ever again."

"Are you threatening me?" she teased.

"Yup. All's fair in love and war."

"And which is this?"

Michael's smile mellowed. "Well it sure as hell isn't war—but don't get any girly ideas about the *love* part, either. If I was in that cafe because my truck broke down, why'd *you* show up? You looked like you'd lost your last friend. Didn't trust a soul in there even though you probably knew most of them."

She smiled secretively. "Just my luck that the only open seat was by a tall, dark stranger, eh?"

"Spill it. A woman who wears shades on a rainy day is concealing something." He held her gaze with his obsidian eyes until she saw herself mirrored in them. And she liked what she saw.

"Okay, so I'd just come from the bank," she admitted, feeling tired and cranky again. "I got behind on the ranch payments when my husband Garrison underwent treatment for liver disease and received a transplant. That, plus the required antirejection drugs, dug us one hell of a hole, financially."

Michael sobered. "I'm hearing all this in past tense."

"Yeah, he . . ." Diana paused, telling herself she would *not* cry while she was enjoying this young hunk's embrace. "Even with all the drugs, Garrison only lasted a few months. He'd been ill for more than a year before the transplant—"

"I'm so sorry, angel." He enfolded her against his sturdy chest, tucking her head beneath his chin. "You don't have to say another word. That's a long hard ride you've been on, and it makes my predicament look pretty damn petty."

"But your family's so pissed at you, you had to leave them," she said. "That's not fair, Michael! Not when you were doing your honest best. I can't say that for the bankers who're now foreclosing on Seven Creeks. All they see is dollar signs from the ritzy ranch-style resort they want to develop after they demolish my house . . . the house Garrison built right after we got married."

"That is just *wrong!*" he blurted. "Surely a repayment plan— debt consolidation—could get them off your back while you recover from your losses."

Diana again gazed into his eyes. They burned with obsidian fire and indignation, and his tight face betrayed intense feeling for her. The way he'd abandoned his own rules heartened her. "Thank you," she murmured. "Your understanding means more than you know."

"You understood me first, sweetheart."

Did she? Michael White Horse impressed her as one of those strong silent types who kept his soul to himself . . . but that didn't stop her from enjoying his body, did it? When she wiggled the tip of her tongue in his ear, he shuddered. Laughed low in his throat, as though he had a delightfully dangerous idea.

"I've got something for you besides understanding . . . that is, if you'd like to change the subject." When he pressed his long body into hers, his rigid shaft spoke for itself.

And wasn't it nice, how he knew when to stop talking about death and hardship and suffering? After all, it wasn't every day she ended up naked beside a hot, good-looking stranger who didn't mind that she hadn't styled her hair or shaved her legs. "I can talk about any subject you like," she replied lightly.

"Like I'm gonna let you *talk*." Michael deftly flipped their positions so he lay half on top of her with a leg cocked over both of hers. His eyes flashed a message she couldn't mistake. His raven hair was almost dry now, and it fell along both sides of her face like a curtain, closing her away from the rest of the tawdry room . . . away from her reality. As he studied her, his long lashes brushed his cheeks.

"You are soooo gorgeous," she breathed.

He nibbled her lip . . . gently tugged it between his teeth and let go. "Thank you. But that just gets me into trouble faster, you know. Trouble like *you*, sugar."

His finger meandered past her midsection to pause in her

curls . . . to make her wait and want. Diana wiggled, unable to control the crazy little bolts of heat lightning that flashed inside her. "You're too good at this, cowboy."

"Nope, can't claim that one. You set me off like a shot the minute you sat down on the stool beside me."

"Really?" She accepted another nibble, reveling in his gentle sense of play. He was all hard angles and darkness and strength, yet he took his sweet time teasing her. "So what got your attention? I—I'm not fishing for a compliment. I'm just really curious about what attracted a stallion like you to a worn-down workhorse like me, who—"

"Stop." Michael kissed her with more pressure while he slid all the way on top of her. "No put-downs. If I say you're hot, you're hot. And if I say you're gonna come so hard you see colored lights and scream my name, you will."

The corner of her mouth quirked. "Nice dodge."

"I'm good at that, too." He kissed her again, slowly, deeply . . . easing his tongue between her lips in an invitation to dance. The angle of his face gave him all the advantage over her, as did the position of his body, but being held hostage played into some of her dicier fantasies: if she was overpowered by this perfect stranger, forced to do his bidding, she couldn't be held responsible for whatever happened, could she?

"It was your attitude," he whispered. "Your refusal to let those small-town, small-time gossips call your shots. They were all gawking at you, and you didn't give them the time of day. Just sucked down your Diet Coke like they weren't even there."

"And yearned for your peach pie."

"I ordered it so I'd have more time to check you out," he confessed with a devilish grin. "But that's not all you were looking at. *Was* it?"

Diana's cheeks tingled beneath his steady gaze. He was gyrating now, subtly shifting his hips so his cock pressed into that bone above her clit. "Ohhhhhhh, you're pushing my buttons again," she moaned.

"Good. Can't think of a single thing I'd rather be doing now. Can you?"

"Yeah."

"Oh?" Michael angled himself up on his forearms to give his hips more leverage. "Don't be shy, Di. I'm good, but I'm not a mind reader."

"Ram that cock inside me and fuck me with it," she challenged in a hoarse whisper. "Don't make me tell you twice."

"Jesus, you little—" He kissed her with a hard hunger that pressed her head deeper into the mattress, accentuating just how much she was at his mercy.

His body outpowered hers in every way, and as he rubbed his chest against her breasts she gloried in the hard male strength of him. Slyly she wiggled beneath him, kissing him wildly yet carrying out her own secret agenda . . . going for down-and-dirty wish fulfillment. At just the right moment, she arched herself to catch his hard tip at her entry. Then she grabbed his ass and opened herself wider.

His head jerked up. In the shadow created by his raven hair, Michael's eyes burned with a dark fire. "You're asking for trouble, lady. Let me grab a—"

"Why?" She gripped his hips. "I've had one man for the past twenty years, Michael. Are you clean? Healthy?"

"Yeah, but—"

"No buts. No woulda, coulda, shoulda," she rasped. "Just all-out, down-and-dirty sex. Isn't that what you said in the car?"

Emotions played over his face in an expression she'd never forget. "Yeah, but if there's a kid—"

"Can't happen."

"You'll either come looking for me or—"

Diana squeezed her knees tightly around him, panting with the effort it took not to lunge upward and claim him. "Are you listening to me?" she demanded hoarsely. "You can give me what most women in this world only dream about, cowboy. No strings—no kids. You in?"

He wheezed. His deep, dark eyes went absolutely still as they sucked hers into a gaze that seemed to span eternity.

Diana thrust upward to take his magnificent cock inside her and he grimaced with the pleasure of entering her tight, heated sheath. He bored into her once, twice—

And then he shoved away from her so violently he nearly fell over himself at the end of the bed. Michael turned away. Went to the window to stare out at the rain.

As he stood in profile, Diana saw his shoulders quiver. He was really, really upset about something.

And what the hell are you thinking? He tried to tell you not to—but you and your big, fat fantasies—

"Sorry," he rasped.

The middle of the bed suddenly felt very lonely. Diana draped her arm over her eyes. "I'm sorry, too. You did the safe, intelligent thing—"

"Last time a girl told me kids couldn't happen, I found out the hard way she hadn't been taking her pills. She wouldn't marry me," he added bitterly. "Which was just as well, considering we lived together about a year and then she said it wasn't working."

"She . . . had your baby?" Diana peered beneath her arm. He stood slumped against the wall, letting his hair fall like a dark veil around his face.

"Twins. Carey and Cait. Guess they must be about six by"—he raked his hair back from his face—"oh, what would you care."

"Try me, Michael. I always wanted kids and couldn't seem

to have any," she whispered. "Those two little girls must be gorgeous. I can see how it rips your heart out that they aren't with you."

He turned to study her, but remained at the window. "When I tried to get shared custody, their mother pulled a fast one. We agreed about visitation and child support arrangements in court . . . but by the time I came home from work, she'd disappeared. Slipped under the radar so fast, it took a couple years for my investigator to find her in San Juan."

Diana let out a low whistle. "Do you get to call the girls, or visit—"

"Hell, no! The numbers Carina gave him were for a gas station and a Laundromat," Michael blurted. "She got a trumped-up restraining order when she thought I'd come looking for the girls. So I've got no chance to tell them their father *wanted* them. That he loves them and thinks of them every single day."

"Oh, Michael. I'm so sorry."

"Yeah, well . . . me, too. So much for keeping the personal stuff out of it." He glanced at the clock. Walked to the foot of the bed and fumbled the cell phone out of his jeans. "Excuse me a minute. Gotta call about my truck."

Diana lay absolutely still, considering his story . . . observing the sleek lines of his body as he paced the small room with the cell at his ear. It was a sure bet there'd be no more wild, impassioned sex now that she'd said the wrong thing, but she didn't have the heart to get into her cold, wet clothes yet.

"Yeah? Mike White Horse—the guy who called you about the black Chevy half-ton?" As he listened, he tucked his hair behind his ear, giving her a glimpse of his taut face . . . a face she wanted to see poised above her own again. "That's what I figured. But you've got this number, right?"

He clapped his phone shut and sat on the end of the bed. After a moment, he laid his hand lightly on her bare knee. "There's only one tow service guy in these parts, and he's been tied up with a couple of nasty wrecks in this rain. And the shop's closed now—"

"And tomorrow's Sunday."

"So he'll call me when he's hauled it in." Michael turned, a pensive look on his face. "I guess I'm bunking here until then. And while I'm not saying you have to leave, Diana—"

"Come home with me."

His eyes widened. "I can't ask you to—"

"I did the asking. Why would anyone want to stay in this low-down—"

"Only if you've got work I can do around your place. I will *not* hang around like some gigolo—"

"Well, damn. I've never had one of those and it sounds kind of . . . adventurous." She grinned, reaching for his hand. "Come on, Michael. I might as well live up to the rep I got in the cafe parking lot. Gladys has us shacking up by now anyway."

He snickered. "If you're sure I can repay you by doing whatever—"

"Trust me. You'll trip over stuff that needs doing before you get to the front door."

She wasn't ready for the sign posted out by the road: TO BE SOLD AT AUCTION. It gave the bank's name and number, with Jerry Pohlsen's name at the bottom.

Diana clenched the steering wheel, determined not to bawl. In the seat beside her, Michael cussed under his breath and grabbed her hand. "I'm sorry, angel. Must be something cosmic, that we're both getting our hearts ripped out today. Again."

She stomped the accelerator, to escape that blatant reminder of the bank's power. They rumbled down the gravel lane toward the house, which sat on a rise overlooking one of the creeks the place was named for. The rain had stopped, and in the last rays of sunlight the ranch sparkled with promise, even to her own tired eyes.

She'd hardly stopped the car before Michael hopped out to gaze around. "Wow, what a great place! Do you have horses, or cattle or—"

"Yes. Past tense again," she replied in a shaky voice. "Had to sell off the stock because we couldn't pay any help while Garrison was ill. Nothing prettier than that pasture with the sun rising over the trees and little Hereford calves grazing alongside their mamas." She turned sadly, fumbling for keys she couldn't see through her unshed tears. Then she rushed up the porch steps, where another auction notice had been nailed to the post. "Those dirty sons of bitches! Posting this at the road was bad enough, but—"

Michael stepped behind her and grasped the sides of the sign. The wood splintered in his grip, but a strip remained on the pillar where the nails were.

"The thought that Pohlsen drove in here! Stood on my stairs to nail this damn sign to my—"

When Michael wrapped his arms around her, Diana let loose. All the frustrations of the one-sided negotiations this morning—the sense that she'd been screwed before she walked in—and now these notices right here on her property were too much. As his warmth enveloped her, she pounded his chest and cut loose with a crying jag like she hadn't had since she'd come home alone from Garrison's funeral.

He held her through the storm. Rocked her, letting her rant and carry on. Made an occasional sympathetic sound, but mostly let her release the despair and fear that had nearly killed her when there simply was no money to pay down her debts. She'd gone into hock, desperately believing Garrison would recover someday.

"Diana," he whispered. "This is a tough topic, but if the bank has taken your place by eminent domain, or they've done you dirty illegally, I know ways to—"

"Unfortunately, it is what it is." She mopped her face with her sleeve. "Garrison's illness drained us, period. He'd have shot himself rather than undergo the transplant and all that expense, had he known it would come to this. But I just couldn't . . . I just couldn't . . ."

"You made the only choice a woman who loved her man

could make, angel. But damn," he murmured into her hair. "There's got to be a way around this. Come on, sweetheart. Take me inside."

Diana unlocked the door and looked warily around the living room. Everything seemed to be in place—and of course, she was silly to think Jerry Pohlsen had come inside after he nailed that damn sign to her porch. Thank goodness she'd picked up the newspapers, so the house looked halfway presentable.

But as she glanced at the careworn furniture . . . the mix of pieces they'd laughingly called "early American attic" . . . Diana sensed her home was the antidote to the spell Michael White Horse had cast over her. Surely, as the CPA for a big-money casino, he preferred swankier surroundings. Probably liked glass and chrome and contemporary artwork, rather than the old paintings that hung on these paneled walls.

"This house feels like such a *home*." Michael stood in the middle of the living room to drink in its atmosphere. Then he squatted in front of the curio cabinet. "Wow, feather paintings! Did you do them, Diana?"

A huge lump choked her. "Actually, my husband did. Painted on turkey feathers, eagle feathers—whatever he found in the fields."

"May I open this and look more closely?"

Diana's fingers went to her lips. It felt like a betrayal of Garrison's memory to have this young, vibrant man—her lover—in the house. And now that Michael wanted to study her husband's hobby . . .

"It's okay, babe." He smiled gently. "I shouldn't have asked."

"There's no reason you shouldn't see his pieces. He showed them at the heritage festival once, but otherwise only a few friends know about them."

"That's a shame. He had a great eye for wildlife." Michael's eyes glowed as he carefully removed the feathers from their dark velvet display blocks. "Look at this falcon . . . and the bison . . . and the elk. These are awesome, Diana."

"Yes, they are. Thank you for . . . for understanding why I have a hard time talking about . . ." Something compelled her toward the bedroom, and as she felt Michael's gaze following her she wondered why she had to show him the largest feather from the wall display in there. When she placed it in his hands, his breath came out in a rush.

"A white horse," he breathed. "A glorious white stallion like you only see in the movies, or—"

"Or like the guy standing beside me right now?" Diana blinked rapidly: Michael White Horse held the large feather as though he treasured it. He looked at *her* then, as though he could cherish her, too, given half a chance.

"Sweetheart, if this was a bad idea, bringing me here—"

"Stay! I'm so damn tired of being alone and—"

He held her against his long, strong body until her despair passed. As evening shadows fell, they ate potato soup at the small kitchen table. Applesauce and peanut butter sandwiches rounded out the meal, over Diana's apologies about not buying groceries for a while. Michael assured her he'd gone too long eating alone to care what she cooked.

Afterward he sat on the couch and patted his lap. Diana was too exhausted—too enthralled—to resist his invitation. Just simple affection: the warmth of his arms around her, the steady rise and fall of his breathing as they sat in the pale light of a single lamp, the softness of his voice, the tender caress of his lips against her temple as he assured her there had to be a way to save her home place. When he scowled as she told how Jerry Pohlsen's wife, Fritzi, already planned to own the first megamansion in the Seven Creeks resort community, Diana knew she'd found a kindred spirit.

But what would she do about him? What the hell had she been thinking, bringing Michael White Horse home with her?

Yet it felt so right to have him here, didn't it? Curled up like a child in his protective embrace, she drifted off to sleep.

Diana awoke with a start. Full sunlight made her squint, and when she sat up in the bed she'd shared with Garrison, it kicked her in the chest to see Michael's duffel on the floor among her clothes. She'd slept in his T-shirt, too, and the pillow she hugged smelled like the mahogany-skinned cowboy she'd met just yesterday. If her husband were here . . . if her mother knew what she'd done . . .

If they're looking down on you now, what makes you so sure they disapprove? You're an adult. You're alone . . .

She grunted. Her mother would lay on the shame about how she'd become a stranger's whore—

A pounding outside made her peer through the window. That handsome stranger was replacing boards in the pasture gate, and he'd stacked the fallen branches from last winter's ice storm behind the stable. Amazing, how the place already looked better. It embarrassed her that Michael was cleaning up after her, yet he understood her despair . . . how she'd holed up in the house, overwhelmed by the outside work during Garrison's illness.

That's not what you're really looking at.

Diana laughed at herself. Michael expertly swung the hammer, making his shoulders bunch and his ass point at her with each drive of a nail. He'd bound his hair at the nape, and it fell down the center of his bare back in a sensual black column. With his hat angled low over his forehead, he could be the cowboy, the rancher, the good-as-gold hero from the movies and TV westerns she'd loved as a kid. Her heart fluttered with hope.

As though he felt her watching, Michael straightened to gaze toward the bedroom window where she stood. He lifted his black hat to swipe his forehead, his gaze never wavering. The heat coiled and bunched in her stomach. When he laid the hammer on the gate post to walk purposefully toward the house, Diana scurried into the bathroom. Her hair was a rat's nest and she needed to shower before he saw her looking so grungy. She should fix him a decent breakfast, and as her mind inventoried the nearly naked pantry she leaned over the sink with her loaded toothbrush.

"Now there's an invitation if I ever saw one. Leaning over, ass sticking out beneath my T-shirt . . . long sexy legs," he murmured. "Jesus, woman, how'm I supposed to get any chores done? I laid awake, wanting you, letting you sleep last night—"

She leveled her gaze at him in the mirror. "Come to think of it, that's the first night of real sleep I've gotten since—"

"I'm glad." As he hung his hat on the doorknob, then unfastened his jeans, his eyes never left hers. "Better rinse your mouth, angel. I'm ready to kiss you into next week—and that's just for starters. You okay with that?"

8

"What's your next trick, cowboy? How 'bout another long hard ride?"

Michael's pounding pulse drove him to pleasure her yet again, to chase away the ghosts that haunted this bedroom . . . to make this visit memorable in a lot of positive ways before he left. He could get way too comfortable in this cozy home, with this delicious woman, working again in pastures and stables and somehow making her dream of keeping this ranch come true.

But he had dreams, too. And they'd all been waylaid by women.

He stroked on another fresh condom. He loved it that Diana watched him from the bed, her eyes and body still eager. She'd sat on the bathroom vanity and wrapped her legs around him the first time, and then surrendered to her aftershocks when he washed her slit in the shower. Her hair hung in damp waves around her fresh face as she sprawled on sky-blue sheets in a sturdy four-poster with the rumpled comforter drifting off one side. They'd done a fine job of wrecking the bed when he'd tossed her there, barely dry from their shower. Her laughter drove his need deeper. This wasn't like anything he'd known with lesser women, and it scared the shit out of him.

Diana spread her legs and teased herself with a finger. "Do I need to show you the spot?" she taunted. "Draw you a map? Take your hand and lead you—"

"Careful what you wish for, witchy woman," he rasped. "Michael White Horse might just rear up on his hind legs and claim you as—"

Diana knelt to point her ass at him, and he was off like a shot. Her cry was that of a wild mare seeking her mate as he entered her. Her muscles sucked him inside and squeezed until he clenched his jaw to hang on to his sanity—to hold his load until he'd penetrated her to her point of no return as well. He suspected she'd never shown such passion for her husband, although she'd loved him deeply. And for this opportunity to show Diana Grant just how high she could soar, Michael felt sincerely grateful.

"Come on, angel," he whispered. "Spread your wings and take me along." Michael closed his eyes and slid his hands higher up her hot body when she stood on her knees. Her breasts bobbed in his palms, so firm and luscious. Her sighs became the words to the song in his heart.

In and out of her he rocked. His thighs slapped hers, still damp from their shower. He chuckled: he wasn't teaching her a thing he didn't need to learn himself. *Never* had he known such stamina or sustained need. And rather than exhausting him, it revived his soul, his spirit. This long hard ride gave him a foretaste of his return to the rodeo.

But he was a fool to think he could mount up and hang on for those frenetic eight seconds without recalling how he'd ridden Diana . . . how she'd shown him the true meaning of triumph over tragedy.

He held her hips as the need to surge overtook him. His cry

filled the room, escalating with his thrusts until she called out his name. Her ass flailed against him and she milked him, squeezed him, until he couldn't writhe any longer. When they collapsed sideways on the bed, he wrapped Diana in his embrace. She smelled sweet and clean—better than any damn saddle bronc. And for a fleeting moment, Michael was ready to ask if he could stay. He could set her place to rights while they fought the bank . . .

But that's not how the script went. This was just down-and-dirty sex with a stranger.

Hah! You still believe that?

Diana swiveled in his arms, beaming at him. "You were wonderful, Michael," she gushed. Her grin looked lopsided, like a little girl's. "I'm going to make you a nice breakfast as thanks for fixing the gate. Just for the fun of it, I think we ought to eat naked. You in?"

He muffled his laughter against her shoulder. "I want *in* every chance I can get, sugar," he replied in a playful growl. "And if eating naked gets me where I wanna go, I'm your slave, woman."

God, but it was good to see that sunshine in her smile. He caught a glimpse of the woman she'd been in happier times— the woman she'd be for him, if he said the word. Diana was that open, that obvious. That trusting and wonderful.

But Carina had been that way before she ran off with his daughters, too.

He set aside those thoughts. Watched Diana as she cracked eggs against the counter and beat them with a fork. The coffeemaker gurgled his name and the salty scent of crackling bacon beckoned him to clear the coffee table so they could eat on the couch. It was all so damn cozy, so *easy*, to be with Diana. Her breasts bobbed when she scraped the scrambled eggs into their plates. The sway of her hips as she walked ahead of him to the living room made him wonder if he'd finish fixing the gate any time soon.

The pounding on the door froze them midstep. Michael saw he hadn't shut the curtains last night before he'd carried Diana to bed. Had he locked the door?

"Hey, now! I know you're in there!" came a mocking male voice. "That bacon didn't cook itself."

Diana's plate clattered to the coffee table. When she glanced around for something to cover herself, Michael drew her against his bare body. "Just nod or shake your head," he whispered. "Do you know who it is?"

She scowled as if she'd bitten into a lemon.

"You could invite me to breakfast," their visitor spoke through the door. His voice had a wheedling edge Michael despised immediately. "Maybe we could strike up a little deal, Diana. I know how you love this place Garrison built."

"Bastard!" she muttered against Michael's chest. He held her tighter, his heart hammering against hers.

"Diana, you all right in there?" Pohlsen sounded concerned, but it raised the hairs on Michael's neck. "Your deadbolt's undone. Garrison would want me to be sure you were safe, so I'm going to—"

As the door swung open, Michael quickly shifted Diana's bare body behind his own. He glared at the thick, middle-aged man who dared to enter this house uninvited. "Don't take another step, Pohlsen," he snapped. "Diana was just fine—until *you* showed up."

The banker's eyes narrowed. "And who the hell're *you*? If Garrison knew some low-life escapee from the reservation was here with his wife—"

"Get out!" Diana remained behind Michael's body as she glared at the banker. "If he knew how *you* were taking over his land, without giving me so much as a chance to—"

"Oh, this is rich!" Pohlsen pointed at them, braying derisively. "Hubby's hardly cold in the ground, and you're playin' house with—hey, wait a minute! You own a black Chevy pickup? The one left alongside the road in the storm yesterday?"

Michael stiffened. "The tow service took it to—"

"Damn straight they did! The sheriff impounded it and had Bernie haul it to the station!" The banker cut loose with another of his irritating laughs. "Guess you better dress and come with me, so's we can—"

"Guess you better follow the lady's orders and *leave*." Michael forced himself to think straight. Diana was depending on him to defuse this unspeakable situation. "It's Sunday. The station's closed. I'll deal with it tomorrow."

"Damn straight you will! We don't like your kind messin' with our women, so I want you *gone*."

An ominous echo rang in the front room after Pohlsen slammed the door. Michael closed his eyes against his anger even as he pitied the woman clinging to him. She was shaking, humiliated, and scared. Pohlsen would never let Diana forget this incident. And Michael knew he'd wonder, every day he was away, if that snake from the bank had slithered out here to antagonize Diana again. There wasn't a neighbor for miles around . . .

"I'm sorry you had to face him—"

"No, *I'm* sorry, angel," Michael muttered. "Any skunk who would open the door and come in can't be trusted."

"But you're naked! And when he said—"

He tipped her face to kiss her. "Maybe the sight of my . . . *equipment* gave him something serious to think about. Or at least a diversion from seeing *you* naked," he teased. Anything to get that beaten, scared-shitless look out of her eyes. She'd put on ten years these last five minutes.

"He had no right to talk about you as though you're a second-class citizen, just because—"

Michael caught her face between his hands. "Guys in these

parts aren't known for their political correctness, sweetheart. And besides, it's to my advantage if he believes I'm just another stupid 'injun.' He won't see it coming when I whip his fat ass with facts and figures that'll save this place from the auction block."

Where had that come from? And why had he gotten Diana's hopes up by shooting off his mouth? He had no idea how to get the bank off her back—and once he reclaimed his pickup, and grilled Bernie the tow guy for hauling it to the police station, he'd be riding the rodeo circuit. Far, far away from this small-town drama. No matter how much he admired Diana, this was her fight, after all.

Her shining green eyes made him swallow hard. "Guess we'd better warm up those eggs," he mumbled.

Diana's sigh told him she'd followed his mental maneuvering. "I'm getting dressed," she announced wearily. "I've had all the excitement I can handle for one day."

"So what's the story about my truck, Bernie? I understand it's impounded at the station now, instead of at your shop." Michael kept his voice low as he spoke into his cell, while seated on Diana's front step. She was inside, putting herself together after a strained breakfast—which had put him in no mood to deal with another small-change local yokel.

Bernie cleared his throat nervously. "Yeah, well, I was gonna call you about that." His voice crackled with the poor cell reception. "Got tied up workin' two bad wrecks in that rain storm, and I was just drivin' down to your truck when the sheriff called me. Said he dang near sideswiped your truck, 'cause it wasn't pulled far enough off the road—"

"The shoulder was half under water—not that I could see much in that downpour," Michael replied tersely. "And it's not like I *wanted* to leave it there! Didn't you tell him I'd called you to fix it?"

"Well . . . when he checked out your license on his computer . . . seen you wasn't from around these parts . . ."

Escapee from the reservation.

"Well, he told me to haul it into town. Didn't wanna hear about it when I told him I was supposed to fix you up so's you could get rollin' again."

Michael considered his options as the outsider here. It wasn't like he had ten other repair shops to choose from. "If *your* truck died alongside the road, and *you* had contacted a mechanic for a tow, would *you* want to pay a fine before the repair guy even looked at it?"

"Well, no, but—"

"Then you'll understand if I deduct my fine from your bill."

Silence. Then a sputtering of words he didn't catch in a burst of static.

"So explain this to the sheriff and get the fine removed," Michael said firmly. "Am I being unfair, Bernie?"

"No, sir, not exactly, but—"

"That's my story and I'm sticking to it. I'll be at your shop tomorrow—say, ten-thirty—for an itemized report of what's wrong with my truck and what your repairs will cost me. See you then." He closed the phone, scowling. Bad enough that Diana had to drive him into town for another round of these shenanigans. He was losing time he'd planned to spend at small rodeos along the circuit, competing to build up points and to get himself back in the competitive saddle.

He focused on the steps—which needed a coat of sealant— to avoid gazing out over the rolling green hills of Seven Creeks Ranch. Behind him, the door opened. Michael braced himself: he was even more likely to succumb to Diana than to his cravings for a place like this.

"You know, I've been thinking." She leaned on the porch pillar beside him. "This delay with your truck means you're missing time in the saddle, doesn't it?" Her hair was neatly combed now and mascara highlighted her eyes; her jeans and plaid shirt looked faded, but they were clean and pressed.

He cleared his throat. "Life happens that way. I—"

"Garrison's truck is in the garage. It's a stick shift. Been sitting there since last fall when he got so sick, because I can't drive it."

Red flags shot up in his mind. Surely she wouldn't loan him her husband's truck, when he wouldn't return to Montana for months. Maybe never . . .

Diana lifted a defiant eyebrow. "What you've done for me—for my confidence—is priceless, Michael. I want you to have—"

"But you could *sell* that truck, to offset—"

"Phooey! *You* know how vehicles depreciate the moment you drive them off the lot," she insisted. "It'd be a raindrop in the ocean of what I owe the bank. It's *so* cool that you want to follow your dream, Michael! Do you know how few people go after what they really want in life?"

Her eyes drilled his, and he couldn't answer her.

"I've learned a thing or three about perspective this past year," she continued pensively. "So *take* the truck—as pay for the work you've done here! We'll figure out a way to handle your repair bill—"

"I'll cover it before I go."

"I'll keep your truck in the garage for . . ." Diana glanced away, blinking. "Well, maybe it'll be incentive for you to swing through here again someday. No strings—I understand that. But it's a nice thing to think about, isn't it?"

Michael let out the breath he'd been holding. Never mind that the bank intended to shove her off this place—and never mind what problems he'd have if the cops caught him driving a vehicle registered to somebody else . . . who happened to be dead. "That's about the nicest thing anybody's ever done for me, but—"

"Good! That's how I intended it!" She grinned as though

they'd struck a deal. "Now you can take off down the road again, like you'd planned. If you leave me a list of the rodeos you'll compete in, I can follow your progress online, right?"

Where did she find the strength—the resilience—to talk this way? It was a sure bet that bastard Pohlsen would screw her out of her home. Most women would cling and beg, hoping he'd stick around and find a way to save their pretty backsides—

And any decent man would sacrifice a few rodeo rides to do that.

But Diana Grant was made of stronger stuff. *Sacrifice* was a situation she felt far too familiar with, and she didn't expect him to tag along. She was playing by his rules. And she was setting him free. She crossed her arms as she gazed down at him, standing firm in her decision. Damn, but he loved her for that!

Michael stood up slowly. When words didn't come, he fished his wallet from his back pocket. Peeled out the wad of fifties that would cover his entry fees. "Take this—no arguments now!" he insisted as she waved away his money. "Get yourself something nice—do something you enjoy! I promise you I'll come back for my truck—"

"*After* you win big at the Vegas finals!"

Michael laughed in spite of the huge knot in his chest. "You've got a deal, Diana. You'll be my inspiration as I ride, okay?"

When she wrapped her small, strong arms around his waist, he realized he'd been roped, thrown and branded before he knew what hit him. Diana had planned all along to lure him back here, hadn't she?

He kissed her one last time Monday morning, knowing he should break away clean—no long, sad good-byes. She'd learned the hard way how to tamp down her anguish. When she reached up to stroke his freshly shaved face, the love in her eyes nearly killed him.

"If you need anything, you've got my number," she murmured, as though *he* were the one in need of a major miracle.

"Thanks for all you've done, and for loaning me the truck, sugar. I'll remind Bernie—again—that you don't owe him a cent, and that he damn well better deliver my truck when it's fixed."

Biting back a sigh, he stepped off her porch. Drove out the long, winding driveway, waving to her. Fought the urge to turn around and declare his original rules null and void, because damn it, he wanted to make it work with Diana! Was he driving away from the one woman who would make his life worthwhile?

He stopped at the gate and got out. Yanked down that auction sign and pitched it into the weeds alongside the road. He waved toward the house one last time, his heart pounding hard in his chest. Already he felt blue, and he hadn't gotten out of Roosevelt county yet.

His sentiments changed color when he reached Bernie's Tow-And-Go. The mechanic had his truck's hood up, but he had no clue about what he needed to fix or what it would cost. After haggling in circles, Michael wrote his cell number on Bernie's work order and shifted his rodeo gear into Garrison's truck bed. And of *course* that jackass Pohlsen pulled into the shop's gravel driveway and sat sideways, blocking his path to the road.

No doubt in his mind the banker would harass Diana about loaning him Garrison's truck. Michael almost demanded to see the loan papers for Seven Creeks Ranch, to determine any irregularities in the bankruptcy and auction proceedings. But guys like Pohlsen thought the world revolved around them. He'd seen arrogance like that after his uncle's cronies began managing the casino, and there was no cure for it.

"Hope you're proud of yourself, suckering that truck out of

her," the banker sneered. "Get out of my town! Good rid-
dance."

Michael tipped his hat tersely. He rolled on down the black-
top road and turned on Highway 25. Got as far as Wolf Point
and saw signs for the Silverwolf casino . . . saw Diana's smile in
his mind, like a powerful talisman.

He pulled into the crowded parking lot. It was time to kick
some ass.

9

It took three days, but Diana finally convinced herself Michael White Horse wasn't going to stroll through her door and into her arms again. By now he was back in the saddle, and had women flocking around him . . . rodeo groupies who'd fly like moths to his white-hot sexy flame. What woman could resist a cowboy? Or long hair that fluttered like a raven's wing when the breeze caught it, as it cascaded over his carved mahogany shoulders?

What the hell are you thinking? her thoughts taunted. *You don't know him from Adam, yet you go to that sleazy motel—beg him to make love without protection. Stick to him like glue, and then send him off in Garrison's new truck! How stupid is that?*

Yet her heart firmly believed she'd see Michael again. She dreamed of him so vividly she awoke in the night, vibrating with need—clenching so hard she nearly climaxed while recalling how he'd felt inside her. It was sheer craziness to think she'd ever have *that* sort of loving again!

But what *did* she have, other than her fantasies? The August auction date wouldn't disappear just because they'd torn down the signs. Diana was so far into denial she refused to count the dwindling food cans in her cabinet. Far nicer to sit on the steps, gazing at the eagle feather with its striking image of a white stallion, bold and fearless and male. Far nicer to tell herself Garrison would understand her need for company and affection . . . and that he would've trusted Michael enough to loan him the truck, too.

She was pondering the two men when tires crunched in the driveway. A shiny silver SUV followed a black pickup that made her heart fly up into her throat. By the time she realized Michael wasn't driving it, it was too late to hide behind a locked door. So Diana sat resolutely on the top step, composing her script for another unpleasant encounter with macho-man stupidity. At least she was dressed this time.

"Mornin', Miz Grant." The guy driving the truck pulled off the driveway and into the grass, about twenty feet away from her. "Finished up on the repairs and brung you back this pickup, like that White Horse fella told me to. Sorry it took so long. Had to order parts from—"

"Thanks. I appreciate you bringing it out to me."

He pulled off his ball cap to scratch his scraggly hair. "Yeah, well, you don't owe me nothin', so—"

"But you owe *me* an explanation!" Behind the mechanic, Jerry Pohlsen stepped down from his big-ass Lexus. He was better dressed than Bernie the mechanic, but he still had no class. Diana squared her shoulders, placing her hand over the painted feather to draw strength from it.

"You're in trouble with the law, first off," Pohlsen spouted as he pointed toward the road. "That sign at the gate—and this one on the porch—are bank property, and you've destroyed them! I'll have to report this vandalism to the sheriff and come back out with more signs—"

"And I guess that'll be one more time *you've* broken the

law," she replied tersely. She'd never had the guts to defy authority—was too much of a good girl. But where had that gotten her?

The banker scowled. "Beg pardon? Where I come from—"

"Is where you better head back to. Like, *now*." Diana stood up, for the psychological advantage of looking down at Pohlsen. "You're trespassing, Jerry. *I* didn't tear down your signs! Nor did I permit you to nail them to my gate and my home like permanent fixtures! And where *I* come from, that's destruction of private property! So leave!"

Her pulse pounded. Where had such sass come from, and what did she hope to accomplish with it? Antagonizing this man could only get her in deeper trouble, because she *did* owe Pohlsen's bank a large chunk of money. But by God, she would not grovel! And she would not cry!

The pudgy banker glanced surreptitiously at Bernie. "Just another way that long-haired redskin had his way with her," he muttered. "*You* saw how he was driving Garrison's new truck—"

Bernie nodded.

"And I told you how I came here the other day and found him . . . playing house with Mrs. Grant, didn't I?"

"Yessir. Nekkid."

Diana's face burned but she held her remarks.

"And now look at what she's got. That's one of her husband's feather paintings. You recall what a fine talent Garrison Grant had, Bernie?"

Again the mechanic nodded. It reminded Diana of a ventriloquist act, where Pohlsen spoke from both sides of his mouth and Bernie nodded like his dummy.

"Can you believe it? She's holding the one with the *white horse* on it as a reminder of her stud loverboy! The one she let into Garrison's house—into his *bed*!" With a thin-lipped gaze at her, he crossed his arms. "What do you want to bet he tickled her bare skin with that feather, Bernie? Can't you just imagine him teasing her nipples until they stuck out, all hard and—"

"Get out," Diana rasped. Her knees were shaking so badly she wasn't sure how she remained standing, but she pointed to his SUV. "And if you come back, I'll call the sheriff."

Pohlsen's eyes widened derisively. "Would that be the sheriff I play poker with on Tuesday nights? The sheriff who serves as a deacon at my church?" When he laughed, his face took on a cruel edge. "At least we know he'll do the right thing if you call him, Mrs. Grant. Especially once I ask him to keep an eye on the new signs I'll post. I have to give public notice of the auction, you see. It's the law."

She was too enraged—too damn scared—to say another word. Somehow she kept pointing at his Lexus until he finally got into the damn thing, with Bernie following like an eager puppy. And somehow she remained standing on the porch until only the dust of the road lingered in his wake.

"Shit head," she muttered. Then she burst into tears and went inside.

The cupboard was bare. The fridge held only condiments. The ache Diana felt had nothing to do with a need for food. She hadn't asked Michael for his cell number, for fear she'd call when he was psyching himself to ride those saddle broncs—but also because she was hardheaded enough to want *him* to call first.

"You and your big ideas," she muttered. She'd been talking to herself more the last few days. But who else was there?

This is insane! Go to town for groceries. It's not like Pohlsen'll be hiding in the aisles, waiting to play demolition derby with a cart.

The banker couldn't take legal action because Michael had destroyed those signs . . . could he? Pohlsen and his cronies were so full of that good-old-boy bullshit, she knew better than to believe his threats.

But a part of her—the part that had depended upon Garrison to handle all the tough-guy stuff—shriveled at the thought of seeing the banker in a public place. By now dozens of folks knew about Michael staying at her place and then driving away in her husband's truck. Most of them would *not* approve, and they'd tell her so when they saw her.

Diana put on a clean shirt. Resigned herself to spending some of Michael's money. When she took the folded bills from the dresser, a white card fluttered to the floor.

Had Michael left her a note? Maybe his phone number? She eagerly retrieved the card, but then sighed. It was a business card from a Will Killiam, an attorney. Like she could afford one of those!

Don't write him off! That phone exchange is from up north, around the reservation, so maybe he does pro bono work.

Her stomach clutched at the idea of taking charity. Then again, beggars couldn't be choosers. As she riffled through the folded bills to count them, Diana's eyes widened. Michael White Horse had given her six hundred dollars.

She wheezed. Counted again, pinching the crisp, folded fifties to be sure they didn't stick together. Sure enough, she had twelve of them.

And what had he planned to do with that money? He's not the type to carry that much cash.

Diana blinked. How did she know that? She'd seen him all of twenty minutes before she'd gone to that motel room, and her mind had swum in a romantic muddle ever since. His story about that woman disappearing with his daughters could've been a ploy to win her sympathy. And how did she know he was really an accountant? And what if he used Garrison's truck to commit a crime? Wouldn't the cops trace the truck back to

this address? Could she be held responsible for Michael's actions if he turned out to be a bad apple?

She caught sight of her scowl in the dresser mirror. When
Michael had stood here behind her, holding her against his
darker bare body, looking over her shoulder with those
sparkling onyx eyes, her whole being had glowed. Now she
looked like a worn-down widow again, old before her time.

Stupid, stupid, stupid, her thoughts taunted. *Why does your
happiness depend upon a man?*

But hey, she had money for food. And surely there'd be
enough left to consult that attorney about how to handle
Pohlsen . . . or who to contact so her home wouldn't be dozed
to make way for a damn resort community. If she stayed here
whimpering, Fritzi Pohlsen would soon be choosing custom
window treatments and gold-plated faucets for *her* new home.
Right here in this spot.

Diana grabbed her purse. That despicable banker and his
high-toned wife would *not* build their McMansion here! This
was *her* ranch!

She walked resolutely to the garage, a woman on a mission.
She stopped at the mailbox, cringing at past-due bills from the
funeral home and the electric co-op. A greeting card awaited
her at the bottom of the pile, addressed in handwriting she didn't
recognize.

Surely this wasn't another sympathy card, so long after Garrison's passing. She almost tossed it on the passenger seat, but
something about the masculine handwriting made her heart
pound with hope. The front of the card showed a lone horse
and rider silhouetted against a desert sunset. When she opened
it, a folded slip of paper fell into her lap.

Diana, my angel, the neat black printing read. *I hit a
couple lucky jackpots at the Silverwolf, and then won big-
time at the Belt rodeo. You were my lucky charm and in-*

spiration, so you should have this. Not since my mother died has any woman shown me such warmth and love without expecting anything in return. CALL TO LET ME KNOW YOU GOT THIS. Michael.

Her heart did a flip-flop as she noted his cell number. She reread the note twice before she picked up the folded paper with trembling fingers. He'd been thinking of her! He'd won at his first rodeo event!

"He loves me!" she whispered as tears sprang to her eyes. Then she mopped her face to be sure of the amount written on his money order.

Forty-five hundred dollars.

"Holy shit! Holy—" Diana flicked the fan up to its highest setting and stared at the paper. This wasn't a check written on some account that might be bogus. This was honest-to-God money.

Forty-five hundred dollars. Plus the fifties she had in her wallet.

When she could get her breath, Diana dug her cell phone out of her purse. She hastily thumbnailed the number at the bottom of the card, and then waited. One ring . . . two . . .

10

When Michael saw the number of his incoming call his heart kicked his rib cage. He trotted behind the chutes toward the guy with the clipboard. "Yeah, Diana? Diana, hold on, sugar!" he wheezed. The crowd in the arena went wild, which told him the first saddle bronc rider had scored well.

He grabbed the hostler's arm. "Hey, put me as the last rider! I got an emergency call!" he rasped, pointing to his cell phone.

The guy's fat mustache curved downward. "Can't just up and change the order of contestants, now that the event's—"

"Diana? Hold on, honey! Breathe real deep and then let it out in little pants! Remember?" He imitated the pattern he'd learned while coaching Carina during childbirth classes.

The man's eyes widened. "All right—I'll tell the announcer you're goin' last. But you surely knew about that baby before you paid your entry fee!" he groused as he hurried toward the booth.

"Baby? What baby?" Diana demanded in his other ear. "Michael, what's going on? Where are you? What's all that noise?"

He grinned as her voice filled him with the only sound he'd wanted to hear these past few weeks. "Diana, I've almost called you every night, but I had to be sure you still wanted—"

"Michael, I'm sitting in my car, at the mailbox, and I'm holding a money order for forty-five hundred dollars," she said in a shaky voice. "What the hell is *that* for?"

"Whatever you want, sugar. No strings," he added quickly, and then wished he hadn't. He *wanted* strings—to wrap around her, to wrap around his own heart—but the loading chutes under a grandstand filled with cheering fans wasn't the place to discuss that. "Angel, I've got to saddle up, so I can—"

"And you're winning! That's so awesome, Michael!"

His heart swelled. He closed his eyes to see her sweet face in his mind. "It *is* awesome. And I'm so damn glad to hear your voice again, sweetheart. I'll call you tonight, okay? Unless you've got a hot date with some stud—"

"Fat chance! I'm going for groceries, but then I'll be home waiting for your call! And, hey—who's Will Killiam?"

He scowled. Why was she asking him *that*? The hostler was back, frantically pointing him toward his chute, where a rangy, mottled bronc kicked the wooden partitions. "Will's my— look, it's a long story and I've *got* to saddle my bronc. Talk to you tonight, Diana. *Want* you, angel."

He punched off his phone and buttoned it into his shirt pocket. Crammed his hat tighter and grabbed his saddle. His pulse raced to the music of Diana's voice . . . damn horse snorted and kicked while he slipped down into the narrow chute to saddle it. Michael slapped the horse's belly, tightened the cinch with a hard yank, and then heard his cue blaring out of the speakers.

"Our last contestant in the saddle bronc competition is Mike White Horse, who hails from Medicine Lake, Montana," the announcer's voice boomed out over the sound system. "Mike has drawn Demon's Dare, a horse with a nasty reputation on the circuit. You clowns and pickup riders better be ready—we're all wishing Mike the best."

He silenced his mind. Breathed deeply. Let instinct take over. He reveled in the scents of sweaty horseflesh and corn dogs and fresh straw. Slipped his foot into the stirrup and swung over the bronc's back, allowing his body to gauge the high-strung mount's skittishness and the likelihood of it making any unexpected moves during this eight-second contest of wills. Guessing how a random saddle bronc would behave was a lot like figuring out a woman's patterns—but rewarding in a different way.

With a last fleeting thought of Diana smiling at him, Michael wrapped the rope around his arm. He took a deep breath and held it.

Whack! The gate flew up as the band played a rousing march tune, and Michael's mount began to spin like a wicked tornado. He let his mind go slack, let his body flow and fly with the bronc's, spinning like a tightly wound top on a horse born to break every bone in a man's body. Some mounts had to be kicked and cajoled to perform, thus raising the cowboy's chance at a high score, but this demon loved his work. Up and back he kicked with spine-cracking strength, spiraling around the arena with a speed and agility Michael had seldom encountered.

When the buzzer sounded and the crowd roared, Michael opened his eyes. He spotted the pickup riders. Let the strap fall from his arm so he could leap off at the best moment in the horse's spin cycle. He hit the dirt with a *whump* and instinctively rolled away from the bronc while the clowns steered the snorting horse toward the gate.

"And there's your winner, folks!" the announcer bellowed. "Our judges have given Mike White Horse a nearly perfect score, based on his riding skill and agility on the tightest sidewinder of a mount we've seen this week! Show him how you liked it, folks! Mike White Horse!"

Michael rolled to his feet to accept his applause. Raising his black hat in thanks, he trotted out of the arena—then fell back against the wooden post at the end of the ramp to catch his breath. Every muscle in his body was crying out from the tension of that ride, but it was a glorious stress: it affirmed that he'd done the right thing, returning to rodeo now rather than waiting. Hell, in a few more years his body wouldn't withstand this abuse.

"Helluva ride, Mike! So what's your secret?"

He opened his eyes: a microphone was in his face, and the guy holding it wore a press pass and a big grin. "No secret," he replied. "Does you no good to be *smarter* than the horse, or to anticipate its moves, because you'll guess wrong every time. Really good rodeo stock is bred and trained to go hellbent-for-leather."

The reporter's head tipped a little as he listened. "But you looked so natural—so unconcerned—while your mount spun in some of the nastiest circles I've seen."

Michael reminded himself rodeo was a family-oriented sport, and smiled cryptically. "I respond to the horse, rather than reacting. Rodeo broncs are a lot like women, because if you think you've figured them out, they'll throw you every time. Respect and adoration—giving the bronc its way—gets you further than dominating it."

The reporter laughed out loud. "Our lady listeners are chuckling about *that* one! Good luck to you on the circuit, Mike! Good to have you back in the game."

And it was good to be back, wasn't it? As he watched the stocky reporter hustle through the dim passageway beneath the grandstand . . . heard the laughter as the announcer and the clowns bantered back and forth between events . . . Michael felt a deep sense of satisfaction that eased a lot of his physical discomfort.

He gathered his gear and headed for the pay window. Strolled toward the proud red pickup with his saddle slung over his shoulder and a spring in his step. He'd treat himself to a good steak and a belt or two of high-dollar whiskey rather than the chili and beer he'd devoured as a younger rodeo contestant.

But first he stopped at a convenience store and put three-quarters of his prize into a money order . . . tucked it into a greeting card that showed a row of blue-jeaned cowboy butts along a corral gate. Diana would laugh at the eye candy before her jaw dropped at another gift from him. He wasn't wild about sending her money and she wasn't keen on accepting it, but it was a give-and-take that served his purpose until he could engage her in the give-and-take they both liked so much better.

"Diana . . . how ya doin' tonight, angel?" Michael relaxed against the bed pillows, closing his eyes to picture her in that homey bedroom with the four-poster.

"Michael! I'm fine! So how'd you ride today?"

He smiled, partly from the second glass of Yukon Jack and water he balanced on his chest, and partly from the way her voice affected his vital parts. "You're talkin' to a winner," he crooned, "but an eight-second ride wouldn't be nearly long enough if I were there with you. Whatcha doin'?"

She giggled tentatively, which made his insides twitch. "I'll have you know I indulged in a steak tonight."

"Glad to hear it. Me, too."

"Before that I restocked the fridge and kitchen shelves. I can't thank you enough, Michael. You saved my life—"

"I doubt that, sugar. You're a tough one."

"And I owe you big-time for helping me."

"Nonsense. Nobody else would've loaned me her husband's truck and told me to go follow my dream, Diana. I haven't nearly repaid you for that favor." He sipped his drink, considering where to take this. "But we're talkin' awfully serious here, considering—"

"Oh! And I called Will Killiam. We set a time next week to look at my . . . financial options with the bank."

Envy kicked his gut like a wayward bronc. Will's business card must've slipped out of his wallet with those fifties—which would teach him to pay attention to what he was doing, instead of gawking at Diana. Killiam's personal power and refined looks won him a lot of cases . . . and women. "Probably should've stayed there to help you myself—"

"He spoke very highly of you, both as an accountant and a rodeo rider," she interrupted pertly.

"As well he should! I've pulled his ass out of a few fires, and he's advised me about some casino situations. He was my college roommate," Michael added, lowering his voice, trying to remain calm. "Good-lookin' sucker, too, so don't go getting any ideas about bartering your uh, *services* for his."

"Michael! Really!"

Shit. This wasn't how he'd planned to talk to her tonight. "Sorry, angel. Will and I know each other's tricks, okay? I didn't mean to imply that *you* would behave—"

"Well, I guess I gave you reason to, didn't I?" came her soft reply. "Michael, I'm *not* the type to check into a motel with a stranger, or to peel off my clothes for—"

"Ah, shucks, ma'am. I was hoping for some down-and-dirty phone sex. You in?" The liquor and his loneliness made him say that. Would she listen?

She sucked air—and sucked away what remained of his rational thought. "You think I'm the kind of woman who . . . well, hell! I guess I *am*!"

In the blink of an eye Diana had switched gears. Transformed herself into the wayward, willing woman he'd hoped to indulge in tonight, and he loved her for it. "So what're you gonna *do* about it?" he challenged in a low whisper. He set his drink on the nightstand, thrumming with sweet anticipation.

Oh, that wicked laugh that came through his phone! "You've already got your pants down, *don't* you, Michael?"

"Who says I was wearing any?"

Diana snickered. "So should I confesss I'd just stepped out of the shower when you called? Had to run through the house all wet and naked to catch the phone—"

"Hope to hell you shut the drapes!"

"Maybe I left them open. So you could . . . watch me."

His cock shot up at that edge in her voice—at the way she directed his mind's eye to peer through the front window from her porch, to gaze at her fine, feisty smile and the body that taunted him. "Oh, I'm watchin', all right," he murmured hoarsely. "And I have to wonder what you're thinking about while you stand there with your foot on the arm of that chair . . . strumming yourself. Grab your tits and squeeze 'em together. Point your nipples at me—"

"Grab 'em yourself, cowboy. And while your hands are busy with my boobs, I'm wrapping mine around your long . . . hard . . . *cock*, Michael. And I intend to get a long, hard ride out of that thing, ya know?"

"Oh, I know how you love to ride it, Diana." His hand slipped down to ease the ache . . .

"But first I'm gonna *suck* it. Gonna suck you till you buck and squirt in my mouth."

"Jesus." He squeezed his eyes shut and his pulse throbbed into a higher, needier gear.

"My lips are running up and down your hot skin, Michael . . . wet and slick . . . while my tongue dances around your tip . . . tickles that little hole where the cum shoots out."

"You're askin' for it now," he rasped. "I just laid you down on the couch and straddled you for sixty-nine. I know how much you love it when I shove my tongue up inside your—"

Her moan sounded desperate, and it gratified the hell out of him. Phone sex was a new game, one he'd always wanted to try, but this! It was blowing his mind, imagining how her eager mouth tightened around his shaft . . . ran up and down him as he thrust into the "O" she made with her lips.

"Deeper," she moaned. "Stick your tongue down inside me and . . . oh, God, Michael! My butt's shuddering so hard I can hardly talk to you."

Was it real or was she feeding into his fantasy? Diana sounded breathless and so damn turned on. Along with all the other pictures flickering through his mind, Michael recalled the way she'd stroked her inner pink lips with that single, purposeful finger . . . the way her pearly juice made her skin shine with need as her thigh muscles quivered . . .

"Diana." He convulsed and had to hold himself back. Would she think he was a pervert if he lost himself during this phone scenario?

"Michael . . . Michael . . ." Her desperation etched a clear picture in his mind: she was writhing beneath him on that couch, wide open and thrusting up to rub his face as he devoured her.

"I'm gonna bring you off," he rasped, squeezing himself. The creaking of his bed spurred him on, and he didn't even care if she heard it. "My tongue's teasing around your rim, and your hard little button is between my thumbs," he breathed. "On the count of three, I'm gonna plunge my tongue inside you and rub everything all at once, really hard, until you holler out. One—"

She started low and hesitant, but he could hear her writhing . . . going with the flow that drove them both so effortlessly . . . until she wailed like a siren. She fumbled with the phone—

He grimaced in climax, muffling his moan like a teenager whose parents slept in the next room. He lay there then, loosely clasping his cell over his chest as he caught his breath. Spent. Totally spent.

"Michael?" Her thin voice, muffled by his skin, reminded him she was still on the line. Made him want to cradle her body, bare and hot and vibrant.

"Sorry. Got busy for a minute," he confessed. "My God, woman. I think I've been struck by lightning."

11

"Oh, good. I thought I'd jarred you out of the flow when I dropped my phone." Diana shook her damp waves around her face. It wasn't as good as having Michael play with her hair after they stepped out of the shower, but she could imagine him gazing intently at her, as though she were the only woman in the world. Never mind that after he won today, he had scads of female fans making all kinds of offers. Right now, while she had Michael White Horse on the phone, whispering in her ear, she could believe she was the only one.

He chuckled. "Okay, tell me straight up—have you ever done that before? On the phone, I mean?"

"No way! Have you?"

"Thought about it, but couldn't see dialing a professional at a nine hundred number. I don't like sex to be a business transaction, ya know?"

"I find that sweetly reassuring." She eased into the overstuffed armchair, feeling wickedly depraved. She sat bare-ass naked . . . sensually aware of the chair's texture and the evening breeze from the window . . . feeling better than she had since

Michael drove off. "Of course, no matter where you go, every woman in sight wants you."

He let out a soft snort. "Tell that to the gals at my uncle's casino. Seems my quest for fiscal information and accountability was a real turn-off."

Diana felt light inside, like butterflies were dancing. "Ah, but giving you sex and giving you incriminating information are two different things."

"I miss you, angel. In a bad way. And it's not just about the sex, either."

She blinked. He sounded genuinely lonely. Sincere about wanting to be with her. "I miss you, too, Michael. A helluva lot more than I anticipated."

"So join me! I can fly you to—"

"You know I have to see to this ranch sale business, and—and—" Her heart thundered so hard she couldn't think straight. Was he offering to buy her airfare? And what would it mean if she went? "Michael, I can't let Pohlsen pull any fast ones or bully me out of my property."

"And I would never, *never* want you to do that." His voice shifted, as though he were sitting up straight again. "You want me to pursue my dream, sweetheart, and I fully expect you to challenge the bank's foreclosure. I intend to help you, too."

She shut her eyes against sudden hot tears. "You don't have to—"

"You didn't have to loan me a truck, either." When he paused, something bumped against the phone receiver. A glass with ice cubes, maybe. "But I don't like you being at the ranch alone, either, like a sitting duck on Jerry Pohlsen's pond. He'll use me against you, every way he can. And I—I love you too much to let that happen."

She fell back against the chair. "Michael, you can't—"

"Not promising we'll always be together. Not saying we'll get married," he explained in a low voice. "But what man wouldn't love you, Diana? You're loyal and sweet and generous. And you have this hot little curve to your ass that drives me nuts, okay?"

Diana let herself down slow and easy from their escalated conversation. "I'm in lust with you, too, cowboy. Before you came along, I was more depressed than I knew. Ready to roll over and play dead, far as letting the bank take the place. That's all changed, thanks to you."

"Good. *Now* will you come join me?" he pleaded playfully. "I'm competing in Cody, Wyoming, over the Fourth of July, and then I'll ride in the Indian Relay in Sheridan. What a rush that is, riding bareback, hellbent for leather, in paint and feathers and a loincloth! I would *love* to have you there cheering me on, angel."

He played her like a violin. Just enough pathos in his voice, just enough pretty words to convince her she could do something so frivolous as leave the ranch . . .

And why is that frivolous? How long's it been since you had a vacation?

Diana couldn't recall. It was long before Garrison got sick, because *he* wasn't one for trips. No place suited him as much as home, sweet home. And while she'd understood that about him—and she cherished their time at this ranch—she *had* felt penned in at times. Curious about what she'd see beyond the Montana state line, and about how other people spent their leisure time. How did they leave the day-to-day stuff behind and go *play*?

Lord knows Michael can show you how to play!

Her body twitched. As she sat naked in the armchair, with her legs dangling over one arm, Diana so badly wanted to believe she'd find a new reason to laugh and rejoice. "All right, I'll think about it—"

"Do you have a PayPal account? I can deposit some money—"

"But I'm meeting with Will Killiam," she continued firmly. "I *have* to know he can turn things around with this bankruptcy, or I've got no business leaving. Like a captain goes down with his ship, I'll go down with Seven Creeks if it comes to that."

"I'd rather have you go down on *me*, Diana. *Soon*, okay?"

Her stomach butterflies danced a jig. So many things to consider, like how she'd get to the airport and what would she *wear*? And what if the locals—and Pohlsen—got wind of her running off to be with Michael again?

"Stop thinking so much," he said firmly. "I want a yes or a no. And if you say no, I'll understand."

"Yes! Yes, I'll come. But how will I—"

"Leave the details to me, angel." He bumped the receiver again, and she pictured him sipping a drink on his bed ... imagined his raven hair hanging past his shoulders ... flowing loose over his smooth, dark skin. She wanted to be the glass he held to his lips.

"All right," she finally breathed. "All right, Michael. You win this one."

"Nobody *loses*!" he said with a laugh. "Get out your calendar, and figure out when you can *come*. And leave it to me to see that you'll *come* wherever and whenever you want to. Are you with me?"

Diana closed her eyes against tears of joy. "I'm with you, Michael. And—and I can't wait to be *with* you!"

"That's what I wanted to hear. Good night, angel," he purred. "And I *do* love you."

Click. His words lingered ... words spoken too soon to seem believable. But she believed. She believed with all her heart.

Diana held the phone to her chest ... let all the sensations settle in. Michael White Horse loved her ... wanted to be with her ... was sending airfare, maybe as soon as the Fourth of

July—which was only a week away! She had a gazillion things to do before then!

Yet she remained in the chair's arms, pretending she was in Michael's lap. It felt so damn good to have something to look forward to! She'd give Will Killiam a call tomorrow—

"Well, Mrs. Grant, I didn't have the heart to interrupt that cozy little phone chat. But since your windows are wide open, I couldn't help but hear it, either."

Diana froze. Pohlsen's voice drifted through the front window, where the breeze fluttered the curtains—which were *not* shut, damn it! She bolted from the chair. Slammed and locked the bedroom door, and then scrambled into her jeans and shirt. Damn that man! Didn't have the heart to interrupt—but didn't have the decency to leave, either! And now he knew of her plans to rendezvous with Michael, and—hell, she was so flustered she didn't remember anything else she'd said! But *he* would.

She glared toward the front window. What she wouldn't give to have a shotgun—just for effect. Jerry Pohlsen's sneak-attack visits were becoming such a habit, maybe she *should* take one of Garrison's guns from the locked cabinet. Violence wasn't in her nature, but Michael had pegged her situation, saying she was a sitting duck on Pohlsen's pond.

She had the right to defend her ranch, and to defend herself. The banker had to know she was here alone, and that it wasn't right to drop over unannounced and then eavesdrop on her conversations.

"Just came by to see that everything was all right," he wheedled. "And to see if you've reconsidered, about turning over your land. You can avoid the humiliation of having your neighbors at an auction if you'll just—"

"I *refuse* to hand over this ranch," she blurted. "So you might as well leave. *Now.*"

His chuckle flickered like the tongue of a snake. "Sounds

like White Horse got you all fired up, Diana. Do you really think he'll bail you out? He's only interested in one thing, and—"

"So are you. Get the hell off my porch, or I'm calling 911."

The banker let out a derisive snort. "If the ambulance and fire truck get here and see there's no emergency, you'll be charged for—"

"Oh, there'll be an emergency, all right. They'll be hauling your ass away on a stretcher after I use it for target practice." Her stomach knotted. She knew better than to make threats she couldn't carry out, because Pohlsen was just weasel enough to call her bluff—and then harass her again.

"So who's this Will Killiam?" he shot back. "If you think some hot-shot lawyer can get you out of—"

"I think that's none of your business!"

His laughter put her scalp on edge. "Fritzi's got a contractor drawin' up plans for the new resort home I've promised her as an anniversary present," he said in an oily voice. "And meanwhile, folks hereabouts've heard about you runnin' with that no-account red man . . . turned your back on all the principles Garrison stood for. Everybody loved him, Diana. They'll have no sympathy for a two-bit whore who's sold out on her husband."

There was no answer to his blatant insult, and Jerry Pohlsen didn't deserve any more of her time or attention. She fought the urge to throw open the door and go out swinging, but that would give him more opportunity to bait her—and who knew what else?

Diana turned out the lights. Stood in her living room, behind a chair. She kept her cell phone in her hand.

"I'm leaving, but I'm not gone," he called out as he descended the stairs. His SUV purred into motion and cruised slowly down her driveway, to taunt her by his presence—his power—for every possible moment.

When he reached the road, she let herself cry. But she'd done so much of that this past year, it didn't have much therapeutic effect. Diana thumbed in the number at the bottom of Will Killiam's business card. She didn't expect him to answer at this hour, but at least she could leave him—

"Hello? Will here."

Diana closed her eyes. "Will, it's Diana Grant. I—I called you earlier about—"

"Yes, of course, Diana. You asked me to help you with your situation there at Seven Creeks Ranch."

His businesslike demeanor soothed her. She hesitated, but her plea came out of its own accord, along with a sob she couldn't suppress. "I—can you come tomorrow instead? Jerry Pohlsen just showed up again, uninvited and unannounced, and I—"

"I'll be there by nine with breakfast. Will that work?"

She exhaled, suddenly exhausted. "Thank you," she breathed. "I can't thank you enough."

She turned off the lamp. Stood alone in the darkness. How would she ever afford a big-time attorney like Will Killiam?

12

"I'll issue a restraining order against Mr. Pohlsen. With information I've gathered, I can postpone the auction date while we pursue other avenues of repaying your mortgage, Mrs. Grant." Will Killiam's grin waxed boyish yet edgy across the kitchen table. "Nothing I like better than going after bastards who break the law because they believe they're above it. If you'll pardon my French."

"No matter what language you speak, it's an ugly situation." Diana bit into a danish pastry, reveling in its cream cheese and apricot filling. "Wow, is this a treat. How'd you know these goodies from Klineschmidt's were my favorite?"

Michael was right: his college roomie was a looker and he knew how to work it. Will wore a crisp oxford cotton shirt rolled to his forearms, a loosened tie, and his sandy brown hair fell in a neat yet trendy fetlock over his forehead. "Inside information never hurts," he replied cryptically. "And that's what we'll nail Pohlsen with, too. Are you comfortable with what we've discussed?"

"What's not to love about muzzling Pohlsen? And postponing that damned auction?" she said, sighing. "He's been swooping like a buzzard ever since Gavin died, telling me I couldn't possibly repay—"

"I'm so sorry about your ordeal," he said quietly. "Organ transplants are miracles, but sometimes they backfire. So much hope and time and *money* at stake, to have your dreams shattered a few months later. And to have your bank threatening your home is unspeakable, Diana."

She could see why women went after this guy. He was so compassionate . . . as compelling as Michael White Horse, in his way. Yet Will was quite different from his college roommate. "I can't imagine you and Michael sharing a room. Totally different personalities and . . . lifestyles."

"Don't let the clothes fool you," he said with a chuckle. "Michael was a shirt-and-tie guy at the casino. Finest number cruncher I know."

"Yet his expertise alienated him from his family and his tribe," she mused aloud. Didn't hurt to snoop for details about the man who was still a mystery in many ways.

"And that's too bad, considering how—" Will stroked his hair back from his eyes, watching her. "I don't know how familiar you are with his situation. And friends don't spill the beans on friends."

His grin was something to behold. Diana nodded as she reached for her third helping of fresh strawberries and melon wedges. "He told me about the gal running off with his twins. Didn't go into detail, but he was pretty torn up about it."

"He was crazy in love with Carina, but she was poison. Here today and gone tomorrow—and it wasn't the first time she'd pulled such a stunt."

"She's had other kids? And run off with them?" Diana's eyes widened.

"Some women can't commit. And some guys are too nice about it." Will gazed around her kitchen. "That wasn't the problem here, though. Everything about this place speaks of love and devotion—which is why this ranch is *not* going to be chopped into resort properties."

That's what she'd hoped to hear, but how could he sound so positive? His card said he was from Missoula, so why would he give two hoots about her ranch north of Wolf Point?

"From what I could dig up about the bank's financial positioning, and the specs in their proposal, Pohlsen and his crew have bitten off way more than they can chew, or construct at a profit," Will continued.

Her stomach clenched. "They've already drawn up plans?"

"I'm afraid so." He leaned forward, smiling kindly. "But having plans and having a done deal are often miles apart—the daydreams of guys who want to throw their clout around. Did you know, for instance, that our friend Mr. Pohlsen intends to run for congress in the next election?"

"Jerry?" She nearly spewed coffee at him.

"His behavior toward you isn't prudent, for a man aspiring to political office. But I've got what I need right here." He tapped his pad with his mechanical pencil.

She still wondered how all this was falling into place so neatly, considering the nightmare she'd endured last night with Pohlsen. "Thanks for taking me at my word, Will. Some folks are pretty good at name calling and finger pointing, and I've been on the receiving end ever since . . . well, since I met Michael."

A sparkle flickered in his eyes. "And how did you two meet? You're not the type he usually . . . falls for."

Would anything she said be used against her if this attorney got chatty with the wrong locals? "I stopped in at the highway cafe because it was raining so hard I couldn't see," she recalled in a faraway voice. "I'd just gotten the sale ultimatum from Pohlsen. Had been crying my eyes out, so I left my sunglasses on when I took the last seat at the lunch counter—which happened to be beside Michael." She shrugged, unable to suppress a grin. "One thing led to another."

"From what he's told me, it was a damn lucky happenstance—which means he and I have discussed the . . . particulars," Will confessed with a quirk of his lips. "Guys do that, so don't get upset—"

"Jerry Pohlsen has broadcast those same *particulars*, after he barged in on us." Diana sat straighter. How should she feel, knowing Michael had divulged some very personal information?

Maybe it means you're his woman now . . .

"I was so damn glad to hear excitement in Mike's voice again—especially when he was talking about a woman." Will lightly gripped her wrist, his hazel eyes shining with gratitude. "And yes, I know he's buying you a plane ticket, and I want you to *go* without a moment's hesitation. The ranch'll still be here when you get back, Diana. And it'll still be yours."

She grinned and let her shoulders relax. "Michael filled me in on *you*, too, you know."

"So you already know I'm the most cutthroat, bad-ass attorney in Montana, and—"

"He told me not to *barter* my services for yours. Had he been within reach, I would've smacked him," she added with a short laugh. "But that brings up the matter of payment. As in, how much will this cost me, Will? Despite the state of my bank accounts, I'm a woman who pays her bills."

"Which I knew from the get-go." He stood, announcing the end of their meeting, and extended his hand. "You haven't seen any results yet—and it might take me a while to set these events in motion—so don't concern yourself with my bill."

"But I can't just—"

"Yes, you can, Diana." He gripped her hand firmly as he shook it, and his gaze didn't waver. "Let me get the debt monkeys off your back, and meanwhile I want you in the stands cheering your heart out for my best friend while he rides those broncs."

As she rose from the table, her cell phone jangled. "Isn't it just like Michael to call now, as though he knows we've been talking about him?" she said with a snicker. Then she spoke into her phone. "Good morning, Michael! Will and I were just talking . . ."

With a signal that he'd wait, Will went out to the front porch. She watched him gaze out over the pastureland as she drank in the sound of her cowboy's husky voice.

"So you ready to fly west, angel? Can't wait to peel down your panties when you get here!"

"But, Michael, I don't know what to pack! Or what to wear! Or—"

"So leave your clothes at home," he purred. "You could be waiting for me in the motel room, naked and spread out on the bed, when I get done riding each day. And then, little lady, this bronc buster would take you for a spin like you've never known the likes of. You with me?"

Diana giggled nervously. Never in her life had she had such a conversation, and it made her feel like she was twenty-one again, on top of a world that held endless possibilities.

"Yeah. Will says to forget about the ranch and Pohlsen, and just—"

"Forget about Will, too. Except for believing he'll do a good job for you."

Diana laughed. "Do I detect some jealousy in your voice, cowboy?"

"I'm saying you'd better get your sweet rear in gear, angel. You haven't checked your e-mail, have you?"

She blinked. "No. Just finished talking to Will about—"

"Will schmill! Print out your ticket, throw some clothes in a duffel, and hit the road, woman!" he teased. "I got you a great getaway deal but it's only good for this afternoon's flight."

"Holy—I've gotta get moving!" She made a kissy noise into the phone. "And thank you, Michael. From the bottom of my widdle heart."

"I love it when you talk dirty," he teased. "Be careful on the road, hear me?"

13

Diana dashed to the computer, skimmed the flight confirmation he'd sent, and her jaw dropped. Michael wasn't kidding! She had *no* time to lose! "Will! Will, my flight's at three-fifty and I haven't started to pack and I need gas in my car and—"

The sandy-haired attorney stepped inside and his smile went directly to her heart. "Seems the least I can do is drive you to the airport—"

"Would you? But I can't ask that favor on top of—"

"If you'll do *me* the favor of letting me stay here while you're gone," he finished. He watched her reaction and didn't miss a beat. "Not only would it save me the hotel bill while I work on your case—"

"Like we have any decent hotels for miles around."

"A point, yes." His hazel eyes narrowed. "It also keeps someone here—a male presence—while you're away. Not that I think Jerry Pohlsen would try anything shifty while you're gone."

Diana stopped in the middle of the living room. She'd always believed in the concept of guardian angels, and Will Killiam had suddenly slipped into that role, hadn't he? "You're a genius. I owe you big time, but I've *got* to get moving!"

While her ticket printed out, she threw all the clean jeans and tops she could find into a suitcase and dropped her cosmetics into plastic bags. Twenty minutes later she was trotting out the door in front of Will. "My face and hair'll have to wait until I get to Cody, so—"

"Somehow, I don't think Mike will mind." Cool and calm, Will opened the door of his Catera. He whipped the car around to drive out—and they were headed straight toward a silver SUV they hadn't noticed coming up the driveway. Diana groaned, but a sharklike grin overtook her driver's face. "Let me handle him. I'm your attorney, after all."

"Hey there, where ya goin' in such a big—well, now, don't *you* look sizzlin' hot?" Jerry Pohlsen leaned down to gawk through her open car window. "And who's *this*?"

"Will Killiam," he said as he extended his hand. "We've spoken on the phone—"

Pohlsen ignored him. "Let me guess. You're still hot to trot for White Horse, and now you've got another man on the string, too? I'm telling you, Diana, these guys are only in this for themselves—"

"Kind of like you, right?" she retorted. "Better watch your step, Mr. I-Wanna-Be-a-Congressman. You're trespassing again, so—"

"It's my right as the president of the bank to—" He scowled. "How'd *you* know I was going to run for congress?"

"We don't have time for this conversation right now," Will cut in, "but I'll be contacting you first thing tomorrow. We have a *lot* to talk about."

Wow, it felt good to hear that! Diana relaxed in the leather seat as Will accelerated down the lane toward the road. Never again would she fear Polecat Pohlsen or let him make her feel inferior or ashamed. She was a single, consenting adult. And right now consenting—*yes*—was the only thing on her mind.

"Yes, Diana, I won my event today. And once again you were my good luck charm," Michael murmured as he took her head between his warm, strong hands. "So *now* I feel like a winner."

When his lips met hers Diana melted against him. Unbelievable, the way her body already anticipated his nuances. She couldn't wait to be lying next to him. Naked. Uninhibited. Totally open to him.

"You're so hot I smell smoke, angel. Better get you out of this airport and into that room." His onyx eyes ignited beneath the brim of his black hat as he steered her away from the baggage claim area.

The vision teased at something deep within her. "I don't get it. I didn't even have time to fix my hair and makeup, but I've gotten all these smiles from guys today."

"Because you look natural," he replied as they strode to the parking lot. "Totally open to whatever a man wants to do to you. What I see is what I get . . . and I see a woman in love." He opened the truck door and kissed her hungrily. "Or at least a woman in lust. And right now I'll take that!"

Diana's cheeks tingled, because yes, even though she'd loved Garrison with her whole heart she hadn't felt this ecstatic—this desired—in years. Climbing into her husband's truck with a younger, hotter man in tight jeans and a fitted chambray shirt would've seemed inappropriate a few months ago, but now it was a means to where she wanted to go. And that was to a motel room with a big, cushy bed.

As he drove, Michael looked at her as though he might pull over to ravish her on the roadside. They chattered about the broncs he'd drawn, but it was all about sex . . . sex as elemental as horses with names like Hurricane and Rampage and

Demon's Dare. Sex that made his face tight and his nostrils flare, until he steered her down the hallway of the modest motel and into his room. Her bags hit the floor and he shut the door by kissing her against it.

"Diana . . . Diana, I've missed you so much," he murmured against her ear. "Just the memory of being in your bed, with your naked body against me, soft and sweet, well"—Michael laughed softly—"I almost called you every night, because I woke up with this . . . need."

"And I'm here to take care of that." She tossed his hat to the desk. "I feel something very hard prodding my thigh. And you know that suck job we talked about on the phone?"

His Adam's apple bobbed above his collar when he swallowed.

"It's time." She unbuckled his belt, gazing into his eyes with a teasing smile. "When I heard you that night, releasing yourself, I knew I had to have you again, really soon. And here I am."

As he yanked down his jeans, she reached inside his stretchy bikini to cup him. His balls felt full and tight and hot. His mahogany face looked downright desperate. "Untie your hair, Michael. Let it drop over your shoulders so I can watch it shimmy like a silk curtain when you shudder and come."

He inhaled sharply. Tugged off the leather thong and then shook his mane loose.

God, but he looked wild and free. She knelt, took his cock in her hands and slowly slid her lips over the length of it. His moan sang to her soul. His head fell back and as his hips bucked slightly, Diana stroked and sucked and tongued him. *Magnificent* did not describe Michael White Horse. He was a fantasy come to life, all muscle and lush skin, and when he placed his hands on either side of her head she let him set the pace that would satisfy his need.

"Just a little more," he groaned. "I don't want to cheat you of—"

"Just take it," she rasped. "I want to feel the thunder roll through your body while the lightning flashes in your eyes, Michael."

His smile lit fires in her secret regions, and when she took him in her mouth again he responded to every lick and tickle. What a power trip! He was hers to make crazy, and Diana slowly set out to do that.

"I—if you don't want me to squirt in your mouth . . ."

She sucked him deeper, then pressed her lips tightly around his thickness to draw them up his hot length. When she reached the tip, she circled it with her tongue until his hips bucked. He grimaced with need.

Again and again she took in his cock and drew her mouth slowly up its shaft until Michael looked extremely desperate. Then, with a series of quick, short thrusts she drove him over the edge.

The thunder rolled, all right: he growled low in his chest and when he looked down into her eyes she saw a flash. It was gratitude but it was something much sweeter, too. He bucked and surged until he'd completely released himself. Then he rested his forearms against the door, forming a dark, mysterious arch above her as he caught his breath.

His smile was so damn gratifying, Diana was ready to go after him again.

"Stretch out on the edge of the bed, babe. I'm gonna give you some of this while I'm still hard." He stepped away to tug down her jeans. Diana laughed and yanked her shirt over her head . . . felt his fingers fretting over the clasp of her bra . . . turned and landed spread-eagle on the bed. What was it about this man that made her so eager to show herself off? She'd been a modest wife—

Garrison rarely tried new tricks. Just wanted release and then fell asleep.

But Michael White Horse was made for hot sex, and he didn't

waste a moment on what-ifs. He lived for the heat of the game, and Diana decided that was a pretty good way to spend her life, too. She watched eagerly as he sheathed himself in black latex.

He spread her thighs. Long, dark fingers drifted into her slit to test its moisture . . . to swirl her juice and watch her face as the sensations flared. He was still erect enough that his intention was clear, and when he tugged her butt to the edge of the bed and up his flexed legs Diana cried out with his penetration. She'd missed him more than she knew.

"Nothing so sexy as a woman who wants it," he murmured. "I smell your heat, and you need a good pumping to take the edge off. *Don't* you?"

"Yeah, that would be—oh, God! Oh, my—holy shit. *Michael*!"

How many fingers had he slid inside her? Her pussy was filled with the in-and-out of an eager hand . . . knuckles that rubbed and fingertips that tickled and firm, warm flesh that found the spots begging for his attention. She couldn't stop writhing. Couldn't stop thrusting and moaning and—

Just when Diana thought she'd go crazy with need, Michael placed his face between her legs. His tongue mercilessly massaged her clit while the roughness of his face inflamed her thighs. With a long, wayward moan she gave up any pretense of control. This man had her where he wanted her, and they both knew it.

Upward she spun, into a spiral of bright lights and spasms that made her body quake. On and on she shuddered. Was it possible to pass out from such intense sensations? She was about to find out.

She speared her hands into his magnificent hair and released her last shred of sanity. When she could open her eyes, Michael was lying between her legs with his abdomen resting on hers and his forearms bearing most of his weight. His hair fell around her face like a canopy of midnight while his eyes shown like stars.

"Now we're both where we need to be," he whispered. "Would it hurt your feelings if we napped? I haven't slept much, thinking about you and how to get you here."

She smiled, feeling sweetly, totally sated. "That makes two of us, cowboy. I woke up in such a lather from a hot dream last night, it could've been me on a saddle bronc."

Was there anything nicer than lying in a lover's arms, surrounded by his strength and warm affection? Diana draped a leg over his lean hip as he cradled her against his chest. All she knew was the gentle rhythm of his breathing . . . the hum of the air conditioner . . . the sense that nothing in this world could ever hurt her again.

The sunrise chased them down the highway toward Sheridan. Michael drove with his hand on her thigh as he chatted about the Indian Relay he would ride in. "You'll love it," he assured her. "It's a competition that dates back to ancient tribal games . . . a relay that pits a team of four ponies and their rider against teams from all over the country. It's just you and each of your horses, galloping around the track at breakneck speed."

"In loincloths, right? What's not to love about that?"

He chuckled. "That's the way most women see it, yes. Since I don't have my own horses here, I'm at a slight disadvantage. But it's still fun."

She nodded, glancing at the passing Wyoming scenery. For a fleeting moment she envisioned the beautiful horses that once grazed at Seven Creeks, but then dismissed her sadness. Mourning the past wouldn't bring back the livestock or the livelihood she had assumed would support her forever. "Do you have horses at home, then?"

"I did when I was a kid. Wasn't a horse I couldn't ride, and I lived for it," he replied wistfully. "But going to college—and crunching numbers—takes you away from that lifestyle."

"So now you've returned to rodeo. Like returning to your roots."

"I've figured out what's important. And what means something to me." He gazed at the road ahead of them, considering how much he wanted to share. "My mother always told me my way with horses was a gift I shouldn't forsake. She's come to me in my dreams recently, to tell me I'm on the right path and that she's proud of me for leaving the casino." He gazed at Diana as they idled at a stop light. "It's cool to see her again, looking young and healthy like I remember when I was a kid."

Diana returned his gaze and saw herself mirrored in his onyx eyes. When his sculpted lips curved in a smile, she hoped she could make him this happy forever.

14

"It's you and me, all the way to the finish line, Wildfire. You'll be my final mount, and we're gonna kick some ass today. Got it?"

Michael ran his hands over the sleek side of this black barrel-chested pony, letting the spunky mount get accustomed to his scent and voice and touch. Wildfire was a fine animal with red feathers woven into his lush mane. A line of bright red hand-prints ran up his flanks to distinguish their team from the others, and Michael placed his palm against each of the painted prints before caressing the pony's firm haunches. His other three mounts stood quietly with their lead ropes dangling, yet Michael had felt the speed and fire they were each capable of as he decided the order in which he'd ride them. They were four of a kind—four aces of spades—but he could distinguish their differences and he sensed their souls.

Wildfire turned to monitor Michael's progress, but showed no sign of distrust or skittishness—a welcome contrast from the broncs he'd ridden these past few weeks. When he'd circled this mount again, Michael gazed deeply into the horse's brown eyes . . . let the gelding assess him, too, as he held its proud head between his hands. These moments of silent communication showed him the pony's spirit while he convinced it to give nothing less than an exceptional effort.

By the time he swung onto Wildfire's back they knew each other well. He circled the practice paddock a few times, urging the black into various gaits and familiarizing himself with the feel of this horse beneath his body . . . two elemental forces melding in a way that made his soul sing the ancient songs.

He shook hands with the three hostlers who would assist him during the relay, and they strategized briefly. All agreed the race wasn't so much about winning as it was for the sheer glory of galloping around the track with an adrenaline rush like no other. As they led Wildfire, Tomahawk, Chief, and Arapaho toward the starting line, Michael found Diana in the stands.

She gazed at him as though he were the only man in the arena.

He raised his hand, a solemn salute of respect; recognition of her as his soul's mate. She might not be so easily tamed as a horse, but the rides she gave him more than compensated for that and her inner mysteries fascinated him. Her golden hair caught fire in the sun and her slow smile warmed a part of him that tightened beneath his loincloth. His pulse pounded hard beneath the red handprints painted on his chest. He felt invincible and proud in ways he thought he'd lost. It would be a phenomenal race. A day of strength and speed and glory he'd missed when he sat behind a desk.

As the announcer's voice blared over the speakers, Michael focused on the race, reviewing his plan: he would lead with Arapaho, followed by Chief, then Tomahawk, and then he would claim a stunning victory atop Wildfire. Not for a moment did he doubt he'd win. He stroked each pony's muzzle a final time, and then nodded at his three hostlers in their red shirts.

Michael mounted Arapaho and took his position alongside

the other contestants as the announcer called their names. His pulse surged, and as he glanced at Diana the look on her face—her direct, sexual gaze—stoked the fires within him. It would be a ride like no other *after* this relay, as well: he couldn't wait to feel her between his thighs as he mounted her fine body.

When the gun fired, he surged ahead with a resounding cry of triumph . . . an elongated calling out of Diana's name, as if she were already making him climax.

Diana gasped at the spectacle playing out before her. Ebony-haired and bare-chested, the Native American riders leaned into the first turn with a ferocity that drove her to the edge of her seat. It was a rush of glistening dark skin and pounding ponies' hooves. War whoops rang out as the riders' feathers and hair flew in the wind. She marveled at the men's dexterity as the pack thundered around the final turn of the first lap, coming toward her. Their proud, lean bodies and intense expressions defined by high cheekbones, sharp noses and raven hair. They made a formidable sight with their team symbols painted on their chests and feathers that matched those entwined in their mounts' manes.

She raised the binoculars. Michael looked so damn good: confident and competitive as he maintained his place near the front of the group. Her palms itched to cover the shiny red handprints on his chest, and to feel the thunder of his heartbeat. His bare thighs bunched as he urged his horse toward the first exchange. She longed for the next time his determined squint would be focused on *her* with such intensity . . .

What does it feel like to be racing a horse with your privates pressed against its spine? The wicked whisper in her head made Diana squirm. While the contestants varied in height and body structure, there wasn't a one she'd kick out of bed.

And what an awesome sight as the riders finished their first lap! Each man vaulted from his galloping pony onto the next mount that awaited him, prancing and tossing its head. With a slap and a cry, the hostlers urged them on while other wranglers recovered the spent horses: the handlers' shirts matched their riders' paint, so it was easy to distinguish the various teams. And it was a miracle no one got trampled during this complicated, colorful, *exhilarating* exchange.

Michael was a study in male grace as he urged his second mount into a tight gallop. Diana followed his progress through this lap and the next with the binoculars. When he vaulted mid-stride onto his final horse, she shot up from her seat.

With a wild cry that sounded suspiciously like her name, Michael shot forward. The frenzied audience cheered, yet all she saw was Michael White Horse riding low and sleek and fast, a raven-haired warrior astride a black. Only the contrast in their coloring distinguished horse from rider as they rounded the first turn. His loincloth flapped and the pony's haunches bunched as they galloped low into the next turn. Unbound manes and red feathers flapped in the wind. Her heart was beating so hard she couldn't breathe. Diana could only gaze in wonder at this primal display of man and animal pitted against time and distance. It was all about testosterone and sweat and adrenaline. And it was the sexiest thing she'd ever seen.

As a fierce whoop rang out above the others, Michael shot forward from the pack as though his life depended on winning. God, he looked glorious! How did he hang on without a saddle? How did he control his mount with only that rope? She was a pretty fair rider herself, but never had Diana witnessed such formidable power—such oneness between horse and rider. Gripping the binoculars, she panted, "Go, Michael! Go, Michael! Bring it on home!"

As he shot across the finish line, the crowd erupted in whoops and applause. With tears streaming down her cheeks, Diana joined in until her throat went raw and her hands hurt.

"And the winner is—Michael White Horse!" the announcer

proclaimed as the rest of the contestants galloped past. "Ladies and gentlemen, let's hear it for this fine rider from northern Montana!"

It was a moment like she'd never known, watching Michael leap from his mount to dance in a triumphant circle with his face uplifted and his hands held high. It gave her a pretty fine shot of his thighs in that skimpy loincloth, too. And when Michael's eyes found hers, they branded her with his potent fire, as though he'd left a smoldering handprint across her heart to match the one on his own. She held her breath, oblivious to the spectators around her.

"Hey, lady, you want to move it already?"

Diana flushed at the stares of the people in her row. She made her way down the grandstand steps, engulfed by the chattering sea of people, her heart still hammering to the beat of those ponies' hooves. Michael had told her to meet him at the truck, and as she gazed out over the vast field full of vehicles, she tried to recall which row it was in. The rest of the week was theirs to enjoy as they headed to San Bernardino, California, and she had no trouble imagining how they'd spend most of it.

An arm hooked around her shoulder and she gasped. Up close, red war paint and feathers looked truly startling. Michael laughed, swallowing her surprise in a fierce, ravenous kiss.

"Let's take a shortcut to the truck," he murmured against her ear. "Time for the real games to begin, angel."

15

"We'll have to pull over. I won't make it to the motel." Michael wedged his hand between her thighs as he steered the pickup into the lanes of traffic leaving the fairgrounds. The fierce heat on his painted face made his eyes shine hard and bright, and the peak in his loincloth left no doubt of his intentions.

Diana giggled. "You sound like a horny kid on a hot date with his—"

"I've been a horny kid my whole life, Diana. Get used to it." His tone was playful but it brooked no arguments: Michael White Horse was a man on a mission, and he'd be penetrating her sooner rather than later. Maybe before they got to the road. Maybe right here while they waited in this bumper-to-bumper line.

She squirmed with wanting. Gazed quickly around the corrals and tan tents on either side of the road that was packed with pickups and SUV's.

The truck jerked sideways and Michael left the line of traffic, headed for the corrals and the grandstand. She gripped the edge of the bench seat, gasping when Michael squeezed the fleshy spot between her legs. Then he cranked the wheel with both hands.

"Hope you don't mind a public fuck," he muttered as he steered between a corral and the stable next to it. "You up for some slam-bam, lady? Some hard-core, straight-up rocket launching?"

"Long as it's your rocket," she breathed. "But I can't believe we're doing this, right here in—"

"That's the nice part about being visitors. You'll never see these people again."

"And you think no one'll recognize you, after you won the relay?" Any respectable woman would walk home before she'd get caught on the fairgrounds in broad daylight with her panties down. But then, respectability lost its luster when it was outshone by Michael's eyes. Diana glanced nervously around them. He'd stopped the truck—Garrison's truck—in the shade of the stable, where a cluster of longhorns stood watching them with interest.

"Unzip," he challenged, "and while I trot around to your side, you can scoot over here. And once I land in that seat, you're gonna whip my loincloth aside and ride, Diana, ride. You with me?"

Her pulse revved as she reached for her zipper tab.

"On the count of three, then! One—" Michael threw open his door and jumped out to scurry in front of the pickup. "Two—"

Diana flung herself to the driver's side. Breathlessly she yanked her jeans off, damn glad she was wearing sandals.

"Three!" Her war-painted lover vaulted back into the truck with his feathers and hair billowing around his face. "I'm comin' in—and then I'm *comin'*. Get over here, woman."

A loud cheer went up from the grandstands. If someone came to investigate a truck in this odd spot . . . if they looked in the window to see her head and shoulders bobbing in that tell-tale rhythm . . .

"Just go with it, honey. Play along like this is the wildest, wickedest dare you've ever taken a guy up on."

"You think it isn't?" As she straddled him, she stifled a surprised cry. Michael had slipped his hand beneath her to insert an inquisitive finger. She held her breath to keep from making any more noise: he plugged her with his thumb and shoved it deep inside her, instinctively hitting that sensitive spot that nailed all her nerves to the same place.

"Don't move." Micheal riveted his gaze on her eyes then; stroked the curve of her ass with his urgent palm as he plumbed her wetness with the fingers of his other hand. She arched above his lap, suspended by a tension that left her too captivated to move . . . too breathless to utter a sound. The temperature inside the truck had risen to a stifling stillness, but the heat around her was nothing compared to the wildfires raging within. Her ass quivered uncontrollably. The spasms racked her body while she stifled her screams against Michael's firm, bare shoulder.

When her vision cleared, Diana focused on his bottomless black eyes. "I love you, Michael. In case you were wondering."

And where had that come from? What business did she have expressing such a dangerous emotion after only a few weeks?

"I already knew," he whispered raggedly. "And I just realized I left all my protection back at the—"

"Like a warrior in a loincloth would whip out a condom right now." Her body ached to feel him inside her, with nothing coming between them. Michael inhaled fiercely, clearly recalling the consequences of a lover's lies . . . daughters born and then torn away from him. His doubts seemed intensified by the red handprint on his face, "Michael, it's all right. In fact, it's downright perfect this way! I can't have your baby, but I can have *you*. Any time I feel like it. You're all I've ever wanted."

Would those words come back to bite her? Had she lost all

perspective because this brazen young lover had to fuck her in the truck?

"I'm gonna *ride* you, Michael." Diana gripped the sides of his seat to steady herself. "I'm gonna lower myself, and then I'm gonna hump your long, hard cock like I'm a bitch in heat. And female dogs don't let go until they're satisfied, you know."

His eyes widened, and when he looked ready to protest, Diana quickly kissed him. From this angle, he was all mahogany skin, midnight hair, and red feathers reclining against beige leather. And with his flagpole pointed skyward, his loincloth had conveniently fallen to one side, like a banner on a breezeless day. She planted her knees on either side of him ... lowered her mouth to taste his need and speak silently of her own. His intake of breath sucked all the air from the truck cab as she slowly positioned her hips above his cock. It throbbed at her opening, skittish yet so ready to claim her.

"Diana," he rasped, "we can go back to the room for—"

She sat on his rigid shaft and sheathed it. *Squeeeeezed.* There was no going back, not from saying "I love you" or from this coupling where nothing came between them. Michael gritted his teeth, his eyes telling stories of love lost and hard betrayal. Yet she raised her hips ... bore down on him again ... hoped her gaze reassured him of her intention to honor her words as surely as he lived up to his. A third time she lowered herself on his cock, struggling to keep it slow—to let him go with *yes* rather than *maybe we'd better not.*

"Faster."

The word slipped between his clenched teeth and she didn't need him to repeat it. Diana pressed against his hot, painted chest, intent on rubbing the right spots inside herself so her body would ignite his. Up and down she drove her hips as she reveled in the feel of his hands grasping her ass. Never had she envisioned herself doing this in her husband's truck, yet the audacity—the tension on his painted face as he succumbed to her—drove her to please him. Or at least to make him explode so hard he'd forget his misgivings.

"More, angel," he breathed. "God, you can't stop now!"

Jubilant, she angled her body so her hips thrust straight down his cock. He slipped his hands under her shirt . . . unclasped her bra to cup her unbound breasts. They writhed as one, joined at the hip as their moans filled the cab. Her head fell back and he set the pace with his hands on her hip bones, until he was driving upward, upward—

Michael convulsed deep inside her. His wetness filled her as she rode him to her own shuddering climax. She felt sultry and dirty and decadent—and *alive*. So vibrant, like the waves of crystalline color exploding behind her eyelids.

When she opened her eyes she gasped. A huge, mottled longhorn had pressed his nose to the window. "We've been caught!" she teased, and when Michael strained to see what was so funny, he, too chuckled uncontrollably.

"Now *that's* one horny devil." Then he sobered, running his warm hands up her sides. "Diana . . ."

"Michael." She gazed steadily down at him, praying he voiced no regrets. Her hands covered his, and she let him express his thoughts first.

He blew a feather from his damp, painted face. "Life's an open road, Diana. And I'm damn happy to be your vehicle." He grinned tentatively. "Trust is something I have to relearn. So keep teaching me till I get it right, okay?"

"You've got a deal." Tears filled her eyes and she blinked them away.

"Did I say something wrong?"

"Absolutely not," she breathed. "Life hasn't been this right for a long, long time."

16

The open road Michael had talked about took them to California, but by a circuitous route with a lot of motel rooms along the way. Never in her life had Diana felt so wicked, so wayward . . . or so damn happy. Never had she lived on the fly, without the maps and plans she and Garrison had sworn by. All she knew was that when Michael looked at her, she felt naked and open to anything he wanted. It was a far cry from her staid, settled life as the wife of a middle-aged rancher—and a huge improvement over haggling with Jerry Pohlsen.

About a hundred miles from San Bernardino, her cell rang. She glanced at the number on its screen, grinning. "Well, hello there, Mr. Killiam," she crooned. "And how are things at Seven Creeks?" She secretly adored the flicker of jealousy on Michael's face when his head jerked in her direction.

"I have some exciting news," Will replied. "But I'm hearing news in your voice, too, Diana. Like maybe things are going very well for you and Mike."

"You're so perceptive—which is why Michael recommended you." Her heart thudded as she made herself wait; didn't jump into the questions whirling in her mind at *his* jubilant tone. "We'll arrive in a couple hours, and Michael rides his first round of saddle broncs at tonight's performance."

"Give him my best—and then give me your take on this." Diana imagined him sitting at her kitchen table ... maybe in the jeans and chambray shirt that did such fine things for his tight butt and broad shoulders. "I've found a way to prevent the sale. Pohlsen'll get hot around the collar, but that's *his* problem."

"Yeah? *And*?" Michael looked ready to snatch her phone, so she glanced out the window.

"A competitive bank wants to loan you the money to pay off your mortgage. When I explained about Garrison's extended illness and expenses, the president put paper to pencil. Didn't take him long to consider this a viable investment."

"Which means?" She swallowed hard, praying this was for real—hoping Will Killiam wouldn't let her fall from this emotional high.

"It means no bankruptcy, so no auction. He'll make the loan at a much lower rate, too, because the real estate market has changed a lot since you took out your mortgage."

"Holy—and why didn't Pohlsen tell me about this option?" she blurted.

Will chuckled. "Not in his best interest. Fritzi wants that mega-mansion in the new resort development, after all."

Diana's breath escaped in a rush. "So—so why would this other banker offer to—"

"Politics. He's tired of Jerry's shenanigans, so he's doing everything legally possible to discredit Pohlsen and prevent the loss of so many productive acres of ranch land in the area."

Blinking rapidly, Diana grinned. "Tell that guy I want to kiss him!" she spouted. "And then tell me what I need to do."

"Just say yes. I can initiate the paperwork and you can sign the loan when you get back," Will replied breezily. "Then you'll have the pleasure of paying Pohlsen and stopping his whole damn project."

"Oh, my God. Oh, my God." She felt downright dizzy as she envisioned this transaction, and when Michael's hand closed over the phone, she let him have it. Diana stared ahead through the windshield, so damn happy she couldn't see.

"What's cooking, guy?" As Michael drove down the highway, listening, his face lost its jealous edge. "Well, hot damn. I'm an accountant, for cryin' out loud. Why didn't *I* think of that?"

"Because your brain's gone between your legs?" Will's voice teased through the phone.

Diana choked on her laughter. It was sinking in, what this *meant*! No bankruptcy! No humiliating auction while the neighbors looked on. No asking Garrison's forgiveness for losing his beloved ranch.

Leave it to reality to catch her off guard. "Just one problem," she mumbled. "How will I repay another bank when I didn't have the money for Pohlsen? I've still got no income—"

"We're gonna take care of that, sugar." Michael handed the cell back to her, his face alight with plans . . . some of which had nothing to do with income. "I've had ideas for your place since I first set foot on it."

Diana gaped. How did this guy talk big business—the rescue of her ranch and her future—while his grin reeked of sex?

"Diana, is everything okay?" Will asked loudly.

She put the phone to her ear again. "More than okay. I can't thank you enough for setting this up, Will."

When she clicked off the call, Michael grabbed her hand. "*This* calls for a celebration! We'll have a great dinner tonight after I ride—bottle of champagne to toast outfoxing Pohlsen! And maybe another bottle for bedtime! And after a hot session in the sack, we'll talk about Seven Creeks profits. I *knew* we'd turn this thing around, Diana!"

* * *

She was still riding the high of Will's phone call as she watched Michael saddle the bronc he'd drawn. It was stifling hot. The crowd was rowdy, and that redskinned cowboy in the black hat seemed psyched for his most glorious ride yet. What a difference his positive attitude had made in her life!

"Next up—Michael White Horse, who's drawn the mount they call Nightmare!" the announcer crooned.

The buzzer sounded and the band began to play. And then something shiny caught the lights as it spun out of the upper level seats.

Diana watched in horror. Just as Michael's mount started spinning like a tornado, the bottle hit its head. The bronc shrieked and bucked out of rhythm. Somehow Michael jumped away from the crazed animal, but when he hit the ground running, the bronc's back legs caught his shoulder. With fiendish accuracy, the horse then spun and trampled its fallen rider before racing away from the frantic clowns and pickup men.

The arena echoed with a stunned silence. Unable to scream, Diana ran for the nearest exit.

17

Things slipped into an eerie slow motion as the rodeo's rescue unit raced into the arena. Diana dodged the guy at the gate and nearly stumbled in the loose sand trying to reach Michael's side. "Michael! Michael, can you—"

"Out of the way, lady! Let the paramedics do their job," a gruff voice ordered. Burly hands clamped around her shoulders, but then the man spoke more kindly beneath the wail of the siren. "You with this cowboy, ma'am?"

Diana nodded rapidly, trying not to be sick when she saw the unnatural angle of Michael's shoulder and the blood oozing through his shirt. As the EMR crew checked him over, she cringed at his groans. This was way too much like the ordeal Garrison had suffered—

Get over yourself! You've got to act in Michael's behalf.

When the paramedics placed her man on a stretcher and rushed him to the ambulance, Diana clambered in after them. The vehicle lurched, and as the EMR guys hooked him up with needles and tubes, she noted the pallor beneath Michael's dark complexion . . . felt his pain as he writhed on the padded table.

She recalled all too well the surreal atmosphere of the emergency room. As the hospital admitting clerk recited the questions on her computer screen, Diana realized how much she didn't know about Michael White Horse. "I'm sorry," she rasped. "He left his wallet in his duffel—at the rodeo—during his ride."

His last *ride*, she thought ominously.

By midnight they'd stabilized him. The ER doctor had set his broken shoulder, and his nose and wounds were bandaged, but until an orthopedist reviewed his X-rays they could do nothing more. When the nurse closed the door behind them, Diana was left to gaze at a man in excruciating pain. Michael's eyes were so black and swollen she barely recognized him.

"Get me outta here. Take me home," he rasped.

Diana grabbed his hand. "You're going nowhere until the orthopedist—"

"No insurance. Lost my coverage when I left the casino."

Her heart quivered. This was a nightmare revisited. "Michael, I can't just wheel you out of here—"

"Give 'em the cash in my wallet and get me the hell out of here, angel." He took a labored breath. "Put me in the truck. Get me to the ranch. Have Will call my mother's brother. He's a . . . shaman."

Diana pivoted so he wouldn't read the terror on her face. How many miles—how many days—between San Bernardino and Seven Creeks? And how the hell would she get him there in a stick-shift pickup she couldn't drive?

Diana gripped the shift knob and gritted her teeth. As the pickup lurched like an animal with a bad cough, she envisioned the pain she was causing poor Michael. He rode in the bed of the truck, on a mattress the sympathetic nurses had found for him. They'd rigged a canopy out of a tarp, and the air conditioning blasted toward her open back window. She had a supply of sample antibiotics and pain relievers, and the best wishes of a staff who had reluctantly released her battered, broken cowboy.

Diana eased her foot off the clutch, praying she didn't bash into the other vehicles in the lot . . . praying for Garrison's angelic assistance as she listened for second gear. Why hadn't she learned how to drive a manual transmission?

Just get into traffic without killing yourself.

Somehow she made the next stop light . . . the next turnoff toward the highway . . . the interstate that would take them a more direct route than they'd come on. She reminded herself that her driving dilemma was far easier than what Michael faced: bad enough that he hadn't made the finals in Las Vegas. If his internal conditions were worse than the ER doc thought, he might not make it home.

A shaman . . . how could she entrust her Michael to a witch doctor?

And who else will heal him? Takes money to go to real doctors.

She grimaced as she hit a pothole and had to downshift. After the first fretful hour of maneuvering through the gears and the traffic leaving San Bernardino, she pulled into a rest area. Diana lifted the bright blue tarp and forced herself to remain calm: Michael's lips were a thin, white line of pain.

"What can I get you? I've got all sorts of pain killers and—"

"Peyote buttons. Bottle of Yukon Jack." He groaned as he shifted on his mattress. His black hair clung to his face in the heat, yet he put on a smile for her. The shiners from his broken nose looked like something out of a horror film. "If we stop every hour, it'll take forever to get home, angel."

She gripped his hand and he gripped back. As Diana climbed into the cab, she cried silently so he wouldn't hear her sniffling through the open window. The truck lurched like a kangaroo with hiccups as she backed out of the parking space. It was going to be one helluva long hard ride. But if she didn't drive them, who would?

Never had she seen such a welcome sight as the gateposts of Seven Creeks. Diana pulled in, too exhausted to appreciate how the truck didn't cough or die going around the uphill curve. She focused on the front porch, and the male figure at the railing. Will Killiam vaulted into the back of the truck before she'd even shut it off.

"Hey, you! Get your ass out of this—" His voice faltered when he saw how horrible Michael looked. "Sorry. Didn't mean to make light of—good God, Mike, why didn't you call me? I could've sent a private plane, or come for you myself, or—"

"Save it." Michael turned his pale face toward them and extended his arm. "Diana and I weren't finished with our road trip."

"Yeah, well"—Will glanced toward the house—"your uncle's got your room ready. Smells sorta like the dorm after we had ourselves a high old time."

Diana's eyes widened and she yanked Will aside. "We should call a real doctor!" she whispered frantically. "I've got the money Michael sent me. He wouldn't let me use it, or I'd have kept him in the hospital—"

"He would've crawled out." Will smiled patiently, yet fear lurked behind his hazel eyes. "He's scared shitless of hospitals. Couldn't stay upright or conscious while his twins were being born. So the sooner we let his uncle work on him, the sooner he'll recover. Trust me."

"Better listen up, Diana," Michael rasped from beneath the tarp. "You can ride me, babe, but you'll never tame this bronc. So where the hell's Uncle Zeke?"

She wanted to razz him, but a man was coming out of the house . . . a man who foretold how Michael would look in forty years. Ezekiel Greentree was shorter and more compact than his nephew, and his raven hair was salted with streaks of gray, but his face appeared ageless. He wore a large necklace of animal fangs and preserved paws, but otherwise he looked more normal than the witch doctor she'd imagined. And she couldn't deny the man's *presence*. He had a sacred air of wisdom from walking in worlds she would never understand.

"Diana," he murmured in a voice much like Michael's. "Thank you for listening. For getting him here, where spirit and herbal remedies will restore him."

"Yeah, well, you'll find a few empty *remedy* bottles back here—" Zeke's grip stilled her. Power and energy pulsed from his palms into hers. "Thank you for coming, Uncle Zeke. He's in your hands now," she said more politely.

The shaman knelt beside Michael to converse quietly, and then tugged the mattress to the end of the truck bed. Will stepped up, but the older man waved him away. With a strength that defied logic—and moves that went against convention about shifting injured patients—Zeke slipped his arms around Michael and carried him effortlessly toward the porch.

Diana gaped.

"Never underestimate the power of a shaman with herbs and spirits on his side," Will murmured. "Let's get you something to eat so you can crash."

"Can't argue with that," she replied.

18

Diana awoke with the sun in her eyes and the salty-sweet aroma of bacon filling her room. She was in her own cozy bed, still bone tired from that god-awful road trip but feeling better than she had for days.

"Michael," she whispered. She padded through the kitchen to peer out the back door, where Zeke had prepared a "sick room" on the deck. The tang of incense and potent herbs drifted through the screen. The healer knelt beside Michael's pallet, murmuring in a low singsong voice as he ran his hands over his nephew's chest and face.

Michael lay eerily still.

Will grabbed her hand on the doorknob. "Uncle Zeke told me to keep the pretty female out of sight while the medicines and the spirits do their work. So why not shower and eat? Then we'll do some work of our own."

She was too dazed to argue . . . amazed at how immaculate the house looked and how kind Will Killiam was. He'd called every day they were on the road, he'd summoned Uncle Zeke, and he'd kept Jerry Pohlsen at bay during her absence. "I owe you a lot for—"

"Nope. I'm repaying Mike's favors over the years." He poured her a steaming mug of fresh coffee. "Clear your head, lady. You've got papers to sign."

"So this loan really, truly gets Pohlsen off my land?" Diana tingled as she held the pen over the loan application. "My next concern is how I'll repay—"

"*Not* a problem." His eyes sparkled with a secret. "Zeke isn't the only guy here who works magic, you know. Your cowboy has a way of making things happen, and he's got plans for this place. Plans for *you*."

"Oh, really?" With an arched eyebrow, she signed on the highlighted lines. "Who does he think he is, to tell me how to—"

Will snickered. "You sound just like him, Diana. I'm glad you'll give him a run for his money, after Carina crept out like a thief in the night. You want me to go with you? Or would you prefer to upstage Pohlsen alone?"

A grin settled over her face. How would Jerry explain to Miss Fritzi that she'd never have her mega-mansion on this pretty hillside?

Diana dressed in a snug shirt that showed off her curves. She let her loose curls drift around her face and applied makeup to set off her eyes and smile: she was a woman on a mission. And as she rumbled down the driveway in the pickup, she realized how far she'd come. No more holing up at home. No more nightmares where Jerry Pohlsen announced they were tearing down her house. No more of that smarmy voice intimidating her to tears.

It was a pleasure to fetch the check from Paul Mathis, the banker Will had set her up with. But it was a bigger thrill to enter Pohlsen's facility, where the tellers didn't meet her gaze anymore, and wait for the polecat himself to wave her into his office.

"So! Did you leave that shiftless cowboy out west?" he joked. "This process'll go much easier now that you're working with me to—"

She thrust the check at him. It was none of his business that Michael lay on her deck with a medicine man mumbling over him. "This pays off my mortgage. Guess I won't be seeing you around Seven Creeks anymore."

His face got splotchy as he glanced at the check. "What kind of craziness is—what makes you think you can just—"

Diana shrugged, ready to dance circles around him. How *fine* it felt to be the one dishing up the dirt! "The ranch is mine again, like it should've been all along," she replied. "Any banker with a *conscience*—any real friend of Garrison Grant's—would've told me I had other options instead of kicking me while I was down and then calling it *progress*."

"I won't change my development plans just because—"

"And I won't listen to your bullshit for another second!" she spouted. She stared him down until he plopped backward into his executive desk chair. "All it took was one lawyer and one call, and your resort's down the toilet with the rest of your crap."

"But how're you gonna make good on this loan, when—"

"That's *my* problem, isn't it? *Your* concern is breaking this news to Fritzi and your political cronies." She planted her palms on his desk and nailed him with a dark gaze. "Fetch my papers. I'm going to watch you mark everything *paid*, and then I'm going *home*. Got it?"

He twitched, rallying his power. "The architects and the contractors have invested too much in this resort to let you get away with—"

"That's *their* mistake, for going along with your underhanded scheme. Good luck running for congress, by the way. But don't count on my vote."

Diana bubbled like champagne as she strode out to the truck—and then she bought a bottle of it, for when Michael could share it with her. All the way up the road she sang with the radio. She'd reclaimed her ranch and that hunk of a handsome cowboy had *plans* for her! Life was *good!* She imagined the ideas Michael might have . . . saw herself as his devoted nurse . . . his wife? Was it too soon to consider that? After traveling halfway across the country with this man, she certainly knew what she'd be getting into.

Like his stretchy little bikini?

She giggled and pulled up alongside the house, but then her heart stilled. Will Killiam stared out across the pasture as though he'd lost his best friend. As Diana hurried up the porch steps, she caught a whiff of something nasty and burnt and medicinal.

Her attorney finally met her eyes. "He's not responding."

"*What?*"

"Zeke's been brewing poultices and god-awful concoctions for Mike to drink. Says he's put our boy into a sort of coma, where his body can heal in the care of the spirit world, but . . . but I'm not buying it." All his courtroom bravado left him. Will looked like a scared little kid. "If this was a bad idea—if I should've called the ambulance instead of letting that old man—"

The door opened and Zeke stepped outside. Diana looked at his impassive expression, trying to read between the lines etched deep into a face the color of clay. "It's out of my hands now. Time will tell if the spirits heal Michael's internal injuries and let him return to us."

"Or?" Diana didn't dare consider other options—not after

she'd busted her butt to get him here from California. Not after she'd tended him at rest stops and resisted the urge to turn off at every blue HOSPITAL sign posted at highway exits. Not after she believed he had *plans* for this ranch.

Zeke didn't smile. "Time will tell."

19

Diana barely endured the next three days. After peeking at him once, she didn't dare look again: Michael White Horse lay with his hands at his sides and his hair smoothed over one bare shoulder. His eyes were closed, and the rings around them shone in sickly shades of greenish purple. From all appearances, she had a dead man on her deck. A naked dead man.

The third night she had vivid dreams of Michael making love to her: bending her over the bed . . . sliding her up the shower wall as the water hissed around them . . . taking her from above as his lustrous hair fell around her. Diana cried out with sweet release in her dream—awakening herself by crying out for real. She wanted Michael so badly, but all she could think about was taking care of Garrison that last week, when he was too ill to respond.

She dressed and left a note on the table: CAN'T STAND ANY MORE OF THIS. WENT TO TOWN.

She tossed her cell phone into the passenger seat. Didn't have a clue where she was going. It was just too weird being in a house where a shaman mumbled to himself as though she and Will weren't there while filling the place with the bitter scent of herbs and smoke. While she wanted to believe Uncle Zeke knew what he was doing, she didn't want to be there if the old guy had to admit defeat. She just couldn't handle that again.

Diana turned in at Klineschmidt's doughnut shop, north of town. The guy at the counter smiled kindly as he handed her a cup of high-test coffee and a bag of apple fritters and bear claws she intended to share with Will when she ventured back. She ate mechanically, staring into the corner of the shop so no one would interrupt her funk.

Halfway through the third pastry, her cell jangled. She wiped the sugary glaze from her fingers . . . saw her home phone number, and was afraid to answer. "Y-yeah?" she murmured.

"Diana."

She went still. The voice was unmistakably Michael's, but it sounded so . . . hollow. Her thoughts raced morbidly. Could spirits call you from the "other side?" "Yeah"? she breathed.

"Imagine my . . . disappointment and humiliation when I woke up with a huge hard-on, calling *your name*," he said in slow, measured tones, "but it was Will and Uncle Zeke looking down at me."

She snorted so hard coffee spewed out her nose. Was it the extreme caffeine, or was her heart pounding so hard because this was Michael! Wanting her! A little bleary, but alive! "And what did they do about your—predicament?" she said, aware the others in the shop stared at her.

"They pointed and made crude remarks. Will you *pleeeease* come home and set these guys straight?" he pleaded in a little-boy voice. "I need you, angel."

She gestured for the guy behind the counter to refill her bag with fritters and bear claws and chocolate-covered eclairs. "Would you believe I woke up in that same *predicament*?" She fished more money out of her pocket, and darted out of the shop without her coffee. She felt too jittery—too giddy—to risk any more stimulation.

"And was I fucking you in the shower?" he whispered. "And then from behind—"

"Over the foot of the bed, yes." Diana couldn't believe what she was hearing . . . how their dreams had meshed in that other-wordly nightscape. "And when I woke myself up hollering for you, you were—"

"Between your legs, letting my hair tease your face."

"Jesus, Michael." Diana cranked the ignition. "I—you looked so *out* of it, and for three damn days I thought you were—"

"Uncle Zeke has great power. Thank you for not running him off. Your house smells like a frat house the morning after a hard-core party."

"Yeah, well, we can fix that. Hang on, Michael. I'm coming home."

Home. What a sweet feeling she thought when she pulled into the driveway of the ranch she'd nearly lost. And what a sweeter feeling, to see Michael sitting upright in a porch chair, wrapped in a quilt. Waiting for her.

Diana ran from the truck, arms extended. He didn't stand up—still had those nasty shiners, and his left arm was bent in a sling again—but the hug he gave her with his good arm made her sob against his shoulder and kiss him wildly. "It's so good to—I thought you were—and I just couldn't go through watching another man die, so—"

"Shhhh," he murmured against her ear. He smiled at her as best he could, considering how messed up his face was. "I was floating, catching glimpses of you yet unable to tell you I was okay. Maybe it was the drugs, but I received some very direct messages while I was in that suspended state."

Diana crouched beside his chair, looking up into his face . . .

a gruesome face now, but when he healed, his nose would look even more hawkish and sexy than before. "Yeah? What sort of messages?"

"Visions. I saw longhorn cattle and sleek horses grazing these pastures," he replied in a faraway voice. "Guys I know from the rodeo circuit told me they needed more places to buy good broncs and bulls from—and they want to deal *me* into this venture. It's not likely I'll ride rodeo stock anymore, but I can *raise* it, angel! They were handing me my next career."

"Right here? On Seven Creeks?" Diana nipped her lip, needing more information. More time to—

"Yup. And in another vision, you were standing here on the porch with me. And your belly was out to here." He curved his arm out in front of him, chuckling.

"Pregnant?" she challenged. "And how did *that* happen?"

"The usual way," he teased. "I felt very proud and protective for having such a profound effect on you. Nothing short of a miracle, the way I understand it. We lived happily ever after, by the way."

Her jaw fell as her mind tried to wrap around all he was saying. After all those years of being married to Garrison, childless yet trying—

"It's a boy."

She dropped the bakery bag. "And you saw all this while you were out of your mind on drugs and—"

"Uncle Zeke knew as soon as he shook your hand."

A jolt went through her—the same startling sensation she recalled from the shaman's first touch. And then another bolt struck her with undeniable clarity. "In the truck . . . after the Indian Relays," she breathed. "It was our first time not to use any—"

"It was your idea, angel. And it gave us the answer we've both been searching for, didn't it?" Michael's smile looked sweet and clear. He raised her hand to kiss it tenderly. "I'll understand if this visionary stuff seems unbelievable, or if it foretells events you don't want any part of—"

"Oh, but I do." Diana's hand found her abdomen, and while she didn't feel any different on the outside, *everything* had shifted on the inside. Michael White Horse had been the agent of that change since the moment she sat beside him at the cafe on the lowest day of her life. And now she floated high and free, like an eagle that soared above the seven creeks of this ranch. "I've wanted so badly to see cattle and horses grazing these hills again, and—and have a baby!"

She fell back against the porch post, laughing and crying at the same time. "All these years I believed something was wrong with *me*, when—"

"Nothing a little lovin' and a long hard ride won't fix." Michael stood up, slowly and carefully. He loosened the quilt to wrap it around them both, and then leaned into her with his bare body.

He was ready to ride, all right.

She smoothed his long black hair, holding his bruised face between her hands. "You are so baaaad, Michael," she teased.

"That's why I need you, Diana. You're so good."

Her heart fluttered and she blinked away more happy tears. "Then it's settled. We're a perfect pair."

"So take me in to bed, and we'll work on that happily ever after," he whispered. "I'm damn tired of sleeping on your back porch."

HOT BLOODED

DELILAH DEVLIN

This is for Kelly who deserves to have a hero there to catch her when she falls.

Acknowledgements

Special thanks to Blake Phillips for the expertise regarding rock climbing he so generously provided!

Thanks to my critique partners and dear friends for polishing this apple until it shined: Cyndi D'Alba, Sasha White and Shada Royce.

More thanks to "Team Delilah," my friends and readers who root for me even when I'm stepping off the ledge.

And hugs for the special inspirations in my life, my sister Elle James and my mom. I love you both!

1

When the first small drops began to fall, Cass McIntyre welcomed the light shower the forecasters had predicted. Already halfway up the route she'd chosen, she'd worked up a nice sweat.

The rain quickly cooled her skin, which was caked in a thick, itchy layer of canyon dirt and chalk. The lazy breeze accompanying the rain fanned the burning cuts on her bare legs and arms, giving her a mental boost of energy.

After another fifteen feet into her ascent—chilled and achy now and getting a little impatient with the worsening conditions—she found a narrow ledge. She unhooked her caribiner clip from the rope, and decided to wait out the cloudburst, a rare occurrence in the Panhandle and extremely dangerous because the rock face she climbed had become as slippery as mud.

She took small comfort in the phrase she'd heard over and over since she'd first moved to Canyon, Texas, that ran like a mantra through her head. "If you don't like the weather in Texas, wait a minute."

Her mistake had been believing that piece of homespun advice.

Not that she was anything more than mildly annoyed at this point. The awe-inspiring view from her perch above the canyon floor placated her restless nature and soothed the deep ache in her chest that had choked her at the start of the climb.

Low-hanging clouds obscured the sunlight and provided an unexpected cooling to a hot spring day. Soft, gray mist filled the Palo Duro Canyon, softening the light and air, the moisture causing a burst of brilliant color to erupt from the fading wildflowers carpeting the rough terrain—bright orange from Mexican hat and Indian blanket, and a cheery yellow daisylike flower whose name escaped her at the moment.

Determined to salvage some enjoyment from her adventure, she settled on the ledge, dangling her legs over the side, and ignored the water soaking through her thin T-shirt and shorts.

Half an hour into the storm that had grown steadily more insistent, she kissed off making the summit and planned a quick rappel to the distant hollow below.

However, as she unwound her long rope from the straps of her backpack for a hasty descent, her narrow perch disintegrated. Rock made fragile by the water splintered into rough shards and gravel that tumbled down the sheer precipice.

Cass dropped the rope and jammed her hand into a crevice in the rock to anchor herself while she reached beside her for her pack. But she was too late.

More of the ledge crumbled. The backpack slid away, leaving her stranded with only the shorter rope she'd used between cams—not nearly long enough to attempt a descent.

"*Jesus.* I don't fucking believe this," she whispered furiously.

Pissed off with her rookie mistake, she pulled the trigger on the cam she'd used to secure her rope above the ledge and wedged it deeper into the crevice. She attached one end of her short rope to the cam and tied the other to the belay. Then satisfied she'd done everything she could to remain safe, she settled again on the last little remnant of her eroding perch.

She'd have to wait for rescue—something she'd never live down. A frequent climber who often provided advice to weekend enthusiasts, she could already hear the razzing she'd get from her fellow park rangers.

She only hoped the team sent to retrieve her wouldn't include the one man she'd come to escape. She could only imagine the black, judgmental glare he'd give her for inconveniencing him. Add this fiasco to last night's and she figured he'd just as soon let her rot on the side of the cliff as drop her a rope.

With nothing left to do to keep her mind from obsessing over mistakes she couldn't undo, Cass sat on the narrow ledge high above the canyon floor with her head bent against the rain, watching it fall like the tears she refused to shed.

Frustration fueled her emotions—not fear or loneliness— she ruthlessly insisted to herself. Cass never cried, and she sure as hell wasn't starting now. She'd gotten herself into this mess. She'd just have to figure a way out.

However, the only plans she could come up with required a little patience and a lot of humility—qualities she didn't possess in abundance. With nothing to do but hunker down and wait, she finally let her mind wander back to what had brought her to this moment.

The ascent of Fortress Cliff was supposed to be a way to blow off steam after a stressful week and even more horrendous night. Stress of a sort she hadn't anticipated when she'd flipped her career with the state police months ago and entered the park service.

Who'd have thought a job patrolling a bit of paradise on earth could put kinks in her neck that only a climb up a rock wall could unknot?

Patrolling campgrounds in the late afternoon and evening to ticket park visitors who made illegal fires, arrest underage drinkers, or search for hikers who'd lost their way on the trails was everything the superintendent had promised.

Fielding complaints from one intensely sexy rancher with an uncanny ability to find her when she did her best to evade him had been an unexpected test. One she'd failed miserably.

Thunder rumbled through the darkening clouds, pulling her back to her present predicament. She couldn't wait out the storm. Her situation was becoming more precarious by the second. She'd have to hope Mavis let the rescue personnel dispatched from the Canyon Volunteer Fire Department know she hadn't checked back in at the park's headquarters. Since rescue would have to come from the top of the escarpment, she needed to give them a sign to help them find her quickly.

Closing her eyes, she cursed softly to herself. She'd have to add one more humiliation to the day—this one a deliberate choice. She eased her arms inside her T-shirt, clumsily removed her bra, pulled it from under her shirt, and thrust her arms back through her sleeves.

Then leaning as far from the rock wall as her harness would allow, she drew back her arm and let the bra fly toward the branches of a juniper tree hugging the edge of the cliff.

Sunlight broke through the clouds by midafternoon. Although the rain had stopped an hour before, chaos still reigned in the park as the rivers continued to rise. All the low water crossings were impassable. Climbers and hikers all along the trails had been stranded. When the Canyon Volunteer Fire Department called the ranch, Adam Youngblood bit back a curse.

The last place he wanted to be today was anywhere near the park and one particular little park ranger. But he headed straight for the headquarters building near the entrance of the park where the rangers had organized search parties to rescue stranded campers and hikers.

Mavis Benson who manned the information desk sidled

close to him with a clipboard in her hands. "Adam," she said hesitantly.

"What do you need, sweetheart?"

"We have a situation."

He glanced at the organized chaos around him and nodded his head. "We certainly do."

She pulled at his shirtsleeve and tilted her clipboard toward him. "Cass—Fortress Cliff—0800" was in purple ink. "She hasn't checked back in."

Adam didn't want to care. In fact, he hated the way his belly knotted at that piece of news. "Have you sent anyone to check it out?"

"They're still assigning teams to sections of the park. Thought you might like to take this one yourself," she whispered, her eyebrows rising.

Adam grimaced, tempted to tell her flat-out she had the wrong man for the job. She didn't know his interest in Cass McIntyre had been obliterated the night before.

However, he didn't want to tarnish the trust and respect shining in Mavis's eyes whenever he entered the building. Mavis was a lifelong resident of the nearby town of Canyon and attended the same church his mother had.

Adam blew out a deep breath and nodded. "I'll take a look around the cliff."

She beamed and handed him the note. "If she's not in any trouble, she's not gonna be happy I sent someone out to check on her."

"Woman's too independent for her own good," he muttered, settling his cowboy hat on his head.

"It's what happens when a woman fends too long for herself," she said with a firm nod. And she should know. The elderly spinster had lived alone for as long as he'd known her, which was all his life.

Forty-five minutes later, after getting his wheels bogged

down in mud twice, he made it to the summit and drove slowly along the rim of the bluff. Just as he'd decided he'd have to park and continue the search on foot, a scrap of white gleaming against the dark green branches of a juniper tree caught his eye.

The closer he drew, the item took shape—two distinctive shapes. He hit his brakes, put the truck in park, and cut the engine.

Adam almost smiled at the thought of Cass resorting to flashing her underwear. But his amusement lasted only a second because he realized things must be grim if she'd signaled for help.

He picked up his radio from the seat beside him and called in his location before stepping out of his vehicle and making his way to the cliff's edge to peer over the side.

His heart skipped a beat when he spotted the top of a blond head, hair pulled into a tight ponytail. Cass sat on a narrow outcropping of rock with her back against the wall and her slim legs dangling in the air.

He drew a deep breath to calm his heart, then satisfied she wasn't in any imminent danger, he scanned the eroded ledge, the last twenty or so feet of rock to the cliff's edge, and the thick trunk of the tree clinging to that edge.

His boot crunched in grit as he leaned farther over the rim, sending a spray of pea-sized gravel downward. "Watch out, below," he called.

Cass jerked her head back, and then turned her face upward. A scowl darkened her features. "Damn. Didn't think my bad luck could get any worse."

"Yeah, well I'm all you've got. Sit tight until I get back."

"Like I'm going anywhere?"

Adam shook his head. The woman didn't possess a lick o' sense bitching with her rescuer. Hell, she had no business climbing on her own in the first place—or hopping into his brother's arms.

He squelched that last thought. No use getting riled up again when he had work to do. If she fell, everyone would think he'd dropped her on purpose.

He backed his vehicle up to a spot directly above her position and grabbed a rope, tied it around his trailer hitch, and then fed the coil through his hand, grasping the prusik knot as he approached the edge again.

Bracing his feet against an exposed root of the juniper tree, he wound the rope around the trunk then lowered the end toward her.

Cass reached up for the rope he dangled above her. "Give me some more."

Adam gave her another few inches, but as she raised her hand to grab it, he pulled it up just out of reach.

Her head tilted until her green gaze met his.

Adam felt a fierce satisfaction that he had her undivided attention.

Her slender brows drew together in a frown. Her lips pouted. "This is not the time to play games with me, Adam. Get me off this goddamn ledge."

"I'd think a woman in your position would be grateful for a little help, not cussin' at it."

Thunder clapped from the southern rim of the canyon, drawing both their gazes.

"We don't have time for this," Cass called out. "Send down that rope."

She was right, but something twisted inside Adam. Seeing her so vulnerable sent an edgy thrill through his body. "Say you're sorry, first."

Her head tilted again. This time confusion and maybe a hint of regret darkened her gaze. "For what? Getting stuck here? Am I inconveniencing you?"

"Wrong response."

She faced the canyon again, and her shoulders slumped.

"You didn't want to hear any excuses last night. Why should I think you want to hear me apologize now?"

"Maybe I'm just curious to see if you know how."

The wind whipped up, tearing at the brim of his hat. They really didn't have time for this.

"I'm sorry," she called out, her tone defiant. "Did you hear me?"

"Yeah, but I'm not feeling it."

"Look, get me off this rock. Then take your pound of flesh."

"Any way I want it?"

There was a long pause, and she peered up again, her scowl screwing up her features. "Any way you want it," she gritted out.

Adam felt a grim smile stretch his lips. Too bad he didn't have any intention of acting on her promise. Taking out his anger on her body would make for sweet revenge.

He dropped the coiled rope again, letting the end dangle in front of her, then fed her more as she tugged it down to attach to her harness. "You're going to have to climb, but I'll take up the slack."

He backed away from the cliff's edge and grasped the rope in front of the tree. Then he pulled until he felt tension on the line, taking up the slack as Cass made her way slowly up the side, not letting up until she hauled herself over the edge and collapsed face-first in the mud.

Adam dropped the rope and strode over to her, leaning down to hold out his hand. She raised her head, mud on her chin and one cheek, her gaze going to his face then dropping to his hand.

She wiped her own against her shorts, and then slid her fingers along his palm, accepting his tug as he hauled her to her feet.

They stood chest-to-chest, and then she wobbled. Adam

clutched her waist and drew her closer, widening his stance so he could feel her taut belly press against his groin.

His cock stirred, something he couldn't hide when there wasn't an inch of space between them.

Just as she couldn't hide the twin points stabbing at his chest.

Her head bowed, but slowly her hands glided up his arms to clutch his shoulders. "This going to be your pound?" she asked, her voice softly muffled.

"I'm still thinking on what I want in trade," he said, forcing his voice to remain even, his tone cold.

She lifted her head, her chin tilting upward in defiance. "What if I don't like what you come up with? I agreed to your bargain under duress. It doesn't count."

Adam narrowed his gaze. "We're a long way from civilization. Not too smart, saying things like that to me when I'm still mad as hell."

Her lips twisted. "What's the matter? Didn't like my apology?"

"It was only a start. Next time, I want you to mean it."

She snorted. "This is ridiculous. I'm through being sorry. Through trying to talk to you like you're a reasonable man. I've been sitting on that ledge for an hour. I'm dirty, hungry, and getting grumpier by the minute. I don't want to do this now."

"I don't want to do this—ever," he growled, pushing her away.

Her eyes closed, a momentary flash of pain tightening her lips.

Good. He'd scored a hit. She damn well deserved it.

"Get in the truck. I'll take you home."

The drive to her place was made in silence thick with tension. He kept his gaze glued to the road before him; she sat with her shoulders angled away to stare out the passenger window.

When he pulled into her drive, she unhooked her seatbelt, and then hesitated.

Adam braced himself, gripping the steering wheel hard.

"It could have been you, you know," she whispered fiercely, "but we've been going in circles for a month now and you never even came close to asking me out. I'm not a nun, Adam."

"You made your choice."

"It was just a kiss."

"And that makes it all right? Get out, Cass."

She opened her mouth again, but he turned to aim an angry glare her way.

Her eyes blinked once, and she clamped her lips closed. The door slammed opened with an angry jerk that rattled the cab. Shoulders straight, she stomped all the way to her front door.

Adam put the truck into reverse, gunned the engine, spinning the tires in a short, sharp squeal, and then peeled out.

Did she really expect him to forget he'd seen her make out with his brother? That he'd be willing to pick up where they left off? He told himself he was glad, even relieved, he'd never made love to her. Their constant sparring had been fueled by his annoyance and her stubborn, prickly pride—never by lust. His brother was welcome to her.

Still, he couldn't quite push aside the feeling that had gripped him when he'd peered over the edge of the steep cliff and found her sitting there, waiting for rescue—vulnerable and alone.

Deep, twisted satisfaction had flared hot inside him.

He'd liked having her at his mercy.

2

Three days later, Cass sat at her desk finishing up reports left from the previous day—or rather, trying to. She clicked on save, closed her computer, and then tilted her coffee cup, noting its half-empty state. She shoved away from her desk with a deep sigh. Truthfully, she'd have used any excuse not to sit there another minute.

She'd been unbearably "itchy"—so restless she'd started planning a new bouldering excursion for her next day off. Physical exhaustion seemed the only relief from what really bothered her.

Adam hadn't relented. Not once. He hadn't called. He hadn't even used one of his flimsy "complaint session" excuses to stop by the headquarters. Apparently, he didn't intend to collect his pound of flesh.

She sighed, acknowledging she was one pathetic creature when she'd settle for a man taking his revenge for the simple joy of seeing him.

Cass refilled her cup at the community pot and headed to the information desk and Mavis.

The lobby was empty except for the elderly, gray-haired woman who was busy stocking the brochure rack with a fresh batch of trail maps.

"Things always slow this time of day?" Cass asked, making conversation.

Mavis continued sliding the pamphlets in their slots. "Most folks settle in the shade about this time. Days are gettin' hotter."

"Gonna be a long summer," Cass murmured.

The older woman shot her a wry glance. "We gonna talk about the weather or what's really on your mind? You haven't said a word about what happened the other day on the cliff."

Cass grimaced. "Nothing happened. He tossed me a rope and took me home."

Mavis set the brochures on the counter. Her soft blue gaze studied Cass's face. "Haven't seen him around here since. Something happened."

Cass released her breath, deciding to confide because she needed someone to talk to. "I think I blew it, Mavis," she said softly. "The night before the storm Adam caught me in the parking lot at The Stone Pony—kissing Johnny." At Mavis's sigh, Cass's cheeks heated. "I know. Not smart. But it happened, and now he won't talk to me."

Mavis's soft, dewy fingers pressed against Cass's as she stood stock-still clutching her coffee cup. "I don't know if there's any way to fix that, hon. Adam doesn't give his trust easy, and he and Johnny are so competitive . . . have been since they were boys."

Which only confirmed Cass's assessment of the situation. Deflated, she forced a smile. "At least he won't be coming around every other day to complain about hikers crossing his fence." She dragged in a fortifying breath and reached for a stack of trail maps. "I'll take some of these with me to hand out. Better head out on patrol and make sure things stay quiet."

Mavis gave her a pinched smile and circled the counter of the information desk. Cass went slowly back to her desk to retrieve her radio and clipped it to her belt.

As she walked back toward Mavis to say good-bye the glass doors at the entrance swooshed open behind her.

Mavis's eyes widened slightly, and she whispered, "Brace yourself."

Cass lifted both brows in question, but noted the smile Mavis quickly flashed and the two bright spots of color that filled the older woman's cheeks.

Cass glanced over her shoulder then stiffened at the sight of the tall glass of firewater that sauntered into the building.

So tall his shadow stretched from the door to the tips of her hiking boots, Adam never failed to make her feel like a little girl in play clothes, although at five-foot-four she was barely petite. Broad across the shoulders, his frame narrowed neatly at the waist before flaring slightly over massive thighs.

Dressed today in a long-sleeved shirt with the cuffs turned to bare his thick wrists, blue jeans, and boots, he looked the quintessential cowboy—except for the long, black ponytail that fell across one shoulder when he removed his straw cowboy hat and the plastic grocery bag he carried.

Completely, *thigh-clenchingly* masculine, he never failed to take her breath away. "Thanks for the warning, Mavis," she muttered.

Mavis chuckled softly as the attractive Indian crossed the floor, making a beeline straight for them.

"Adam Youngblood," Mavis called out cheerily. "What can we do for you, sir?"

He halted in front of the desk, scanned Cass with a quick, impersonal glance, and then turned his attention to Mavis. He leaned over the counter and pressed a kiss against Mavis's papery cheek. "How's my girl?"

Mavis blushed. "What's got your back up today, handsome?"

"More hikers crossed my fence."

While irritation prickled because he seemed set on ignoring her, Cass still shivered at the gravel roughening his voice.

"Sorry to hear that," Mavis murmured. "Did they cut the wire this time?"

"Yeah, and I have proof they came from the park. They left this next to the hole they dug." He slapped the plastic grocery bag of trash on her desk. "Do you recognize the brochure?" he asked, pointing to a crumpled trail map at the top of the heap of soda cans and energy bar wrappers.

Although she wished she could remain as impersonal as he, and even though part of Cass's training had included units on public relations and role-playing exercises where she'd practiced how to diffuse aggression from unhappy park visitors, she raised one eyebrow and broke in, answering innocently, "Looks like one of our brochures. The latest printing, actually. You can tell from the pricing for the campsites. They just went up."

His glance cut downward, catching on her slight smile. His eyes narrowed. "I found it inside my fence," he bit out, "next to a freshly buried Batman lunch box with a fishing lure inside it."

A GPS hiker's cache box, Cass guessed. "Seems you've got a new lure and a lunch box, Robin. Congratulations."

He blinked, and then his face was suffused with ruddy color beneath his darkly tanned skin.

Cass wondered if she'd been a little too glib, but he'd pissed her off by ignoring her. "I take it you're here to make a complaint?"

He eyed her and let out a short, annoyed grunt. "My boys have better things to do than pick up trash, fill in holes or fix fences when a hiker decides it's too much bother to climb. And we damn sure don't have time to rescue them when they run out of water. What are you going to do about it?"

Cass smiled sweetly, pretending he was a stranger. "Since this seems to be a common occurrence for you, sir, I'm sure you're aware we aren't responsible for visitors' actions outside the park. Have you posted sufficient signage to alert people they're entering private property?"

His nostrils flared around a sharply indrawn breath.

Mavis muttered something under her breath and eased away from the counter.

"I'm also *assuming* your property borders the park," Cass continued as though she hadn't noted his deepening glower. "GPS hikers tend to take the most direct route to their destinations, regardless of whether they're trespassing."

Another deep breath and a sharp-edged glance told her she was pushing him to the end of his patience, but she couldn't resist one more jab at his arrogance. "You know, there is a solution. You could simply deed that section of land to the park. It'd save you the headaches and be a great tax write-off."

His black scowl, while intimidating, caused a ripple of pure heated excitement that raised gooseflesh on her skin. She couldn't help wondering for the thousandth time what all that dark intensity would feel like up close and personal.

He clamped his hat on his head and turned to Mavis. "This isn't over." Then he strode to the door, thrusting it open with so much force he rattled the glass surrounding it.

"I'll make sure to enter your concerns in my report," Cass called after him.

Shaking his head, he stomped out of the building.

"You tryin' to piss him off?" Mavis said wryly.

Cass felt a smile stretch her lips. For the first time in days, righteous anger and an electric thrill of arousal warmed her whole body. "Tell me I'm good," she murmured, her gaze never leaving him as he swung open the door of his pickup.

His glance met hers through the glass and narrowed.

Quick as a fire licking at dry buffalo grass, her anger sparked hotter and she strode quickly to the door.

"Do you think that's smart?" Mavis's quavering voice called after her.

"I don't give a damn about smart."

She shoved through the doors and flew down the steps to approach him as he stepped onto the running board and slid into the cab of his truck.

"What'd you mean, it's not over?" she asked.

Adam's black brows lowered. "You're blocking my door."

Cass held his glare with one of her own. "I'll move when I'm good and ready."

"You aren't big enough or mean enough to keep me if I wanna go."

"I'm an ex-cop and I've taken down men your size before."

His lips twitched once then flattened. "What is it you want, Officer McIntyre?"

Cass stepped up onto the running board, not caring who might see. She leaned close and whispered harshly, "For fuck's sake. I was drunk. I wanted you. It was dark—he looked like you. I closed my eyes and let it happen. I've apologized. Be a man and suck it up."

Adam's jaw tightened. "Not too good at taking hints, are you?"

"You know we have something," she continued, anger starting to make her shake. "You're just too damn stubborn or stupid to admit it."

His eyelids dipped, and his expression made a subtle shift, from obstinate to calculating.

Encouraged, she came closer.

Adam's eyes flicked over her, and then came back up to lock with hers. "I don't think anyone's ever talked to me that way before," he said softly.

"Shocking," she whispered, near enough now to catch the scent of his skin and hair—soap and his particular brand of musk teasing her nostrils.

His glance cut away. "I need to show you something. You have to see the damage they've done this time."

It was on the tip of her tongue to remind him again that the park wasn't responsible, but she caught herself, realizing this might just be his way of starting a conversation with her.

"Let me tell Mavis—"

"Just give her a wave. She knows," he drawled, nodding toward the glass doors where Mavis stood staring out at them.

Cass stepped down to the ground, gave Mavis a short wave, and headed around the truck to open the passenger door.

Once inside, her heart began to beat faster. She folded her hands in her lap and barely resisted the urge to stare at him. Was he giving her another chance or was this really all about the hikers?

The drive out of the park and around the north rim of the canyon was made in silence. Adam left the paved road and followed a long gravel trail across a bleak grassy plain, leading to a long stretch of barbed wire. The top two strands had been cut.

He parked next to a scraggly mesquite tree and got out. She followed on his heels, climbing over the fence and heading to the edge of a dry creek that sliced through the flatland and emptied into the canyon.

She slid in gravel and sand down the side of the arroyo and tromped toward a mound of fresh dirt. "This is where they buried the cache?"

"Yeah," he said, setting his hands on his hips.

She didn't know what he expected her to do. She'd seen the hole. Now what? She lifted her gaze to his face to find him staring steadily back.

Cass licked her lips. "Did you bring a shovel? Maybe they left something else behind that will identify the trespasser."

One dark brow arched. "Not going to tell me it's not your concern?"

She shrugged. "I'm trying to be helpful."

"Why?"

"Because . . ." She shrugged, deciding to be honest and to hell with pride. "Because I'm glad you asked me to come."

His gaze swept down her body, slowly, deliberately. His bronze skin darkened; his eyelids dipped. "About our bargain . . ."

Cass inwardly cringed when his gaze settled between her legs in an obvious insult. She swallowed hard. "Have you decided what you want?"

"Yeah. You. Now."

Of course, here and now in the dirt and broad daylight. She shifted uneasily, knowing this was another test. "Here?" she asked weakly.

"If you meant what you said, why hesitate?"

She glanced around the ravine—at the rocky sides, the gravel floor. "Doesn't seem a likely place . . ."

"The truck, then?" he said, his tone suspiciously agreeable.

"But it's in the open—anyone driving by could see us."

"Yeah, so it is."

Cass stood still, the hot sun beating down on her head, not a hint of breeze to cool her fevered skin.

Despite her misgivings, her body already grew ready to accept him. Her breasts felt heavy, her nipples beaded, becoming more aroused by the scrape of lacy fabric covering them. And deep inside, heat curled, tightening and dampening her pussy. *Any way you want it*, she'd promised him.

She spread her hands. "What's your preference?"

"The truck."

Cass decided not to give him a chance to accuse her of stalling. She turned on her heels and headed back up the side of the ravine, Adam right behind her.

When she reached the truck, he opened the passenger door, inviting her to stand between him and the door with a sweep of his hand. "Undress and give me your clothes."

Her gaze swept his hard, implacable features, a frisson of unease sliding down her spine. She'd be naked. At his mercy. What would his reactions to seeing her be? Would his icy reserve thaw? If not, how could she allow him to touch her? She gulped down her nervousness.

She could do this without letting him know how uncomfortable she was, how badly she wanted to bolt. Sure, she could.

Her hands raised shakily to her shirt, which she pulled from her pants, a little unnerved by his disconcerting stare, and glanced beyond his shoulder to the lazy, cliff side trail. She undid her buttons while his dark gaze honed in on every little movement of her hands.

Christ, she was going to get fired. Someone was going to note how long she'd been gone and her condition when she returned. She'd lose her job and have a devil of a time finding another as sweet—just because she wanted to fuck this man.

She shrugged off the khaki shirt, and then opened the front fastening of her bra and let it slide off her arms.

His nostrils flared, his eyelids lowered as his gaze dropped to her breasts. "Everything else but your socks and boots."

She unstrapped her equipment belt and dropped it on the floorboard of the truck, then closed her eyes and unfastened her uniform shorts, shoving them down as best she could without bumping against his body.

Her green shorts slithered down her thighs, leaving only her lacy underwear for modesty.

Again, he arched an eyebrow.

She briefly closed her eyes then rolled the lace off her hips until it fluttered to the ground.

Adam leaned down, not as worried about touching her, and his face glided along her belly then her thigh. He picked up her clothing and tossed it into the truck. "Sit on the edge of the seat and spread your legs for me."

Cass had been pretty stoic up to this point, but her courage fled beneath the cool challenge he issued. "What about you?" she blurted.

"Is there a problem?"

"Why am I the only one naked? Are you doing this to humiliate me?"

He shook his head, his soft tsking raising her anxiety. "I don't want to fuck you, Cass. Not yet. Are you going to do as I ask?"

Only he wasn't really asking, was he?

Although humiliation burned her cheeks, she slid backward onto the hot leather seat, clamping her legs together so she wouldn't leave a slick, telltale trail. Her bottom burned, but she bit her lip, determined not to let him see her wince, and opened her legs.

Adam leaned into the cramped space, locked his glance with hers, and then flattened his hand between her breasts and pushed.

She fell back, gasping as stinging heat bit her skin, but Adam cupped her sex with his warm palm and pressed, completely filling her mind with the enormity of what she was doing. She closed her eyes.

A mistake. One she recognized immediately, because something slick and soft trailed along her inner thigh, starting at her knee. Her leg jerked at the contact. A trickle of cream slid from inside her, something he couldn't miss due to the moist contraction of her inner muscles.

A sexy, rumbling chuckle gusted against her skin. Long, thick fingers thrust inside her and stilled.

Cass's eyes shot open and she looked between her legs.

Adam's eyes were slitted, his jaw tight. "Tell me, Cass," he rasped. "Would you have been as eager for Johnny to eat your sweet pussy?"

Air hissed between her clenched teeth, and she tried to sit

up, but he slipped his fingers from inside her, hooked his arms beneath her thighs, and pulled her ass past the edge of the seat.

"Don't. I don't want this. Stop," she gasped, still trying to squirm away.

His hands came over the top of her legs, and his fingers parted her wet folds. His head lowered, his nostrils flaring as he inhaled. Then his mouth opened and his tongue stroked the length of her folds.

"Adam! Damn it, stop," she cried out, pushing against the top of his head to force him away.

A futile attempt, because he forced her thighs higher, wider. His tongue stabbed at her center, lashing inside and swirling.

Cass grabbed for his hair, pulling hard. But a wicked flick at her clit caused her back to arch. Her hips pulsed, driving her cunt against his mouth. "I fucking hate you," she whispered, misery and arousal strangling her.

His tongue retreated. "Maybe. But you want me." His thumb flicked the burgeoning knot at the top of her folds, scraping deliciously. "Say it. Say you want me, Cass."

Her belly shivered, curving upward, driving her pussy higher.

His thumb slid away and fingers stroked her labia, easing along the outer edges, gliding downward in the wet trail trickling between her buttocks. The roughened pad of a thumb caressed her small furled hole.

All the while his hard, steady gaze remained locked with hers, waiting.

Cass felt her lips tremble. Her body began to shudder. Arousal wound tight around her womb, and a deep, convulsing ache set her hips plunging up and down. "I want you," she answered. "You already know that. Please, Adam, fuck me."

As though she'd released him from restraint, he surged upward and pressed her thighs against his chest. "Hold them. Keep them high."

Cass clutched her thighs and widened them, bracing one foot against the top of the door frame and the other against the window.

She whimpered now, not caring that she was ready to fly apart and he would see it all—the deep, agonizing desire making her tremble and beg, both entrances exposed. Pure, primal need ravaged what was left of her pride.

Adam cupped her buttocks briefly, squeezing the globes, massaging them while he settled on the running board on his knees.

Then he rubbed her asshole again with his thumb, holding her gaze while his darkened, and pressed inward.

Cass couldn't look away, didn't care that his intrusion burned. She billowed her cheeks and puffed until the painful burning eased, and he thrust deeper. Then she ground her teeth together, because he was already stroking her pussy with his long, thick fingers, coating himself in creamy honey.

Three fingers plunged inside, and she tensed, her feet pressing hard against the truck as she raised her head to watch him.

His gaze lifted to hers again, grim satisfaction curving his lips and feral heat stretching the skin tight across his sharply etched cheekbones.

She didn't care about the sight she presented him, twisted like a pretzel, red faced and quivering. She was ready to explode. She panted, beyond speech, a throb like a primitive drum beating against her chest.

Adam slowly lowered his face between her legs. A thumb scraped the hood stretched taut over her clitoris, exposing the moist, red nub. His mouth opened and warm lips latched around it, sucking hard while he plunged thick fingers deep in her ass and pussy.

Cass screamed, throwing back her head and rolling it on the hot leather while her orgasm spiraled deep inside her cunt, radiating outward, setting thick, rhythmic convulsions rippling along her channel.

He continued to suckle and thrust, long after her body sagged against the seat and her breath became jagged, tortured gasps.

Fingers withdrew, his lips relaxed, and then his tongue gently stroked over her damp folds.

When at last he backed away, Cass couldn't move for long moments. Tears slowly slid along the side of her cheeks, and she turned her face aside to swipe at them, hating that he saw this too.

Adam dragged down her legs, and his fingers closed around one hand to jerk her up. "Get dressed."

She closed her eyes, savoring the hint of tension in his taut, gravelly voice.

She'd gotten her satisfaction.

Adam could roast in hell if he thought she owed him a thing.

3

Cass followed the curve of the park road, passing water crossing number six and slowing as she drove past the camping area at the west end of the park.

She'd made the circuit through the canyon nearly twenty times already. The sun was lowering beyond the edge of the rim, a huge orange ball sliding into shimmering layers of mauve and red, a sight that usually filled her with wonder. Today, she could only muster a sigh.

Adam hadn't called last night. She shouldn't have expected him to. After he'd finished with her, nothing in his demeanor changed to make her think he'd relented.

She'd come to the conclusion that the pleasurable torture he'd inflicted on her was his brand of revenge. Completely diabolical. Even cruel.

She'd been as wrung out as a dishrag after coming, legs wobbling, hands shaking as she'd dressed. He'd stood with his back to her, arms folded over his chest, until she was through.

Then he hadn't said a word on the long drive back. Not one.

The scent of sex, *of steamy pussy*, had permeated the air they breathed despite the cool breeze blasting from the AC.

And if she'd looked a little ragged when he dropped her at the headquarters building, Mavis hadn't noted it—or at least had known better than to offer a comment.

Yes, the older woman's eyes had rounded, a sparkle of excitement gleaming in the soft, faded blue, but one glance at Cass's anguished face and she'd left her alone. Cass had spent the rest of the afternoon and evening in her car, patrolling, ignoring minor infractions because she hadn't the emotional strength to do her job.

Today was better, but only because she felt hollow, as though something vital had been carved from her chest.

Just as she passed the restroom beyond the campground, a woman burst from the door of the lady's side, her arms waving.

Cass muttered a curse, wondering if a snake or a scorpion had wandered into the showers. She pulled to a halt and got out of her car, approaching the heavyset woman whose chest heaved like two pontoons on a choppy sea.

"There's a young man in the women's shower."

Cass lifted a brow. That was different. "Ma'am, let me handle it. You stay outside while I sort this out."

Cass checked her sidearm—because she never knew when she might actually have to use it—and straightened her shoulders, pushing through the door and walking past the restroom stalls to the shower area. "Sir, I'm going to have to ask you to leave," she called out.

She halted as a tall, lean man stepped from the stall, a grin curving his lips. Cass fisted a hand on her hip. "Johnny, what the hell do you think you're doing in here?"

"Do I have your attention now?" he asked, leaning a shoulder against the tiled wall. His dark eyes glinted with humor—and a hint of something wicked. "Missed you, Sunshine," he drawled.

Cass firmed her lips into a straight line, immune now to his considerable charms. Although alike in build and smoldering good looks, his conceit spoiled the view when she compared him to his older brother. "Like I said, *sir*, you have to leave. Now."

"You didn't return my calls," he said, in a lazy, drawling baritone. "What was I supposed to do?"

She closed the distance between them, coming so near she forced him to step backward into the stall. "I would have thought you got my message loud and clear the other night," she said, dropping her voice into a feminine snarl.

Johnny's lips curved. "Before or after you kissed me?"

"You kissed me, dumb ass," she reminded him, narrowing her eyes. "And I damn well know you saw Adam before you did it."

His smirk was a sexy twist of firm lips. Something he'd likely practiced in front of a mirror. "So it's all my fault?"

"No. My lips were right there, too," she growled.

"So why are you so mad?" His calculated smile slipped for just a second, revealing a hint of authentic confusion.

He seemed so much like a boy trying hard to be a man that her irritation with him faded. She leaned away from him, mad at herself for taking out her disappointment on him. Whatever his beef with his brother, the hurt was older and deeper than any kiss in a dark parking lot.

"Johnny, go home," she said, suddenly tired.

"Come out with me. Tonight."

Cass shook her head, staring at him. "Are you out of your mind? Don't you know when to leave well enough alone? I won't ever go out with you again. I'm not your girl. In fact, I'm already feeling sorry for her."

Johnny's dark brows lowered into a fierce scowl. "Well, if you're waiting around for a chance at Adam, you're going to be alone a long time. He'll never come near you again. Not after I've been there."

Fury blazed hot and fast, and she leaned in again, slamming her chest against his, body-checking him to force him hard against the tiles. "Then you don't know him as well as you think."

Johnny's gaze widened above hers. "You've seen him? You slept with him after he saw us together?"

Ready to end the conversation right then and there, Cass reached for the spigot and turned on the cold water, stepping back to avoid the worst of the spray that splattered him, soaking into his clothing. "Get the hell out of my park."

She turned on her heels, hands fisting at her sides. Outside the restroom, she nodded to the heavyset woman and stalked to her car.

Once behind the wheel, she didn't look back once. She drove through the park, found a deserted parking lot and pulled to the far end of it before she cut the engine. She rolled down the windows, settled her head on the backrest and closed her eyes.

Damn it, how could she have been so stupid to ever have trusted him? Johnny Youngblood carried a chip on his shoulder when it came to his brother. The little flicker of attraction she'd felt had been a reflected heat. His eager attentions had only soothed her disappointment over Adam's unwillingness to pursue her.

Johnny had played on that insecurity the morning of their date. She'd been supervising a crew clearing debris from an eddy in the river flowing through the park when he'd caught up with her.

Cass hadn't thought anything about his showing up. She hadn't been aware of the brothers' strained relationship since he'd accompanied Adam only once to file a complaint. She'd offered him a wave as he pulled his vehicle off the shoulder of the road.

She'd have been lying to herself if she didn't admit her breath had come a little faster—something about the Youngblood men did that to her.

With the same dark, exotic good looks—tall, muscular physique, long black hair, razor sharp features, and eyes so black the pupils were indistinguishable from the irises—Johnny had been nothing but a substitute for the one man she'd really wanted.

That morning on the roadside, Johnny gave her an easy smile, but the gaze he aimed her way told her he had something on his mind. She'd accepted his request to speak with her privately, and allowed him to take her arm and tug her away from the crew and their curious glances.

"What's on your mind today, Johnny?" she'd asked. "Got more trespassers?"

"I'm not here on ranch business. This is strictly pleasure."

She'd given him a reserved smile, wondering where this was leading.

Johnny had lowered his head to hers, which gave her a moment's pause, but what was he going to do? Kiss her? The thought had her grimacing. She'd been thinking a lot about one particular pair of lips. Still, she didn't step away from Johnny. Instead, she waited for him to get to the point.

"My brother's always been a little slow to make a move on a woman."

She'd shot him a startled glance, surprised at his intimate comment, but shrugged it off. Maybe Adam had confided in him. "He doesn't strike me as the shy type," she said, not wanting to jump into an awkward conversation but unable to stem her curiosity.

"I don't get why he does it. He doesn't trust easily."

"I can understand that. He must get hit on by desperate women all the time," she'd said, trying to lighten the conversation.

"I've seen the way he looks at you," Johnny said, his expression charming in its earnestness. "It's not hard to miss he likes you."

She'd pretended indifference to that little tidbit of exhilarating news while she'd glanced away, unable to meet his gaze with a blush creeping across her cheeks.

"He doesn't much like the fact you wear that uniform. He likes his relationship with the Palo Duro Canyon folks to remain strictly adversarial."

"Seems strange he'd volunteer to search for lost hikers with the fire department," she'd murmured, again wondering where this was leading.

Johnny shrugged. "He doesn't have a thing against the folks who come and use the park the way it's intended. He just gets frustrated when they decide to wander off the trails. We've had to rescue them off our property when they ran out of water, fix fences they don't want to climb. They dig holes in our land to hide their little prizes—"

"I get why he'd be pissed, but there's not a lot we can do about it other than to warn hikers to stick to our marked trails."

"He knows it. It's partly why he hasn't asked you out—but he hasn't been able to stay away either. I think he likes having excuses to come over here."

"You think he's looking for excuses to see me?" she'd blurted, then wished she could take it back because he'd smiled at her eager response.

"You're very pretty."

Cass snorted. "Most days I'm not wearing a lick of makeup. I have skin peeling off my sunburned nose and these uniform shorts don't do a thing for my hips."

"Adam doesn't seem to care. He still comes back all riled up every time he sees you."

She was always equally "riled"—deeply aroused by his visits. Heat filled her face. Cass gave him a sideways glance. "Why are you telling me this?"

"Because I'm going to ask you out."

She'd blinked, and then shook her head. "Why would you do that if you think your brother might be interested in me?"

"Adam needs a little shove in your direction, don't you think?"

She'd seen the wicked glint in his eyes and read it as humor. If only she'd guessed the joke would be on her. Instead, she'd grown excited about the idea of shaking up the quiet Indian.

So, she'd agreed to meet Johnny at a bar in Canyon after her shift ended, ignoring the feeling in her gut that told her this was a really bad idea. As the afternoon stretched into early evening, she'd grown increasingly certain she'd made a mistake.

On the verge of calling to break their date, she'd found Adam's battered pickup at a trail head, and the tall, dark rancher leaning against it with his thumbs hooked in the pockets of his jeans.

She parked beside him, feeling guilty and hating that she did. A deep breath calmed her rioting heart and she stepped out of her park truck as he straightened away from his and approached.

Adam stalked over to her, trapping her against her vehicle, his expression so intense she'd felt her heartbeats escalate. She had thought, for just a moment, that he intended to kiss her, but he'd backed away, his face molding into a flat, emotionless mask. "Heard you and Johnny are steppin' out tonight."

Nervous and trying not to show it, she'd sucked in a breath, prepared to tell him that she'd changed her mind when he'd snorted, his mouth twisting into a grim line. "Told him you'd be a damned fool to even consider it."

All concern for his feelings in the matter shriveled. Her back stiffened. "Why's that, Adam? It's not like I have anything better to do."

His gaze sharpened, cutting from her face to glide down her

body and back up again. "I'm not sure who deserves a warning more," he murmured.

She'd lifted one brow, anger slowly burning a hole in the pit of her stomach. "We're both of age."

"Be sure of what you want," he'd said, his words clipped.

Then he'd turned on his heels and stomped away before she'd had a chance to untangle her tongue. Who in hell did he think he was?

If she'd been wavering about the good sense of going out with his brother, Adam's warning had shoved her straight into Johnny's waiting arms.

However, as much as she'd love to place all the blame on Adam's stubbornness for what happened later that night, she couldn't. She had only herself to blame.

Still, if he hadn't been so arrogant, if he'd asked her not to go, she might not have ended up in The Stone Pony's parking lot, staring over Johnny's shoulder when Adam quietly stepped out of the darkness to pin her with a cold, hard glare that sent her stomach plunging.

But if Adam Youngblood was a stubborn man, she was downright mulish.

Rather than end the embrace she'd been trying to escape, she'd clung to Johnny as his lips left her mouth to glide down her neck.

While Adam's eyes narrowed to angry slits, something wicked rose inside her. She'd honed in on his anger and sharpening features and found herself responding to Johnny's unwanted attentions as though she'd been eager to accept them in the first place while Adam's bitter gaze drilled her.

Her head tilted, giving her assent for Johnny's lips and tongue to trail wetly down her neck. Her body relaxed against the wall he'd shoved her against, and she let him nudge apart her legs to rub the hard column of his cock against the apex of her thighs.

Only after Adam had turned sharply away and melted into the darkness had she peeled her arms from around Johnny's body and given him a shove to get him off her.

He'd growled and taken her lips again, and she'd resorted to a trick her older brother had taught her in high school, slipping a hand between his legs to grasp his balls and twist.

Johnny, cursing and bent at the waist, didn't stop her as she left him braced against the brick wall.

Coward that she was, she snuck away, clutching her purse to her chest. When she opened the door to her car, she found Adam sitting in the front seat.

"I did warn you," he said softly.

Cass had felt small, dirty, and wished she could have pretended she didn't care what he thought. She decided not to comment and stepped to the side as he unfolded from the seat.

"A storm's brewing," he murmured. "I'd stay off that rock tomorrow."

She'd looked at the midnight sky. Where all the stars of the Milky Way should have shone, a dense blackness blanketed the sky.

"I didn't mean for anything to happen," she whispered. "It was just a kiss . . ."

One dark brow lifted in a derisive arch. "Long night. Must have found plenty to talk about."

"That's all we did. Talk. Dance."

His face turned away from her.

"Adam . . ."

"Seems you made your choice."

Heartsick and filled with remorse for what she'd allowed to happen, she'd driven home where she'd showered and changed, and then made the decision to climb despite his warning.

Anything not to dwell on his expression as he'd turned away. His jaw had been tight. Hatred had glittered in his dark eyes.

Despite his prediction, she'd gone climbing the next morning anyway, desperate to escape her own reflection in the mirror. Only to meet with disaster. Adam her witness, again.

Cass started her car to make another circuit around the park. Climbing hadn't been the answer. She could have climbed Everest and not been able to escape her own misery.

At the sight of Johnny's white SUV grinding to a halt in front of the ranch house, Adam straightened in the saddle. "Javier, I'm calling it a day," he muttered.

He lifted his right leg over the saddle and slid to the ground, tossing his reins to his foreman. Without a backward glance, he strode toward the house.

At Johnny's bedroom door, he didn't bother knocking. He opened it just as Johnny dragged his wet T-shirt over his head.

Johnny shook his long hair and aimed a glare at Adam. "Ever consider knocking?"

"Where were you today? Thought you were checking fences with Mitch. Funny thing was, he said you put him in charge and left."

Johnny shrugged. "I had some business in town to take care of."

Adam eyed his wet clothing and lifted one eyebrow.

"What can I say?" Johnny tossed his wadded shirt toward the clothes hamper, and then gave Adam a smile. "The woman thought I needed to cool off. She's all about the job when she's got that sidearm strapped to her leg."

"You talking about Cass?" Adam asked, keeping his voice even.

"The woman's a firecracker," his brother replied, flashing a brief, wolfish leer. "Looks like it'll take both of us to keep her satisfied. Good thing I don't mind sloppy seconds."

Adam didn't think—he couldn't because his head felt ready to explode. He took two steps closer and swung his fist at Johnny's smiling face.

Johnny landed on his ass next to the bed, rubbing his chin. "What was that for? I'm willing to share."

"Keep away from her."

"Why? You don't want her. You can't make her happy."

"Johnny, I'm warning you. Keep away. I'm not gonna step aside like I did with Pam."

"Pam was a horny bitch too. She liked stringing us both along."

Adam shook his throbbing hand. "Any time you want to sell me your half of the ranch . . ."

"I'm not leaving. It's my home too. Get used to it. And don't tell me who I can fuck."

Adam jerked away, afraid he'd have to take another swing and wouldn't be able to stop. He headed out of the house to cool off on the porch, cursing Johnny and wondering what had happened between him and Cass, whether he'd kissed her again, and if she'd let him do more. And how could he blame her?

He'd left Cass wound tighter than a spring. He should know. They'd walked on the edge of arousal for weeks. Yesterday, he hadn't been able to stay away—even knowing she'd betrayed him.

While he hadn't planned to have sex with her, she'd pushed him past his endurance when she'd stepped up on his truck and gotten in his face to plead with him.

Smelling sweet but with that bulldog tilt to her chin, it had been all he could do not to yank her across his lap and kiss her right then and there.

Instead, he'd driven away with her on a lame-ass excuse, anything to get her into his truck and alone. When she'd submitted to his demands so readily, he'd been surprised.

Christ, the taste of her and the sweet sounds of her moans had stayed with him all night long. But so had the shattered look on her face when he'd withdrawn and demanded she dress.

He didn't want to care that he'd hurt her. Despite his brother's taunts, and his own past experience, he believed her explanation. They needed to talk and get some things straight between them—and he needed to know what the hell had happened between her and Johnny today.

Adam dug in his pocket for his keys, and then remembered if Johnny saw her at the park, she'd be working until late. Their conversation would have to wait until tomorrow because he didn't want interruptions.

His fists tightened, and he glanced back at the house, bitter regret washing over him that things remained so strained between himself and the only family he had left.

For the sake of their relationship, he ought to just end things now with Cass, but he suspected Johnny wouldn't stop there. His brother seemed determined to come between him and anyone he chose.

It's why he'd taken his time to get to know her. No use bringing a woman around who could be swayed by his brother's easy charm.

However, he should have warned her rather than letting her be used. Johnny didn't give a damn about Cass. The only thing he cared about was taking away everything Adam cherished.

4

Late afternoon the next day, Cass stood at the foot of a hoodoo, eyeing the bouldering pads she'd placed at the base of the rock to cushion a fall.

She'd decided to try free climbing. The tall rock spire would provide the physical and mental challenge she needed to keep other thoughts at bay—ones that included sensual memories of heated kisses and invasive thrusts.

At the moment, conquering a pillar of stone seemed the lesser danger to her well-being.

Already she'd scaled an inverted angle, using just her fingertips to hold her weight. The fingerless gloves kept the sweat on her palms from moistening her fingers. A dusting of white chalk gave added insurance.

Because her hands ached, she planned a climb up a straight, sheer wall, supported with toeholds this time. The last climb she planned for the day and a short one. Once again, storm clouds threatened in the distance, and she'd learned her lesson.

Footsteps sounded from around the corner of the spire

where she stood, and she wondered if another climber, curious about her route or perhaps eager to join her, was coming.

Any other day she would have enjoyed the company, but today, she sighed in resignation and cupped a hand over her eyes to watch the person's approach.

Her hand dropped to her side when she spotted Adam. "I'm off duty. You'll have to take up your complaint with Brody James."

"I'm not here on ranch business."

"Well, then you've wasted a trip because we don't have anything else to talk about."

His glance went to the dusty pads and up the side of the tall hoodoo. "A ropeless climb? I knew you were crazy, but this is insane."

"Trying it for the first time without pads and some practice would be insane."

"Have you fallen?"

She lifted her shoulders. "That's what the pads are for."

"Should you be doing this alone?"

"I prefer to climb alone. And I know my limits."

"You could break your neck and no one would even know."

"I could fall in the shower and be just as dead. Who the hell would care?"

Adam's chest lifted with a deep breath. "Maybe I would."

"Maybes aren't good enough for me," she said flatly. "Not anymore."

Adam's lips tightened, and then he blew out another deep breath and looked away. "Look, we need to talk."

"We're talking," Cass said, keeping her tone mild. "Mind if I head up while you get whatever you came to say off your chest?" She turned and sank a hand into the chalk bag hanging beside her right thigh and dusted both hands thoroughly before reaching up to grasp a rocky outcrop.

Adam stepped forward and grabbed her wrist to draw it down and turned her body toward him. "I've got another idea," he said, pulling her against him. "You don't have anyone waiting on you at home. Johnny's not going to show up at your doorstep because I sent him on an errand in Amarillo—I'm taking you home. My home."

Cass wrestled her hand away and took a step backward. "I don't want to go. I'm set for another hour of climbing before I'll be ready to leave."

"Who says you have a choice?" Adam growled.

She shot both eyebrows upward. "You're kidnapping me? Seems a little primitive."

"It's an old family tradition. Only question is, are you going to make a big enough fuss that I have to retrieve rope from my truck and tie you up?"

Cass had to admit that the thought of being his "captive" for the night was intriguing, as was the fact he didn't seem willing to budge from this rock until he had his way.

Still, the man had put her through hoops. He didn't deserve to have her capitulate without giving him a good fight. "I don't get it," she said, bracing her hands on her hips. "Since you never called me after you had your fun the other day, I thought I'd be the last woman you'd ever want to be near again."

"I didn't call because I had to work some things out. Then you had work, and so did I. There hasn't been a good time."

There he went again—making it sound as though she was an inconvenience. "Next time, how about checking my schedule first before you plan on a kidnapping, because I already have plans."

Adam's face suffused with angry color. "Do you always have to be so goddamn obstinate?"

Cass huffed. "You've got some nerve. Like you're the model of malleable."

"I'm warning you," he ground out, "I'm not feeling very civilized."

Didn't look it either. With his hair pulled back in a ponytail, a bleached-out cotton shirt and jeans hugging his solid body, he looked downright elemental, as primitive as he claimed. Just how far would he let her push him before he acted on his instincts?

Cass raised the back of her hand to her forehead, and fluttered her eyelashes. "Why, sir, you shouldn't say such things," she said, in a deep southern accent. "You'll make me swoon."

"Damn it, Cass."

She couldn't seem to help herself. A delicious swell of rage and lust quivered through her. "You're going to have to do better than that, Adam. I've wanted to talk to you for days, and guess what? I'm over that urge now."

Adam stepped closer, crowding her against the sharp-edged rock. "Are you?" He gripped her hips and lifted her high enough that the ridge of his thickening cock ground between her thighs. He pinned her with his hips grinding her into the rock, then slapped both palms against the wall above her head.

Pressed so close she could feel his heart beat against her chest, she stared into angry black eyes. "What a surprise. Both Youngbloods like shoving a girl against a wall to have their way."

A breath billowed his chest and Cass clamped her lips together to stop goading him because his bronze skin darkened, and his features tightened into a feral mask.

With a jagged edge digging into her back, she didn't have room to fill her lungs with air. "This doing it for you?" she gasped. "'Cause I can tell you, all I'm getting is bruised."

"This goes a long way toward soothing my *primal urges*," he drawled, his mouth hovering above hers.

She grimaced, pretending those lips weren't working on her urges as well. "You get 'em often?"

His mouth came closer still. "Only when I'm near you."

"Oh," she said, feeling a little faint. But whether from lack of air or the dark promise in his eyes, she wasn't sure.

His mouth slammed into hers, and Cass melted against the rock, gasping into his mouth as his tongue stroked inside hers in swirling laps that reminded her of how he'd made her come on the seat of his pickup.

When he lifted his mouth, he asked, "Gonna let me kidnap you?"

Adam watched one side of her lush mouth curve upward, and felt a heavy, sensual thrum course through his body. He had her now. Despite anything her mouth might say he could see the flare of hunger in her eyes.

"You asking me if I want to be kidnapped?" she asked, in a tone thick with sarcasm. "Seems more like a date if you expect me to agree."

"Can't give you any false signals," he muttered, stepped back and dipped down, snaking an arm beneath her ass and then straightening.

She didn't fold over his shoulder the way he expected her to, not that she ever did the expected. Her body remained rigid as he approached his truck. He knew she was doing it just to be awkward. He had to admit her feistiness was a big part of her attraction.

"Are you still mad about me kissing Johnny the other night?" she asked, her tone teasing.

"Furious," he replied, although a smile was beginning to tug at his lips. "But we're not talking about it now."

"Because it doesn't matter who I kiss?"

"Cass . . ." he said, his voice rising on a warning. "Do you ever think before you open that pretty mouth of yours? You don't provoke a man when he's already committing a crime to get you where he wants you."

"You want me in your truck?"

He rolled his eyes. "Yeah, I'm kidnapping you to my truck." Rounding the corner with her, he headed down the trail to the dirt parking lot where he'd left his vehicle. The trek wasn't long, but the sun was beating down, and while she was slender, she was also muscular—not as light as he'd expected. Not that he was in the mood to listen to complaints. There were sexier sounds he longed to hear, and soon.

"What's this about ancient tradition?"

"It's a Comanche thing. We raid to get women."

"Wouldn't think you'd need to resort to that."

"Believe me, I'm not hard up. But you're a special case."

"I'm special?" she said, sounding happy. "Sounds serious."

"Cass . . ."

"Yes?"

"Shut up or I'll get the duct tape out of the glove box and make it official."

"Gonna bind my hands?"

The little witch sounded excited at the prospect. "No, that pretty mouth of yours."

"You think my mouth's pretty?"

"I say that?" he teased.

"Uh-huh. Twice."

His truck was parked beside hers, and he dropped her into the front seat and held out his hands for her keys.

"Think I'm just gonna sit here while you lock up for me? And what about my gear? It's not cheap."

Adam groaned, and then popped open the glove box and reached inside for the roll of tape.

Her eyes widened.

So she hadn't believed him? Good. He didn't want her too confident. He grabbed her hands and raised them above her head, and then used the duct tape to strap her wrists to the gun rack behind her head. When he finished, he stood back and grinned.

Her lips were flattened, her eyes shooting daggers his way.

"Should have kept your mouth shut," he said, shaking his head. Then he loped back up the trail to gather her pads and gear.

When he returned, her head was resting on the headrest which arched her back. The soft outline of her breasts jutted outward, and Adam felt that same dark satisfaction he had the day on the cliff. He could do whatever he wanted with her, and she'd be helpless to resist.

There must have been more of his ancestor's blood racing through him than he'd ever imagined—or maybe it was just the woman.

Cass's head swiveled his way, and then snapped forward; a scowl darkened her eyes. Her lips pulled into a pout.

Adam began to whistle as he dumped his burden into the bed of his truck and came around to the door. Once inside, he didn't look her way, knowing that ignoring her would drive her wild.

He gunned the gas, and the truck leapt forward. From the corner of his eye he watched her grapple with her bindings and slam her feet against the floorboard to keep from being thrown around the cab. Again, a smile threatened to ease across his mouth, but he fought the urge. No use letting her know he was enjoying this so much.

The trip to his ranch took only minutes, but it was long enough for the storm to catch up with them. The clouds opened. Rain whipped sideways in a gusting wind.

He parked in front of the porch rather than the garage, not wanting to wrestle her that far to get her into the house. He shoved open his door, hurried around to hers and slung it open before she had a chance to think about her next move.

Good. Let her stew and wonder what he had in mind. Although she had to have a pretty good idea what priority number one was from the instant erection that had poked her taut belly when he'd held her against the rock.

He stood in the opening of the door, rain beating down on his head and shoulders, and stripped away the tape. Then with his hands spread to grip the opening and prevent her escape, he said, "Going to come along peaceably or do I have to carry you inside?"

"Why'd you bring me here?"

He noted the muted excitement shimmering in her eyes. "Afraid I brought you here to exact revenge?"

Her chin rose, but the glance she gave him from beneath her lashes was pure invitation. "Depends on whether your brand of revenge is sweet or not."

Heat stirred in his sex. "Get out of the truck," he growled.

She eyed him warily. "You're going to have to give me room."

He backed up half a step and she slid to the ground, her body gliding down the front of his. She stood in thin-soled climbing shoes, and he was reminded again just how small she was. He tended to forget that fact when he was in her company because she was so damn ornery.

"Don't suppose you're going to offer me a warm bath and meal?"

"Maybe later."

Her gaze skimmed his face. She opened her mouth to say something then seemed to change her mind because she clamped her lips closed.

"What? No comeback?"

"Think I'm going to argue with my kidnapper?"

"So long as you know who's in charge here . . ."

A shiver shook her slender frame, and he wondered if she was chilled or aroused. Only one way to find out.

With steam rising off their heated bodies, he pulled her hips flush with his and bent toward her—and then waited. He was too tall to press his mouth to hers without a little cooperation. He left the choice up to her.

Cass licked her lips, blinking against the water streaming down her face. Her tongue flicked out to capture moisture beading on the bow of her upper lip.

Adam rubbed his thumbs on her belly, increased the pressure of the fingers spanning her hips, and let the distinctive bulge at the front of his pants prod her into responding.

Cass's mouth parted. She ran her hands up to his shoulders and slowly pulled herself up.

Her kiss held a world of promise—at once sweet and carnal, it had him shaking in seconds, his hands clamping on her hard enough to bruise, but she didn't protest. She raised an inch higher and groaned into his mouth.

Adam devoured her, his tongue tasting her lush bottom lip, relishing her growing desire, which she confirmed with a sexy inward stroke of her own. He clutched her buttocks and rutted against her belly, letting her know exactly where this was leading.

Cass didn't demur. She boldly opened her mouth and waited until he stroked his tongue inside again, and then clasped it with her lips and sucked on it, giving him a hint of where she was willing to be led.

Adam lifted his head, then bent and swept her up into his arms. She tucked her forehead against the corner of his neck.

"This still about revenge?" she asked in a small voice.

"It's about a lot of things. Some not very nice. Does it matter?"

"No."

Her body tightened inside his embrace, and for a moment, he thought she'd changed her mind. Last thing he wanted to admit was how much he didn't want that to happen.

Adam strode toward the porch steps and set her down next

to the door while he fished his keys from his pocket and opened the door, all the while watching her from the corner of his eye.

Her arms were crossed over her chest; her bottom lip was sucked between her teeth. She was thinking hard, but the nipples outlined so revealingly beneath her thin T-shirt were dimpled, the tips erect. Her thighs squeezed together, sliding forward and back.

She wasn't backing down. She was as hot for this as he was.

His own body was tight, his cock heavy and throbbing. He twisted the knob and swung open the door, pausing to give her a glance. "You first."

"Bet that will be the last time I hear that tonight," she said, her voice tight.

"Don't know what kind of men you've been with, but based on your sparkling personality I'd say you've been disappointed a time or two."

She slipped past him, entering his house quickly, and then slowed as her head craned around the room. "I don't think I'll be disappointed," she said, her voice halting as her glance landed on the multicolored rug stretched across the wooden floor. "I have no expectations. Remember, you brought me here. Against my will."

"The house not what you expected?"

"It's . . . colorful."

Adam gave a quick glance around and shrugged. "Our mother liked bright colors. Haven't bothered to change anything."

"You don't have to. It's nice. Warm."

"It's orange and yellow and red. Hurts the eyes first thing in the morning."

"That is such a guy thing to say. I'd suppose you'd be happier if everything was brown."

"What's wrong with brown?"

She lifted her hands, fingers spread. "Thank you."

"For what?"

"For reminding me you're not any different than the rest of your sex."

"You think so? So, any man will do?"

Her tongue wet her bottom lip, and then she lifted her chin. "Didn't the other night at The Stone Pony tell you anything?"

His body went rigid with the reminder of what he'd seen. Her plastered against Johnny's chest, his brother's hands roaming her back and the curve of her bottom. Her unblinking stare, challenging him even as she tilted her head to let Johnny glide his lips along the silky skin of her neck.

He curled his fists and strode straight for her.

Her eyes rounded, and then her head turned as she sought an escape. She launched herself toward the hallway door, and he followed. She'd save him some trouble if she'd just go to the end of the hallway and try to hide inside his bedroom.

Glancing over her shoulder, she shoved open a bathroom door and stepped inside, but he'd lost what was left of his patience and wrapped an arm around her waist to pull her back into the hallway.

She bucked against him, pushing down against his arm, but he hugged her closer and stomped toward his own bedroom door. Blood pounded at his temples, his muscles bulked out, spiked by a rush of adrenaline and sensual anticipation.

He kicked backward to slam the door closed and slung her on the bed.

Cass scrambled backward across the mattress, started to roll to her belly to crawl away, but he was already on her, turning her, his hands going straight for her waist. The belt slung over her hips went first, along with the bag of chalk that fell with a soft thud and a cloud of pale dust. He tucked his fingers under the elastic of her waistband and pulled, dragging down her shorts and panties over slim legs and knocking her shoes off in the process.

Her arms flailed at him, her hands going straight for his hair, pulling hard.

He grabbed the bottom hem of her shirt and pulled it over her head. Her sports bra proved more challenging, but he managed to rake it off as well. Then he came down on top of her, still completely dressed and soaked to the skin. He used his chest, thighs and hands to pin her to the mattress.

Cass bucked beneath him, her breaths rasping harshly.

He let her fight until she tired, quivering beneath him. Her eyes were fierce slits. Her lips trembled around shattered, breathy sobs.

Adam had never subdued a woman with force before. Had never felt the urge before now. Lying on top of her, her legs spread beneath him, her body shuddering under him, he felt heat build between his thighs, thickening his already rigid cock to the point of pain.

He brought her hands together above her head, and clutched them with one hand. Then he lifted his hips just high enough for him to rip open his belt, the button, and then the zipper of his pants.

His cock sprung from the opening, landing on her soft, hot belly, and he could only feel relief and driving tension that wouldn't let him take the time to push his pants past his hips.

He braced his knees in the mattress and rooted for a second between her legs, then speared inside.

"God. Fuck!" He'd dreamed about fucking her, countless nights, waking to find his own fist wrapped around his cock. Now, surrounded by her heat, he couldn't stop, couldn't slow the arousal cramping his balls. With only three hard thrusts he tensed, his breaths hitched, and cum shot in burning spurts inside her.

Still he couldn't stop rocking against her for long seconds afterward. Only when he came to a complete halt did he admit this hadn't been about sex, hadn't been about her attraction—pure, burning revenge had held him captive while he took her.

She'd led him on a cock tease, however unintended, for weeks while he'd fought his desire for her. Then to see her with Johnny, his arms and hands surrounding her, he'd tasted the bile burning in his belly long after he'd left her in the parking lot, hours after he'd gone to bed and stared at the ceiling, wondering how he'd put this attraction behind him.

His head sank to the mattress beside hers. The slight trembling of her belly against his, the gusts of her shallow breaths, would have told him she'd been very near to orgasm if the soft, waning convulsions rippling along his softening cock hadn't clued him in.

He couldn't shake his anger with her, with Johnny, which she'd sparked with her careless words. Couldn't let go long enough to see to her pleasure—because he wanted her to hurt.

Adam slid from her pussy, clenching his jaw at the loss of her warm, wet heat. He backed off the mattress, not meeting her eyes, then turned and dragged his shirt over his head. His boots and pants followed, but he didn't face her.

Standing with his hands on his hips, he wasn't done being angry. But now he had shame beginning to creep along the edges of his conscience.

"Adam . . ." Cass said behind him, so softly, so choked, he wondered if he'd made her cry, and he closed his eyes. "I'm sorry."

5

"I'm sorry," Cass repeated, hating the jagged texture of her voice. "Truly. Nothing happened between Johnny and me. It was just a kiss."

Adam stood with his back to her, naked but unmoving. The shock of the three violent thrusts, and then his abandonment, rammed home the point he'd meant to punish her. And she deserved it for ever thinking she could manipulate him with such a childish game.

One hand lifted from his hip and tugged at the rubber band fastening his hair, and his fingers slipped through the thick strands, combing it. The long black tangles hit him squarely between the shoulder blades. Her fingers itched to thread through them, tug them hard, and make him wince and growl.

But would he give her the chance? And if he did, would he forgive her and let her try to make things right?

"I'm taking a shower," he said, his voice a raspy whisper. "Use the one in this room. I'll go down the hall. Find something of mine to wear."

He walked away without looking back, and her stomach

clenched. Moving as slowly and carefully as an old woman, she scooted off the bed and made for the bathroom. She flicked on the light and gripped the counter beneath the mirror and stared at her own reflection.

No wonder he hadn't wanted to linger. Her hair was plastered flat to her skull. Her features were washed clean of color but smudged with mud on her chin and cheek.

She'd likely left his bedding dirty and admitted a grim satisfaction over the fact. It had been his idea after all—that quick in and out that had left her shaking with unfulfilled desire.

Her nose wrinkled as she opened her legs. Semen smeared her thighs, and she realized neither one of them had given a thought to using a condom. She wasn't going to mention it. Hoped nothing would come of it, but she was damned if she'd let herself seem even more vulnerable in his eyes. She'd already apologized with tears thickening her voice.

She grabbed a towel off the rack beside the shower, tossed it over the top of the stall and stepped into the tub before she turned on the tap.

Cold water warmed then scalded as she scrubbed. At the end she leaned against the cool tiles and let the water slip over her skin, soothing her, lulling her into a peaceful frame of mind where his hard glare couldn't hurt her.

When her toes and fingers wrinkled, she turned off the water and dried herself, wrapping the towel around her body then entering his bedroom cautiously.

She didn't know if she was relieved or disappointed to find it still empty, but she rifled through his drawers for a T-shirt and pair of shorts with a drawstring waist, which she cinched tightly around her own narrow hips.

And then only because she didn't want him to think her a complete coward, she cracked open the door and slipped through it, heading to the living room.

He stood in the growing shadows, staring out the large picture windows. Outside, jagged bolts of lightning ignited the clouds and streaked toward the ground.

She didn't want to pull his attention toward her, but the suspense was killing her. "Are you taking me home now?"

His shoulders stiffened. "I will when I'm done with you."

Cass swallowed and lifted her chin, assuming a more defiant posture than she knew she could sustain. "The storm can't last long."

"Planning on walking back to Canyon?" he replied, his voice taut and grating.

"You really mean to keep me here? You could have gotten more enjoyment from a knothole than me."

A muscle along the sharp edge of his jaw flexed. "I got what I wanted. Think I should care that you didn't enjoy it?"

If he didn't, why did he look so unhappy? Pushing aside her own hurt, Cass thought about that for a moment. It wasn't over yet.

She took a deep breath, gathering strength for the storm she knew could erupt again with one misstep. His fuse was just that short. "I could really come to hate you."

"Then we'd be even."

Her breath hitched on a sharp gasp. Sure, she'd felt pain, but she exaggerated her reaction. "I'll fucking walk to town," she bit out.

"Not until I say so."

"Don't you think people will be looking for me eventually? Do you think I won't tell them what you did?"

His gaze swung to lock with hers. "Gonna complain because I fucked you and left you hungry?"

Shock sucked air from her lungs; an indrawn breath fanned her fury. "Don't think I won't tell them that you—" She halted, not able to lie and say the hateful word.

"That I raped you?" he said, silkily. "Is that what I did?"

She shook her head. He'd done something. Something just as damaging, just as hurtful. He hadn't forgiven her.

"Will you tell them I kidnapped you?" he continued in his silken rumble.

"If it wasn't that before, it is now. I want to go home."

His hand shot out, and she flinched away, but he was faster, fisting her hair to pull her face toward him, forcing her onto her toes.

Cass reached instinctively for his shoulders to steady herself and felt the flex of hardening muscle. She wet her lips, her gaze snagging on his mouth.

"Do you? Do you want to go home?" he whispered. The steady, emotionless tone of his voice flayed where a shout wouldn't have. "I'll take you home now. If you ask me to."

She read the warning in his voice. If she said yes, then they were done.

Something in his dark, pitiless stare had her back straightening, her remorse curdling. If this was all about revenge, then maybe it was high time she took a little of her own.

But she wasn't going to speak her surrender. She held his stare, her lips firming into a straight line.

His grip tightened in her hair, and he dragged her higher.

Her scalp burned, but so did her lips as his mouth devoured hers. She opened her mouth to gasp, and he thrust his tongue inside, sliding deep, sweeping her tongue, the tender roof, curling to lap behind her teeth. He tasted her so thoroughly she felt as though he ravaged her again, more so than when he'd stroked his cock in three short bursts inside her.

When he drew back, his gaze held hers. "Be sure of what you want," he said, repeating the words he'd spoken before she'd stepped out with Johnny.

Then, as now, she knew exactly what she wanted. Him.

Deep inside her, cramming every bit of his cock deep and hard, shafting her long after she'd shattered like glass.

Still standing on tiptoe, she met his heavy-lidded glance. "My wants haven't changed a bit," she whispered, leaving her answer ambiguous. Why give him everything when he didn't intend to cherish her surrender?

His grip relaxed, and her heels met the floor again, but her knees wobbled and she sagged against him. His arms slowly enfolded her, and for a moment, she surrendered to his embrace, drinking in the clean spicy scent of the soap he'd used to bathe with.

"Are you hungry?" he asked, his deep voice rumbling beneath the cheek she snuggled against his chest.

She nodded, not trusting her voice. Was she hungry?

Adam dropped his arms and stepped back. "The kitchen's that way," he growled, lifting his chin toward the door.

Cass studied his expression for a hint of humor, but the implacable mask was firmly in place. She followed him into the kitchen, cautioning herself not to jump at anything sexually ambiguous or she was sure to be disappointed.

She took a stool at the marble counter and watched as he drew bread from a cupboard and roast beef, tomatoes, and lettuce from the refrigerator. The sight of him, barefoot, hair dampening the back of a plain brown T-shirt that stretched around his biceps, and butt-molding blue jeans, was as mouthwatering as the scent of the meal he prepared. She hadn't eaten more than a couple of granola bars since breakfast.

She slid from the stool and strode toward the refrigerator. "What do you have to drink?"

"Coke's on the bottom shelf. Beer's in the door."

She chose a couple of beers, hoping a little alcohol would ease the tension between them.

Sitting side by side at the counter, they ate in silence. Cass was aware of every movement of his jaw as he chewed and watched from the corner of her eye as he upended the beer for a long draw.

"Not gonna eat?" he muttered.

She blinked and took a bite of her sandwich. With the amount of calories she'd burned today, she should have been starved, but sexual awareness seemed to have interrupted the synapses that sent that message to her brain.

She was on sensory overload, sitting beside him, feeling dwarfed by his size, admiring the bronze tone of his skin, the dark hairs dusting his arms, and remembering how the large hands cupped around his sandwich felt stroking her skin.

Suddenly overwhelmed by the moment, she set down her sandwich, took a drink of her beer, and then pushed the bottle and plate away. There was no use pretending she could keep this casual, or pretend she wasn't waiting for him to take her to the bedroom and exact another sweet revenge upon her body.

She cleared her throat. "Are you about done? I'll clear away the plates."

"That can wait."

Cass held still, willing her heart to slow its frantic beating.

His fingers closed around her wrist, and he pulled her from her stool, led her out of the kitchen and back down the hall to his bedroom. This time, he walked inside, switched off the overhead lamp and pulled apart the curtains covering a wide window.

The sky was an inky black with occasional smudges of light illuminating dark, roiling clouds. The window faced the long gravel road that led from the wrought iron gate at the entrance of the property to the garage on the other side of the house.

Adam came back to her, pulled her toward the window, and turned her to face it. He stepped behind her, his hands resting on the notches of her hips. "Think we'll even notice when Johnny comes home?"

She jerked, knowing she wasn't the only one being punished for the other night's misstep. "Why would I care?" she asked, her voice raw and scratchy.

"Right answer." His hands cupped her breasts beneath her shirt and squeezed.

Cass leaned against his chest as he caressed and plumped up the mounds, gliding his thumb across the aroused points. His hips pressed into her, his clothed cock rutting against her buttocks.

Cass's breath came faster. She clutched the sides of his thighs and held him tight, letting him know wordlessly again that she was willing.

His hands slowly glided down her belly, then came up under her shirt. Callused palms skimmed burning skin as he shoved up her T-shirt and tugged it over her head.

She closed her eyes as his palms settled on her breasts again, massaging, thumbs flicking her ripened nipples until she rolled her head on his chest and arched her back.

Hands skimmed beneath the shorts and pushed them over her hips to drop to the floor. Naked, with him fully clothed behind her, she wished she had the nerve to turn and undress him as thoroughly, but she waited, letting him set the pace, giving him what he demanded of her—surrender.

"Lean over and grab the windowsill."

Cass turned and tilted her head, trying to read his expression, but found herself frustrated as usual. "I'm too short standing on the floor . . ."

"Did I say I wanted to fuck you?"

Jesus Christ, she'd fallen in love with a sadist. So, why was her body starting to quiver?

He stepped back and so did she. Then she extended her arms and bent over, gripping the edge of the wooden casing.

His feet nudged hers wider apart, and once again, she was opening for him, her folds parting with a moist sigh.

Two large hands cupped her ass, lifting her buttocks and spreading them. "Think you deserve a spanking?" he whispered.

"No!" she bit out, but stopped herself from saying more. Every time she opened her mouth she got herself into deeper trouble with him.

"Did you like what I did the other day?" Fingers slid between her folds, and he had his answer in a rush of cream that soaked her inner channel.

His soft chuckle had her gritting her teeth, but still she stayed silent, waiting for him to decide how he wanted to take her.

One hand lifted, and she braced herself, shoulders stiff, her head held high. The flat of his hand landed against the length of her pussy in a stinging slap. Her cunt tightened.

He did it again, the sound making her wince because it was wet and dirty. Air hissed between her teeth. Fingers stroked inside her, then withdrew. Another slap and her knees trembled.

Cass gripped the casing harder and lowered her head between her arms, because no amount of passive resistance would make this any less humiliating to take. He'd discovered a part of her she didn't know existed. A part that craved the sting of his physical mastery.

Soft licks stroked along her spread folds, and she moaned because she loved the things he'd done to her before with his wicked tongue.

"I haven't been able to get the taste of you out of my mouth," he groaned.

"Try gargling," she gritted out, her voice soft and thin, so unlike herself, she wished she hadn't said a thing.

His lips pursed around her clit and suckled then let go with an audible pop. He repeated the action again and again, until she was ready to scream because he never let the urgency inside her build.

"I'd like to fuck you like this. Watch your sweet cheeks jiggle. But you're right. You're too damn small."

"On the bed then?" she panted.

"Kneel on the edge."

She straightened and turned toward the bed, startled to see him still fully dressed. She'd forgotten. "Would you like me to undress you?"

His nostrils flared. "Go ahead."

Cass had never been timid with a man, but Adam made her nervous, because she really cared whether she pleased him and hoped at the end of it all that he'd forgive her.

Now, he stood still, his eyes glittering in the darkness, watching as she slowly approached him.

She stepped close, her gaze drifting down his broad, solid chest, and she reached out to grab handfuls of cotton and drag his shirt upward.

His arms lifted, and she stood on the tips of her toes to tug the shirt over his head. Next, she opened the button at his waistband and slowly pulled down the zipper at the front of his jeans. The scrape was as loud in the silence that surrounded them as her own choppy breaths.

Her fingers slid beneath the denim at his hips and pushed, peeling his jeans downward to his ankles.

Cass knelt to hold his pants as he stepped out of each leg, and then she looked upward, getting her first full-frontal view of his cock.

It jutted upward from a ruff of crinkly black hair. The crown was blunt and round, the shaft thick and ridged with veins.

Her breath gusted against him, and his cock jerked. Cass couldn't resist, she encircled him with her fingers and rubbed her cheek along his length. Steamy, satiny heat glided along her skin, and she inhaled his musky, clean aroma.

She cast a questioning glance upward, but couldn't tell from his thinned lips and narrowed glance whether he was pleased with her interest or impatient for her to climb onto the bed.

Her own arousal sharpened. And anger drifted to the surface again. Adam wanted her surrender. Wanted her dancing to his tune until he figured she'd paid enough for the cost to his pride.

Well, she had plenty of pride of her own, and she needed to recapture her own weakening spirit. If she was ever to convince him she was his match, his mate, he had to see her as equal in pride and ferocity.

She allowed a little smile to curve the corners of her lips, then pointed his cock upward and dove beneath to lap at his balls.

He murmured something soft, probably filthy, but she didn't care. She licked his hard, round balls, stroking her tongue slowly over sparse, prickling hair. She cupped them, lifting the sac to her mouth and opened to swallow him inside where the steamy moisture of her mouth enclosed him. She suckled, gently at first, then more vigorously, rasping the skin with her tongue, tugging with her lips, until his fingers thrust into her hair and held her close.

She murmured, deep in her throat, telling him how much she loved the flavor of his skin, how much she savored the masculinity he surrendered to her care.

When she released them, she pressed a kiss against each ball, and then glided her lips, cheeks, and nose up his shaft.

Coming higher on her knees, she pointed him toward her mouth and locked her gaze with his, then rocked forward, just far enough to suck the crown between her lips.

Her mouth stretched, and her next moan was for herself, because already her pussy moistened as she imagined the blunt thickness pressing inward, crowding into her channel, stroking deeper than he had before when his clothing had interfered.

Both her hands surrounded him, gliding up and down his

shaft, twisting in opposition as she nibbled on the satiny head. Her tongue swirled inside her mouth, capturing the pre-cum leaking from the thin slit, then greedily burrowing inside.

"Fuck. Cass." His fingers pulled her hair, trying to force her to rise, but she sank forward, opening her jaws to swallow him. When his cock bumped the back of her throat, she suctioned hard and withdrew, then sank again, and again, until his hips began to pulse forward, and he fucked her mouth.

She worked him with grasping fists and mouth, until his glides were no longer gentle or shallow. Until her jaws ached, and her fingers cramped, but still he didn't come.

A glance at his face, and she knew that wasn't part of his plan. His face was tight, and his lips were drawn back against clenched teeth.

She came off his dick, mouthing the crown, moistening the tip with her saliva then kissing it before clutching at his hips and rising unsteadily to her feet.

She stepped around him and crawled onto the bed, kneeling at the edge, so that her ass was high enough now for him to stand behind her and fuck her.

His palm slapped her wet pussy once, making her gasp and tilt higher. Then fingers swirled and quickly withdrew.

Cass leaned on her elbows, staring straight ahead and waiting for him to stroke inside.

A large hand closed on one side of her hip, and the thick, round head of his dick rubbed up and down her folds.

Cass held her breath as he slid into her. She clenched her fists around the coverlet beneath her as he slowly worked his way inward with short, steady thrusts.

Her pussy tightened and relaxed around him, caressing his shaft as he tunneled inside. The tender tissues of her inner walls burned, unused to the thickness cramming deep, but moisture seeped steadily around him, easing his way.

Both his hands gripped her harder now, pushing her back

and forth while his cock sank and retreated, ramming deeper with each glide until at last his groin and balls slapped wetly against her. His strokes strengthened, coming harder, sharper, making her ass jiggle the way he'd wanted it to.

Cass rolled her face into the bedding, biting her lips to still her cries, but ripples were already working their way up her tender inner walls, and she knew she wouldn't last long.

She'd waited too long for this moment, dreamed of it, fingered herself in the dark countless nights while imagining how she'd feel.

Yet every imagining fell short of this blissful reality. Her pussy had never ached this way. Her body and her heart had never felt this full.

"Adam," she groaned.

"It's okay," he rasped. "Come for me. Come now."

And she did, pleasure spiraling inside her, coiling tightly around her womb, setting off electric jolts of pleasure that grew and grew—until she was exploding in a burst of heat that made her back bow beneath the tension, and had her mouth opening around a keening scream.

Adam slammed into her, hammering her pussy, crowding closer as he shoved her farther up the bed, leaning over her when her knees collapsed and she sagged forward, unable to move.

His release came with frenzied jerks and a long, agonized groan. Scalding moisture spurted inside her.

Finally, with her legs draped over the edge of the bed where they'd slipped from beneath her, his body came down on top of hers, his hips still rocking, his cock churning in thick cream and cum. Cass dragged in deep, ragged breaths through her mouth, trying to calm her heart.

His mouth glided along the tops of her shoulders, sucked the skin at the back of her neck, and then his head dropped to the mattress beside hers.

They lay in a sprawl, half on and off the mattress, and Cass's lips twitched.

She opened her eyes to find him staring, his own mouth relaxing into a sheepish smile. "Did I leave you hungry this time?"

"I think you killed me."

Headlights flared in the distance, and she turned toward the window. A thin, thready moan slipped between her lips. "He'll see."

Adam didn't pull away to jump up and cover them. His body tensed against her.

"I hope he does."

6

Adam lifted his torso from her back, braced his weight on one arm, but didn't move his lower body away. He stared out the window.

The lights glared across the glass, slowing, then cut away sharply as the engine revved and the truck sped past.

"Was that necessary?" she whispered, her voice muffled because she'd dropped her head to the mattress.

"Completely." Adam wrapped an arm around her waist, hauling her up against him.

A door slammed in the distance, but Cass couldn't muster the strength to be concerned. Footsteps stomped the length of the wood floors, pausing outside Adam's bedroom door.

Adam turned them both and sat on the edge of the bed, bringing her with him and spreading her legs either side of his knees, while keeping his cock lodged inside her tight pussy.

The door slammed open, bouncing against the wall. Adam slipped his fingers between Cass's legs and thumbed her clit.

Cass reached between her legs to cup her palms over his hand, trying to push him away, but he didn't budge. She grasped his wrists and squeezed and tried to bring her legs over his knees, but he spread them farther and she sank, lying against him, more of her sex exposed than before.

Boot steps scuffed the floor, nearing them, circling the end of the bed until Johnny stood in front of them. He eyed Adam with a tight, impassive expression etched on his face, then his gaze dropped to where Adam's fingers and dick disappeared. "Didn't think you'd bring her here, bro," he said softly. "Not after the other night."

"She's mine," Adam said, his voice even, although his body tensed beneath Cass's. "I didn't leave her any choice."

Johnny's gaze rose to meet Cass's. "All yours? Or are we sharing?"

"Adam, please," she said, pushing at his wrists. "Is this a test?" she asked, squirming hard now. "I told you, the other night was a mistake. I never wanted him."

"Are you sure?" Adam whispered in her ear. "Or am I swimming in lies," he said, swirling his fingertip over her hard nubbin and she quivered.

Her pussy gave an involuntary caress, clasping him to hold him inside, the moist sound adding the punctuation to his terse statement.

Cass whimpered. "Stop this, both of you."

"Brother," Johnny said, widening his stance in front of them. "Better kick me to the door now, or I'm gonna get a little taste of what I'm giving up."

Adam nudged her face until she met his gaze. "You said it was just a kiss, that he was a substitute for me."

Cass's gaze clung to his, willing him to listen, hoping this time he'd believe. "That was the truth. I never wanted him."

Adam's jaw tightened, then he turned to Johnny. "The lady doesn't want you. Get out now."

"Think she wouldn't have fucked me if I'd gotten to her first?"

"You don't do it for her. And I won't let you have her. Now, get out. We aren't finished."

Johnny's fists curled at his side. He shot Cass a hot glare, and then turned his back on them both. The door slammed closed behind him.

"Was this all about him?" Cass asked, her voice shaking. "Did you want me because he wanted me too?"

Adam didn't answer right away. The truth would hurt her. He let his head fall back while his arms closed tighter around Cass because she was fighting him in earnest now, her fingernails scraping his thighs. Her body bucking and, at last, dislodging his cock.

He rolled to the side, turning her, coming over her and dragging her up the bed until they lay in the center of it, his body stretched over hers.

"He had to know he'd lost the game," he ground out.

"This is a fucking game?" Her arm swung wide, her fist landing against the side of his head.

"His game," he said, and then cursed as he reached to catch her fist before the next punch landed. "Johnny won't ever leave us alone if he thinks there's a chance of coming between us."

Her body bucked again, her thigh jerking to the side, then her knee coming back to slam at his hip. She was strong. He'd have bruises. But damn if the fire in her eyes didn't turn him on.

Wrestling Cass was like holding a wet fish inside his bare hands. Finally, he locked her feet with his ankles and stretched her hands high above her head, and waited until his weight pressed the air from her lungs and she ceased to have the strength to fight him.

"Think I won't sink my teeth somewhere?" she said, her voice shaking with fury.

"You don't want to injure me. Not seriously."

"And how did you come to that wrong-ass conclusion?"

"You could have gone for my balls a time or two there, reached right between my legs and had me. You didn't want to hurt me."

Her chin jerked up. "I twisted Johnny's balls. To get him off me the other night."

"But you wouldn't have done that to me. Not even if I'd goaded you hard enough."

"Why did you do that?" she whispered. "Why did you let him see me that way? Couldn't you have just waited until morning when we both strolled out the door? Why humiliate me like that?"

"I had to send him a message he could understand."

"What he said about sharing, you thought I'd go for that?"

Adam sighed. "I'm not perfect, Cass."

She snorted.

"I had to let him see that, but I didn't like sharing the view. I was jealous. And I'll admit I can get damned ugly when I think about you with him."

"This 'who's-got-the-bigger-dick contest' didn't start with me, did it? You brought me into the middle of it tonight, I deserve to know why."

"You through fighting me?"

She sniffed. "Depends."

"I'm going to let you go. Throw any more punches and I'll go find that duct tape again."

"You're as big a bastard as your brother."

The tears in her voice bled away his strength. His gaze dropped away from hers, and he climbed off her, lying on his back. If she decided to leave now, he wouldn't stop her.

Cass sat up on the edge of the bed, her back to him. "I still want to know why."

It was easier this way, not having to meet her gaze. "My brother and I hate each other's guts. Our father set us competing with each other for everything. Sports, grades, for a truck, a horse, his love. Guess I won, because he left me controlling interest in the ranch."

"Sounds like a right bastard."

"He was. Can't say I was all torn up when he died. I got engaged to a girl in Canyon."

"A blonde?"

Adam's jaw tightened. "Yeah, she was pretty and tiny, like you."

Cass's head shook. "And you judged me for using Johnny as a substitute."

"Those are the only similarities you share. Pam was sweet."

A short, harsh laugh gusted from her. "I take it Johnny interfered."

"He seduced her. I found them both in my bed."

Her hand tightened around a fistful of sheeting. "This is looking more and more sordid by the second."

"I didn't want to fuck you because of Pam or Johnny. I wanted you for me."

"But you couldn't help using the situation to make a point with your brother either."

"No. I want him gone. I want him to know—"

"That he lost?" Her head turned, her liquid gaze unmanning him completely.

Adam's chest deflated. Saying it out loud, admitting his own less-than-honorable intentions, made him feel ashamed. "I'm sorry, Cass."

"And I should listen to you now because you were so ready to hear my apology?"

"I never meant . . ."

"Can't say it, can you? You meant to hurt me. You meant to rub your brother's nose in my pussy." She stood, her gaze raking the floor until she found her clothes and scooped them up. She held them in front of her, and then raised her face again. "I think I'd prefer to have him take me back to the park."

Adam swallowed hard. Unable to force another word past his burning throat, he watched as she walked to the bathroom and quietly shut the door behind her.

He stared at the ceiling as the water started, finally looking at his actions from her point of view and coming to the same conclusion—he was a bastard. He'd used her, just as Johnny had intended to do.

Problem was, now that is was over, he didn't know how he'd let her walk away. He hadn't started out to pursue her. Hadn't wanted to act on the attraction that sparked between them, because he'd cared enough about her to want better for her than bringing her into his battle with his brother.

Now, it was probably too late to make amends. She'd never trust him again.

Adam scrubbed a hand over his face then rose. He dressed in the darkness, turned on a light so she'd know she was alone when she came out, and closed the curtains.

Then he strode down the hall to his brother's bedroom only to find it empty.

Johnny was in the kitchen, nursing a beer at the kitchen table. His eyes narrowed as Adam approached.

"She wants you to drive her back," Adam said quietly, feeling the familiar tension build in his shoulders and arms.

Johnny started to smile, but Adam held up his hand. "Leave her alone. She's had enough of us."

His brother set his beer on the table. His expression sliding from a self-satisfied smile to a thoughtful frown. "I'll take her. And I won't mess with her."

Adam nodded, and then turned to leave.

"Pam wasn't the one for you," Johnny said quietly behind him. "You know that don't you?"

"You saying you fucked her as a favor to me?"

"She wasn't the one. Pam liked stringing us both along. I let her. Didn't know how else to show you."

"You saying you didn't get satisfaction from proving it to me. In my bed."

"Didn't say I didn't enjoy it. But Cass isn't Pam. I kissed her. But I had to back her up to the wall and make her take it. She didn't expect it. Just bad luck you happened to be there. Her bad luck."

"You saw me there."

"Of course. When she cupped my balls, I thought she'd changed her mind. But she damn near twisted them off. She's perfect for you, man."

Adam grunted. "Nice to know, but a little too late to change a thing."

"I wouldn't give up if I were you. She's strong. Tough. She can take your shit."

"I don't need your advice."

"You've never wanted to hear a thing that came from my mouth, but I'm telling you. She loves you."

"It's too damn late."

"Maybe it is. I'll take your girl home. Then I'm heading to San Antonio."

Adam turned to his brother and shot him a questioning glance.

"There's a spread up for sale I've had my eye on for a while. Get the money together. I'm out of here."

"Because of Cass?"

Johnny snorted. "Because it's time to be my own man. We both have to let go of the past."

Cass hugged the passenger door all the way to the park. She'd ignored every attempt at conversation Johnny had made. She'd turned her head away when he'd asked if she'd like music. Folded her arms across her chest when he'd asked if it was too cold.

"Okay, I get it. I'm the last person on earth you want to talk to," he muttered.

Cass snorted and hit the switch to lower the window, preferring the scent of rain-freshened air to him.

"I'm sorry you got in the middle of this," he said softly. "Didn't realize how much we were hurting you until I saw you in his lap."

Cass stiffened, hoping like hell he wasn't about to start talking about everything he'd seen.

"You're better than he deserves."

"Damn straight," Cass muttered.

Johnny let loose a soft, sexy chuckle, and Cass eyed him with disdain.

"I know I don't have anything you want," he said with a crooked smile. "And to tell you the truth, I'm not that into blondes. Just wanted you to know that."

"But you don't mind screwing with a girl's heart for revenge," she muttered.

"Since I know I never touched yours, I'm assuming Adam told you all about Pam." He nodded, his lips tightening. "She was sweet. And easy. Adam was at an age when he thought it was something he was supposed to do. Find a wife. Start having kids. Pam seemed eager for the sex anyway—and it might have worked. But I saw her flirting with another man. Much as I dislike my brother, I had to do something."

"You couldn't have just told him?"

"And he'd believe me?"

Cass huffed a breath. "He has trust issues."

"Didn't start with me, I promise."

"Your old man."

"Yeah. Played us against each other. Thought it would make us tougher. Things between me and Adam were always tense, but after Pam . . ." His glance left the road as he gave her a look wiped free of his usual sly humor. "I didn't understand why he brought me to the park to meet you."

"Must have been a test. See if I'd fail."

"That's what I thought too. Figured you must have been booby-trapped or wired to explode. Never figured he'd let me around anyone he cared about."

"Well, surprise, surprise. You were right."

"But I wasn't. I think maybe the test was for me. I failed, Cass."

"And I feel so much better knowing he used me to figure out if you could pretend to be a decent person." Cass shook her head, feeling even more dejected. "That's my car. Turn in here."

Johnny drew his truck to a stop beside her vehicle, and she pulled at the handle to open the door.

His hand closed around her upper arm.

She stared down at it, and then lifted her gaze to his.

He let go his grip instantly. "Cass. Don't quit on him. He cares about you."

"For all I know you're saying that because you know we'd make each other miserable for the rest of our lives."

"Not true. I may not get along with him. But he's all I've got for family. I want him happy."

She studied his gaze, read regret, and hoped for his sake that it was real. "You two could have been amazing together, if you weren't so busy tearing each other apart."

"I'm just figuring that out. I don't know if Adam will ever come around to that way of thinking though. I fucked everything up."

"Yeah you did. But don't let him off so easy. What he did tonight . . ." Her lips tightened and her glance fell away.

Johnny cupped her chin and turned her face toward his. "Take heart. I saw his face after you jumped into the shower. He knows he screwed up and he's scared."

Cass's eyes filled with tears, which she quickly blinked

away. If Adam felt only a fraction of her own despair, then there was hope. "Good. I'll let him stay that way awhile."

"You do that," he said softly. "He needs to appreciate what he has in you."

She opened the door and slid to the ground, the beginnings of a smile tugging at her lips.

Johnny honked the horn, and she lifted her hand without looking back. She wasn't ever looking back.

7

"More flowers?" Mavis asked, leaning over the tall vase filled with daisies and orange-red roses to take a sniff.

"Uh-huh," Cass said, pretending interest in the report she was finishing up. "Take 'em to the information desk. They'll cheer the place up."

"And he'll drive by again and think you didn't like them."

"I don't want flowers from him."

Mavis snagged the note nestled in the flowers. "'I'm sorry.' How many times has he said it?"

"I'm not counting," Cass lied. "I'll believe it when he means it."

Mavis clucked. "You're a hard woman, Cass McIntyre."

Cass grinned. She wasn't. Not really. She'd discovered she had a big sappy center when the first bouquet arrived and she'd burst into tears.

"Quit lollygagging, girl. Brody's already got his hands full with trouble in the park."

"Really?" Cass said, hitting SAVE and closing down. She reached into her drawer for her radio. "Forgot to turn it on."

"He's waiting for you at the Mesquite Camping Ground. Said something about a party getting rowdy and finding something interestin'."

"Why didn't you say something?"

"I did, but you were off dreaming. Must have been the flowers."

"I told you. I don't care about the flowers."

"No, but you can't say the same for the man who sent them. Can you?" she said grinning.

Cass frowned, but couldn't hold the expression for long. Her lips twitched into a smile. "I'll see you later, Mavis." She added dryly, "Better go rescue Brody." She swiped her keys from her desk and headed to her vehicle, eager to get outside in the sunshine and away from the sly winks and asides she'd been getting from the rest of the park's staff once the flowers had begun to arrive.

Adam hadn't missed sending something beautiful to greet her each morning for the past week.

Not that she thought for a minute that reconciling would be smooth riding once she returned the many calls he'd left.

She'd pricked his burnished hide, burrowing deep—even though she knew he'd tried hard to fight the attraction that flared hot between them like dry tinder in a forest fire.

That she wielded that kind of power over such a powerful and masculine man thrilled her to the core. Not that she'd make it easy for him to work his way back into her good graces and her bed. The man deserved to wonder whether she'd ever forgive him.

However, her defenses were slowly crumbling away, rather like that ledge she'd found herself perched upon. She wasn't sure she'd last another day.

She found Brody standing at the edge of the road, waving her down. "Heard you've got your hands full," she called out as she dropped to the ground.

"Yeah. What took you so long? Mooning over roses?" Brody growled, a quick smile followed that sank dimples on either side of his cheeks.

Cass gave him a blistering glare, but chuckled. "What do you have?"

"A party getting out of hand, which I'll handle, but I have something else that's right up your alley."

Cass lifted an eyebrow and followed him onto the bridle trail. A freshly dug hole sat in the center. A shovel and plastic box sat next to it.

"Found it just like this. Looks fresh."

Another cache box. Cass knelt next to the box and lifted the lid. Inside lay a folded sheet listing a set of coordinates and a shiny compass for the next GPS hiker to claim.

Brody cleared his throat.

She glanced up as he pulled a small plastic case from his pocket and held it out to her. "Your mission, should you decide to accept it, Agent McIntyre, is to find the next prize."

Taking it, Cass glanced at the GPS tracker and the note she held, and then met Brody's amused expression. "What's going on here?"

"Where do you think those coordinates will take you?"

Cass entered them in the tracker and pointed it toward the northern rim. The blip on the contour map within the small computer's screen looked as though the point lay smack in the middle of Adam Youngblood's property.

"Thought you might like to take this one," Brody said with a wink.

Cass rose from the dirt, eyeing him with suspicion. Something was afoot. "It's off park property. Why should I?"

Brody rolled his eyes. "Give a guy a break," he said. "Follow the trail."

Cass pocketed the tracker. "All right, I'll bite. I'll get this back to you later."

"You do that. Good luck."

Cass glanced over her shoulder as she left and saw the huge smile he quickly wiped from his face. Something was definitely up, but she fought the giddy rush of hope that rose inside her at the thought of what, or *who,* would be waiting for her at the end of the trail.

Wouldn't you know it, the coordinates led her straight back to the cut fence she'd seen before when Adam dragged her out for a little afternoon delight.

Cass parked beneath the mesquite tree and cut her engine, then made her way across the fence and dried out grass to the edge of the arroyo. She followed the blip to a curve in the creek bottom and glanced around.

No telltale mound of dirt lay in the vicinity, and no sexy rancher waited for her on the spot. Thinking she'd been the butt of a bad joke, she turned to head back to her truck and found Adam standing in the center of the trail behind her.

Her heart thudded against her chest. She held up the GPS and note. "Your idea?"

Adam shook his head. "Mavis's. It was the best of a dozen we threw around. She was disappointed I didn't latch on to her plan to resurrect the old Comanche tradition of kidnapping." His lips curved into a rueful smile, which faded quickly when she didn't return it.

"You two have been plotting?" she said, keeping her tone even. "Why?"

"You won't return my calls."

"Maybe I wasn't ready to talk to you."

Adam's chest lifted then fell. The light dimmed in his eyes. "Guess this was a bad idea, then." His gaze slid away. "Did you like the flowers?"

Cass tilted her chin. "What girl wouldn't?"

One dark brow arched. His eyes cut back to lock with hers. "I meant what I wrote on each card."

The deep texture of his voice and the need evident in his taut features convinced her. A curl of tension, a delightful hint of anticipation unfolded inside her. "Apology accepted."

A swallow moved his throat, and he took a step closer. "Johnny's gone."

"Would it be callous for me to say I'm glad? I didn't know how I'd look him in the eye in the light of day."

"I'm hoping he won't be gone that long. Is that a problem?"

"Depends on whether you can look at him and me and not go primal."

His mouth twitched. "Seeing you look at me like that is all that takes."

"Like what?" she said, breathlessly.

His hands closed around her upper arms and pulled her toward him. "Like you can't wait another second to have me slidin' up inside you."

Cass snuggled her hips closer, and Adam widened his stance. His cock hardened against her lower belly. "This place still isn't ideal," she muttered. "You couldn't have set the coordinates on your bedroom?"

"I didn't want you running the other way."

Cass closed her eyes and leaned her cheek against his shoulder. "I'm through running. I'm through fighting, unless we both enjoy it."

Adam's chest shook. "I'll always win. I'm bigger than you."

"I'm meaner, but I'll let you win."

His arms crept slowly around her waist. "Because you like being at my mercy?" he asked, his cheek nuzzling her hair.

"I like being completely open. Vulnerable. Maybe even a little afraid."

"I won't ever hurt you again."

"Don't make promises I won't let you keep."

"You liked being spanked?"

"A *well-aimed* slap can be very . . . inspiring."

"The truck?"

Her head lifted and she wrinkled her nose. "I'd just as soon not burn my ass again."

"Come home with me now?"

She smiled, then groaned and settled her forehead against his chest. "Can't. I'm on duty. I can't just leave."

"You're covered."

Her head tilted back to enjoy the wicked smile that curved his firm lips. "Mavis?"

"She's already planted a cover story. You went home sick. She caught you throwing up in the ladies room."

Her eyes widened and she punched his arm. "They're all going to think I'm pregnant."

"Is it a possibility?"

Cass's mouth opened to deny it, but then she remembered. "You didn't use a condom. I'm not on the pill."

He shrugged. "I'm healthy."

"So am I."

"Would it be so bad?"

"Depends."

"You're always qualifying your responses. Would it?"

"Depends on how you'd feel about it. I'd hate to make Mavis look like a liar. Sweet old lady like that." Cass smiled, relaxing as Adam's hands moved from her waist to cup her cheeks. She rose on tiptoe to meet his kiss. "Need a damn ladder," she murmured when his mouth lifted from hers.

"Not when we're horizontal, sweetheart."

Cass smiled, feeling a little misty eyed and trying not to let him read the deep contentment she felt standing inside his embrace. She wasn't ready to give him everything he demanded—not yet. And not because he hadn't atoned for hurting her. She'd done her share of harm to his heart and pride.

Cass wanted to savor the journey. Not in a million years could she have conceived of wanting a man so fiercely.

If all she'd felt was a strong attraction she could have milked it for pure pleasure then walked away. But she hadn't planned on his relentless pursuit, which had amused and mystified her. She'd landed hard on a slippery slope and come dangerously close to losing everything.

As Adam bent to capture her lips again, she clutched his shoulders and rose to meet him halfway. She'd thought climbing cliffs was the ultimate thrill, but claiming Adam's heart just might prove the greater joy.

Adam pressed Cass's hands to the pillow beneath her head and leaned back, sweeping her naked body with a possessive glance.

"All mine," he whispered, dropping a kiss on a pale pink nipple.

"To do anything you please," she agreed, letting his hair sift through her fingers.

He nuzzled the side of her round breast. "I've been a bastard."

"Uh-huh."

"I'm just realizing I never kissed these," he said, dipping again to latch on to one tight peak.

Cass moaned and one thigh lifted to ride his hip.

He took the hint and came over her, releasing her nipple and scooting upward until his face hovered above hers.

Their kiss was a slow, sweet melding of lips. When they came up for air, he was already nudging between her slick folds. Her gaze clung to his face. Trust, pleasure, and a poignant yearning were reflected in moist, green eyes and soft, parted lips.

Warmth filled his chest. He cupped her face and leaned his forehead against hers. "I love you, Cass."

"I love you, too." She smiled, the moisture in her eyes trickling into her pale hair.

Her hips undulated, tilting upward to ease his entry. Liquid heat surrounded his cock, and he began to move inside her.

Cass sighed and wrapped her legs around him, then slipped her arms beneath him to scrape her fingertips down his spine.

Adam shuddered. The moment was perfect. Pressed against soft, warm skin, he plunged into a pussy so tight and wet it felt like a moistened fist clutching at his shaft. His mind drifted, imagining many more days and nights spent sinking between his woman's thighs, claiming her heart and body.

"This is nice, but I want all of you."

Adam buried his face against the soft corner of her shoulder to hide a smile, fiercely glad Cass was every bit as possessive of him.

He leaned away, coming up on his knees. Her legs fell away and he hooked his arms beneath her knees, lifting her ass off the bed.

Cass reached between them, grasped his cock in her greedy fist, and fit his cock to her entrance again. Then she reached above her head to brace her hands against the headboard and gave him the look that had intrigued him from the very start. Her chin tilted upward. Her eyes glittered with challenge.

Adam's eyelids dipped and he formed his lips into a small, tight smile. He thrust hard, grinding inward at the end, then withdrew and slammed back inside. He did it again, and again, watching her tanned face tighten and flush a deeper pink and her breasts jiggle with the vigorous fucking.

"Dear God, Adam!" she said, between clenched teeth. "More!"

A laugh gusted from him, and he dropped her legs and urged her to turn and come up on her knees. He blanketed her back and kissed her sweaty nape. "How do you want it, sweetheart?"

She reached one hand behind her to caress his cheek. "Nasty. Hard."

He pressed a kiss to her shoulder and straightened. Then he pushed between her shoulders until she sank to her elbows and her sweet ass rose in front of him. Adam grinned. Cass never did the expected. He wouldn't either.

Gripping both cheeks, he squeezed, then let them go and delivered a stinging slap to each.

Cass's face sank to the bed. "Please, please, please . . ."

He grasped his cock just below the crown and circled her opening, moistening the tip.

"Don't play. Fuck me. Now!"

Adam dropped spit onto the tip and smeared it with his thumb, then rubbed the tip against the small furled hole above her pussy.

"Adam?" she asked, her voice thinning, alarm making her thighs and buttocks tense.

"Breathe slowly, relax. You trust me, don't you?" he rasped, enjoying the way she trembled.

Her back rose and fell with her shallow breaths, and Adam took that as permission to continue. He placed his cock against the entrance, pressed both thumbs against either side to open it, and flexed to push inside.

His breath hissed between his lips as intense pressure closed around him.

Cass's head sank harder against the bed, and her fists clutched the coverlet so hard her knuckles whitened.

"Breathe," he whispered. "Let me in."

"I can't," she moaned. "Burns."

"Is that so bad?" he asked, quickly dropping a hand beneath his cock and fingering her pussy.

Scalding cream soaked his hand, and Adam spit against his fingers to lube his shaft, wishing he'd thought ahead of time to have a tube of lubricant handy.

But he couldn't stop now. Unless she asked him to. One word and he'd withdraw even if it killed him.

However, Cass continued to moan beneath him. He toggled

her clit and began to circle on it. When a small sexy convulsion tightened around his fingers, he pushed a little deeper into her ass and withdrew, screwing deeper and deeper in increments.

Her clit ripened, hardening until he could pluck it. He gently dug his fingers around it until he felt a slight narrowing at the base and squeezed.

Cass went rigid beneath him.

"Too much?" he whispered urgently.

"Fuck! Adam . . . Adam!" Her hips jerked, and then jerked again.

Encouragement enough. He plunged into her ass, deepening his strokes as he held her clit firmly and rolled it between his fingers, judging her comfort with the manipulation by the tenor of her thin, whimpering cries.

The tight ring of muscle cinching his cock was just enough to prevent his coming. He needed it, because he was plunging through hot tissue, his fingers drenched in liquid silk.

Cass's breath caught and then she cried out, thrusting back to meet him. When she shuddered to a halt, he let go of her clit, gripped her hips and hammered her ass, until his own release erupted. He closed his eyes, his fingers sinking deep into her flesh as he thrust her forward and back.

When the agonizing pleasure faded, he held her still, his chest dragging deep breaths into starved lungs, and his concern turned from his needs to hers.

He pulled slowly out and eased her hips to the side on the mattress, then came down beside her, wrapping his arms around her. "Are you all right?" he asked, sliding his cheek along her shoulder.

Her hand came up, aimless, wavering, and he reached up to grasp it and bring it to his lips. "Did I hurt you?"

"A little warning next time," she said, her voice weak. "I can't seem . . . to catch my breath."

She hadn't answered. Damn. He untangled himself from her and strode to the bathroom where he washed and soaked a cloth in steaming water. When he came back, she was in exactly the same position he'd left her.

Carefully, he cleansed her, and then pulled the sheet up to cover her.

"Aren't you coming back?" she asked.

When he gazed down at her face, he noted the fatigue that deepened the brackets beside her lips.

He should have felt guilty, but again, bastard that he was, he felt a flush of exultation that he'd exhausted her, that he'd claimed another piece of her.

"You're mine, Cass."

Her eyes opened, her gaze tangling with his. "I'm yours." A smile turned up the corners of her lips. "But I'm sore."

"I'm sorry," he rumbled.

One brow curved. "No you're not."

"You're right," he grinned. "Did I hurt you?"

"Why should I answer that? When it's not going to make you feel anything but . . . *manly*?"

Adam lay on the bed, his back against the headboard, and pulled her up against his chest.

Her head tilted, her cheek sliding on his chest. "I could get addicted to this feeling."

"To being sore?"

She wrinkled her nose. "Don't be a jerk." Her face relaxed and he could have sworn it began to glow. "I could become addicted to your loving. My whole body feels completely boneless, but I've also never felt so alive."

"Better than clawing your way up to the top of The Fortress Cliff without ropes?"

"You're scarier. I could take one wrong step . . ."

"Then you have no worries, Cass. I won't let you fall." He kissed her forehead. "Sleep."

She snuggled closer and closed her eyes, falling to sleep in moments.

Adam reached out and turned off the lamp. As he closed his own eyes, he wondered how long Mavis could string along the "sick" excuse, because he wasn't letting Cass leave his bed until she said yes.